NOTHING TO GAIN

SCARLETT FINN

Also by Scarlett Finn

GO NOVELS
GO WITH IT
GO IT ALONE
GO ALL OUT
GO ALL IN
GO FULL CIRCLE

EXILE
HIDE & SEEK
KISS CHASE

WRECK & RUIN
RUIN ME
RUIN HIM

THE BRANDED SERIES
BRANDED
SCARRED
MARKED

FORBIDDEN PREQUEL DUET
ALL. ONLY.
ONLY YOURS

THE FORBIDDEN NOVELS
FORBIDDEN DESIRE
FORBIDDEN WANT
FORBIDDEN WISH
FORBIDDEN NEED
FORBIDDEN BOND

BOMBSHELLS & BILLIONAIRES (ROXIVERSE)
NOTHING TO HIDE
NOTHING TO LOSE
NOTHING IN BETWEEN: ONE
NOTHING TO DECLARE
NOTHING TO US
NOTHING IN BETWEEN: TWO
NOTHING TO SAY
NOTHING TO GAIN
NOTHING IN BETWEEN: THREE
NOTHING TO YOU
NOTHING TO THIS PREQUEL: ONE WILD NIGHT
NOTHING TO THIS
NOTHING IN BETWEEN: FOUR
NOTHING TO DO
NOTHING TO NO ONE
NOTHING TO FEAR
NOTHING TO DENY
NOTHING TO BEAT
NOTHING TO THE WEDDING
NOTHING TO TELL
NOTHING TO IT
NOTHING TO SEE
NOTHING TO WIN
NOTHING TO OFFER
NOTHING TO PROVE

LOVE AGAINST THE ODDS STANDALONE COLLECTION
SWEET SEAS
HEIR'S AFFAIR
RESCUED
MAESTRO'S MUSE
GETTING TRICKY
THIRTEEN
REMEMBER WHEN…
RELUCTANT SUSPICION
XY FACTOR

KINDRED SERIES
RAVEN
SWALLOW
CUCKOO
SWIFT
FALCON
FINCH

MISTAKE DUET
MISTAKE ME NOT
SLEIGHT MISTAKE

LOST & FOUND
LOST
FOUND

THE EXPLICIT SERIES
EXPLICIT INSTRUCTION
EXPLICIT DETAIL
EXPLICIT MEMORY

TO DIE FOR…
TO DIE FOR TRUTH
TO DIE FOR HONOR
TO DIE FOR VIRTUE
TO DIE FOR DUTY
TO DIE FOR LOVE

RISQUÉ & HARROW INTERTWINED
TAKE A RISK
FIGHTING FATE
RISK IT ALL
FIGHTING BACK
GAME OF RISK

ONE

"WOMEN PUT UP with you because you buy them diamonds."

Xander Gauge was used to his buddies not pulling their punches, but even that was damn on the nose for Lance.

"Geez, tell me how you really feel why don't you," Xander said, taking their food from the room service cart to slide it across the suite's dining table to each of his friends.

"It's true," Ethan said, grabbing a fork, using it to gesture around the penthouse suite. "You don't even have an apartment. You move from five-star hotel to five-star hotel. Luxury is your norm."

"There's no point buying somewhere," Xander said, sitting at the circular table with his friends. "Which city would I settle in?"

"Exactly the point," Ethan said, jabbing the fork his way before spearing a vegetable.

Narrowing his eyes, he shook his head. "What's the point?"

"The point is, without a lot of gravy, a woman like Courtney Sarandos doesn't go with a guy who only calls her once a month."

What the hell did that mean? Ethan was busy with his food when his brows rose, but Lance was ready to explain.

"Diamonds are the gravy," Lance said. "We're just saying no other guy would get away with treating women the way you do."

Almost offended, Xander couldn't believe his ears. "I'm respectful of women. What the hell?"

"You're respectful when you're with them," Lance said, adjusting to twist more toward him. "Nine times out of ten, how do you get a date?" Xander didn't respond. "Your people call their people, right? Or the other way around. There's no… spontaneity."

"I'm a shit date. Is that what you're saying?"

Both Lance and Ethan shook their heads. "You don't go through what the rest of us have to," Ethan said. "For you, it's like browsing a catalog. You see someone you like and get Topher to figure it out, then the beautiful, incredible model just appears in the restaurant or outside the event, just there, like you called and ordered her to your bed."

"Okay, that's not true."

But his friends were on a roll. "Women agree to go out with you because they Google you or their people know who you are. They hear 'rich' and 'not an ogre' and they give you a shot," Ethan said. "You don't need to run the gauntlet like the rest of the population."

"It's not like you two are out trawling dive bars every Friday night. You clean up good too… You should, I pay you enough."

Lance opened a hand at Ethan. "And that's before we even get to how they fall over each other to be perfect for him."

"Oh, yeah," Ethan agreed. "Bet they get up to all kinds of kinky shit trying to impress him."

Exasperated, his mouth opened wide before he got to seeking words. "What the hell are we talking about now?"

"You don't live in the real world, buddy," Lance said, eating some more. "Get used to it."

Ethan leaned over his plate. "You date them while you're in town… At most, they get a date a week, maybe every other week, depends how busy you are."

"We're all married to our jobs," he said, not appreciating how his friends singled him out.

Neither of them listened. Was he on mute?

"A month later," Ethan said. "You blow out of town with a 'see ya, babe.'"

Lance laughed. "But still they're calling, asking when he'll be back."

"Yeah, and when he eventually makes time a million weeks later, they're happy to be sitting there waiting… On their backs and ready."

"Okay," Xander said, dropping his flatware in a clatter on his plate. "What am I? A gigolo now?"

"Sort of the opposite actually," Ethan said, frowning at Lance, who was nodding.

"We're saying," Lance said. "They're so eager because in the interim, Topher's been on it, racking up the spend on your Cartier account."

"I don't—" Xander stopped talking when his friends laid knowing looks on him. "Okay, it's possible, just possible, we have accounts with a couple of jewelers."

"And it's never him that actually chooses the thing," Ethan said to Lance.

"No, Topher does that… or he just gives the jeweler a price bracket and an address."

Both guys turned to him again. "You don't live

in the real world."

"And no woman would put up with you if it wasn't for the sparkly, expensive perks."

"I'm fundamentally unlovable," Xander said. "That's what you're getting at."

Again, his friends laughed, leaving him in the dark.

"Buddy," Lance said, slapping a hand on the table. "How many women in the last…?" he thought about it for a second, "let's say five years… How many of them have brought up marriage with you?"

"All of them want a future," Ethan said. "Usually after they've been dating him for ten minutes."

"All of them *love* you, if you want to put it that way."

"Not that they actually have a damn clue who he really is."

Lance nodded. "He doesn't know them either. When does he have time to get to know someone?"

"How did all this come from my telling you I ended things with Courtney?" Xander asked.

"You ended it because she wanted a ring, and you just didn't have the time."

"They'd been dating six months," Ethan said. "He always needs a regular date over the holidays. And he leaves a little time after, just so they don't get suspicious."

"Shit, who have you been talking to? I was getting this same rhetoric last Saturday at Reid's engagement party too," Xander said. "Courtney and I were dating six months, so what?"

There was a thread of pity in their next bout of laughter. "He doesn't even know if that's an appropriate timescale," Lance said. "The minute women talk commitment, moving in or marriage, you are out of there."

"I should stick around?"

"No," Lance said. "They don't love you. They want to be with you because you're rich."

Ethan shook his head. "If you weren't rich, your relationships wouldn't last a week."

"What's his average?" Lance asked Ethan. "About ninety days, right?" Ethan nodded. "By ninety days women who've only been out with you a handful of times start talking about the next step."

"Which is right about when you break it off… because you don't know how to have a real relationship."

"And the women you choose don't either. The money's what they're interested in."

"Because no regular mortal woman would put up with you."

"Nice," Xander said, nodding slowly. "So all the women I date are shallow?"

Lance shrugged. "And vapid most of the time."

The guys didn't mean this. Couldn't… Except he knew them well enough to read their sincerity.

"You're wrong," he said while suspecting they could be right on the money. "Yes, I have experience with different kinds of women—" His friends' sudden blast of laughter cut him off. "What? What the hell is wrong now?"

"You date exactly the same woman over and over," Ethan said. "Every one of them is cookie-cutter glossy magazine perfect."

"Gorgeous, glamorous, money-obsessed."

"I'm surprised you could even tell them apart. No real woman spends six hours getting ready to meet for dinner."

"Real woman, real woman," he said. "Who is this real woman?"

"A woman who doesn't know you're worth the gross national product of a small country," Lance said.

"A woman who holds down a job. Who pays her own bills… and doesn't have an entourage constantly reminding her how gorgeous she is."

"How come this is all about me?" he asked, leaving the table to go to the wet bar. If ever there was a moment for a drink, he was in it. "I don't see either of you rushing to put rings on anyone's fingers."

"We have real relationships," Ethan said. "Women actually dump us."

"Yeah, they bust our balls when we don't call or show up too. Women hold us to account."

"And they expect us to share." Share? His surprised attention sprang from the decanter in his hand paused in midair over the glass. The conversation had taken a sharp, interesting, turn. "Our feelings," Ethan groaned in explanation, glaring at him. "Not the fun kind of sharing you get with all the models lined up waiting to take their turn in your bed…" Rather than stop at a regular measure, he tipped just a little more into the heavy-based crystal tumbler. Solidarity had to come from somewhere. If not his friends, liquor would do. "I bet you lose count sometimes."

If that was envy in Ethan's tone, he didn't know what the hell he was talking about. "When do I have time for these orgies?"

His friends carried on, still not listening apparently.

"Yeah, we have to talk, get sensitive," Lance said. "We can't just grunt a few words about our shitty day and then get our cocks sucked."

"This is a great conversation," he said, swinging the glass to his lips. "We should do this more often. Next time we'll rip one of you apart."

The weight of his friends' expectation hung in the air as he gulped the much-needed alcohol. Now, apparently, they wanted to listen. Instinct demanded he argue. To tell the guys they were wrong. That he did have real relationships. That the women he dated weren't superficial and two-dimensional.

Except if they were wrong, he wouldn't have complained about every woman he dated being quick to bring up marriage. Even the younger women, those in their early twenties, they all eventually talked about serious commitment.

His friends weren't wrong about the quality of his relationships either. He didn't connect and share. For months, maybe years, everything had felt mechanical, like he was going through the motions. At work, he knew what was expected of him. New investments, listening to pitches, the excitement of a risk, those were the things that warmed his blood.

But in his personal life… When was the last time he'd listened when a date was talking? Really listened? He couldn't remember. They'd go for drinks, for dinner, and they'd tell him about their careers or their friends. He'd hear them. The words went in. They just didn't linger. He'd respond appropriately but couldn't recite any of his own mutterings. Conversations like that didn't stick.

Professional Xander could be bold or harsh, whatever was required. Personal Xander spent most of his life numb. Work was always on his mind. Dates felt like a waste of his time. During them, he usually focused on how quickly he could get back to work or some situation connected to the business. When was the last time he'd been enraptured by a woman? The last time he'd been in the moment with one? He couldn't remember that either. In fact, he had no memory of ever being consumed by a personal relationship the way he was by a professional one.

Lowering the glass, he exhaled. "God, it's depressing."

Rather than commiserate, his friends smiled and

nodded in agreement. Even his friendships were professional. Ethan Atwell was his CFO, keeping a tight rein on the many strands of Venture International Incorporated, VII, colloquially known as "Seven." Lance Payne was his Chief Operations Officer, working his ass off to keep the wheels turning in the ever-expanding juggernaut.

"Want to talk some more about the Summit Sponsorship?" Ethan asked.

That inspired such interest, he took a step toward the table. "Yes. God, please."

"No, no, no," Lance said, not so quick to move on. "We don't identify problems and then ignore them. Did we get as far as we did by giving up?"

"What are you thinking?"

Ethan might be interested to know; he wasn't as eager. That light in Lance's eye was ominous. He'd seen it before. Inspiration had struck his buddy. In business, that worked out for him. Lance's ability to think fast on his feet made him good at what he did.

"We practice our people skills," Lance said, rising to go over to the file box in the corner. "For ninety days, he's got to make it work with a real woman."

"What are you going to do?" he asked. "Cut my allowance?"

"No, you keep your money," Lance said, retrieving a file. "You just can't tell her about it. You don't tell her your real name or what you really do. She's got to believe you're just a regular Joe."

"Why would I agree to that?"

"The business won't suffer," Lance said, mirroring him in his approach to the table until they came to a stop on opposite sides. "You do what you do, just… I don't know, rent a shitty, regular Joe looking office with crappy furniture and a fake plant… You do what you do remotely. We'll pick a random city in the

US. Topher will rent you an apartment, basic, one bed."

"You want to set me up in a drug den?"

"No," Lance said on a snicker. "You can live in a nice, safe neighborhood. The aim is to prove our point, not to get you killed."

"Your point that I can't keep a woman happy without money," he said to his friend's shrug. "Aren't we getting a little old for frat boy games?"

Thirty-five wasn't exactly ancient, he just didn't have the patience for screwing around like he used to. Which was maybe the foundation of his buddies' point and why it was breaking through. His professional life was soaring, yet he was unsatisfied. Going to bland hotel suite after bland hotel suite, his personal life was a revolving door of blah. If it wasn't some corporate function, it was a charity event, or a date with a perfectly fine woman.

He was the job. Nothing more. He loved the job. But he was good at it, maybe too good. The challenge used to be his favorite part. He'd gotten so good, it was almost impossible to fail. Seven was so huge now that even he couldn't control every nuance. That was when he'd set up the Summit Sponsorship. The program invited start-up companies to pitch ideas for investment. It was supposed to help him recapture the high of the early days. Sometimes he got glimmers of that stimulation, but there was no exhilaration anymore, no real thrill.

"If you're scared…" Lance said, smirking.

Deadpan, he looked at Ethan. "And now he thinks he can bait me into it."

"I think it's worth a cool million."

A million dollars was nothing. Why would he play along for the sake of such a measly amount—Lance held up a file and then tossed it across the table.

He didn't have to open the file to know whose it

was. "BlueGold," he said, recalling their disagreement earlier in the day. "It's a dud."

"And we'll never know," Lance said, his smile becoming much more satisfied as he folded his arms. "Because you make the calls."

"You want us to stake our professional judgment on a personal bet?"

Lance shrugged. "You make it ninety days committed to the same woman, a regular woman, who doesn't know about your personal wealth, and we'll never talk about it again."

"If I don't, you get the million investment."

"And we find out who was right, you or me."

The Summit Sponsorship always brought disagreements. He called the shots. So they'd never found out if the companies Lance and Ethan went to bat for without his support would've been a good investment or not. It was a bone of contention that could often lead to different companies coming up in conversation throughout the year.

They accepted pitches at any time if they could fit them into the schedule. Some they heard alone, but they made recordings to playback for each other too. It wasn't often that he, Ethan, and Lance got to be in the same place at the same time. Once a year, they issued their decisions. At that time, it was necessary for them to get together.

Ninety days in one place would be impossible. "I'll still need to travel."

"Yeah," Lance said. "We'll tell her you're a traveling salesman or something." Ethan laughed; he wasn't as impressed. "You're a consultant... You know those guys pop in and out all over the place, doing as little as possible."

"*I* consult," he said, still not smiling.

"Yeah, but you're a fucking billionaire. When you

give people advice they piss in their pants."

Their seated friend just enjoyed himself while he and Lance stared each other out.

If this was a challenge, he couldn't back down. How tough could it be? He liked to be proved right.

He took a breath. "Ninety days?"

"Ninety days."

"A random city?" Lance nodded, his smile growing. "The business won't suffer?"

"You're not that important," Lance said, starting around the table. "We'll cope. The place won't fall down without your micromanaging." If he could micromanage something as vast as Seven, he probably would. Still pondering, he turned as his friend approached, offering his hand. "Deal?"

He never shook hands on a deal without intending to give it his all. The personal wasn't all that different from the professional in that regard. Could he do it? Ninety days as a regular Joe...

Slapping his hand onto Lance's, they shook. "Deal."

Ethan's laugh rose again. "Never could refuse a challenge... Damn, this is going to be interesting."

TWO

A RANDOM CITY.

Picking the city had been as simple as typing the request into a search engine. Yep, there really was a website for everything. The first metropolis that came up was Honolulu. Sea, sand, a slower pace… He wouldn't have minded spending some time in the sun. Except Lance ran it again, stating two thousand miles from the US mainland wasn't ideal.

Seven had business hubs all over the world. Any of them might need his attention at any time. Most everything could be done online or by video from any corner of the globe.

Still, he suspected Lance wasn't interested in their deal granting him a three-month vacation surrounded by women in bikinis. Hence why his friends settled on the Midwest choice.

He might say organizing an office and apartment was easy, except he hadn't been the one to do it. Topher, his assistant, had traveled ahead, dealt with everything, and met him at the airport to hand over the essentials. It was odd for them both that Topher was the one taking the jet while he stayed put with nothing more than a set of keys and a roll of twenties.

Out in the world on his own. He could do this. Live a regular life, couldn't he? It couldn't be too hard. People did it every day of the week. Not people like him, but people with fewer opportunities and less cash. His "people" were still on the end of the phone. Employees and buddies. Nothing was permanent, but this was a challenge. He couldn't help but relish those.

Lance thought it was a big deal, that this would be a stretch, but he wasn't worried. No matter the circumstance, he always rose to the occasion. One way or another.

Apparently, the apartment was kitted out with everything he'd need. Clothes, food, all necessities, and rent paid for six months; the landlord didn't offer three-month leases. Topher was efficient in everything and usually got the details right. Usually.

From the airport, he caught a cab to his block. His block. He couldn't remember the last time he'd had a block… or an apartment. Had he ever?

Before checking out his new home, he headed into the coffee place across the street. It wasn't like he was a complete moron; he knew how to order coffee… Though he'd probably want something stronger after seeing the place Topher leased for him. With Lance calling the shots, it was smart to be wary. His friend never passed up an opportunity to have a little fun at someone else's expense.

Inside, assaulted by the scent of java, a dozen people lined up at the counter. He moseyed over to wait behind them and took his phone from his pocket to dial Lance. This was going to happen, he just had to know where to start.

As usual, he answered within a couple of rings.

"Missing us already?"

"I'm here," he said. "Now what?"

"Whoa, bad attitude. You were much more positive at dinner last night."

"I had someone cleaning up after me last night," he said, though hard work wasn't something he shied from. "I don't want this to be a waste of time."

"Then you better get started. Clock doesn't start ticking until you meet her."

He'd figured that. "Right. How do I do that?"

Lance laughed. "You want me to tell you where to put it when you get her on her back too? Pick up a woman, how difficult is that? Oh, wait, right… you've never had to pick one up."

He sneered. "I can pick up a woman."

"Really?" Lance asked, making no secret of enjoying himself. "You can't even find one. Can you only notice attractive women photoshopped in a magazine? Shit, man, sometimes you've got to take a chance and date a woman you haven't already seen in a bikini."

"Never knew you thought of me as such an asshole."

Lance laughed. "You know I love you, man. Whatever happens. But she won't just crash into you and introduce herself."

The line moved, so he did too. A person coming the other way tripped. There wasn't time to react before freezing liquid cascaded down the front of his pants.

THREE

OOOOOO! RAINIE TAIT caught herself against the arm of the guy in the line who'd just taken her frappé to the groin.

Leaping back, she gasped at the dark stain seeping down the front of his pants.

"Oh my God! Oh my God, oh my God. I'm so sorry." Thrusting the plastic cup at another guy in the line, she grabbed for the napkins stuffed in her purse and dropped to a crouch to try mopping up the stain. "I'm sorry. I'm sorry. Oh, I'm such a klutz! I'm so sorry."

No matter how hard she rubbed at it, the stain didn't go anywhere. The poor guy had picked his fancy tan chinos out the closet that morning oblivious their paths would cross. Maybe if he'd known, he would've gone with a darker fabric.

Flattening her palm on his thigh, Rainie pushed up and down, trying to scrub his pants dry to no avail.

"Bill me for your dry cleaning," she said, still working on the stain. "Do you dry-clean chinos? I don't know… I'll buy your detergent… Want me to get it now?" She surged to her feet so fast that her balance wavered, and her body bounced off his. Wow, he took up a lot of space. Something about him did. His presence? It was… hmm… His height? Those shoulders had sure seen some hours in the gym too. "I'm Rainie, by the way, Tait. Rainie Tait. I work literally around the corner at Viva Marketing. Eric Donal, he's head of my division. I don't know him really, but you can call Stacey, she's my supervisor…" Remembering the stain, she leaped aside. "You should go wash up, in the restroom." But, uh… "You'll lose your place in the line…" That was easy fixed. She hopped in front of him. "I'll keep your place, right here." Taking his arm, she tugged him out of the space. "Go clean before it sets. Go. Go." The guy's mouth opened like he might say something. There wasn't time! She yanked his arm again. "You'll be sorry if you don't get it now. Hurry. Hurry!"

Pointing to the back of the room, to the restrooms, she urged him to go. When he took her suggestion and turned to head over there, she breathed out.

The people in front of her were staring. She glanced behind and found they weren't the only ones watching the performance.

"What?" she appealed to the gawkers. "It was an accident."

Those in front seemed surprised she'd addressed them. That was the problem with social media society. People thought it was okay to get in each other's business. To watch and comment and share. Voyeurs. That's what the world was full of. Watchers.

Staying in the line, waiting to get up front, she admired the cakes behind the glass. They were so pretty. Each looked yummy… Admiring them, she played the game of deciding which she would eat first, which would be second and third, and so on. She never ordered the tasty treats. They weren't supposed to eat at their desks. Coffee was permitted, providing it was covered.

She and Stacey worked in client relations. Details were their job. Anything customers needed. Setting up meetings and rendezvous. They did necessary research and once in a while got to travel to meet with clients. They were the invisible middle-people between the customer and the brains of Viva, who put the marketing campaigns together.

If there was one thing she sucked at, it was being invisible. Her memory was great. She cared about things others might consider ridiculous. Bonuses in her professional position.

In other areas of life, she wasn't so perfect. As her most recent accident proved. If there was ever a chance of doing something stupid, she'd find it. Tripping over air was her specialty. It only happened every once in a while. Whenever it did, she managed to make it a doozy. Maybe she wasn't the most finessed or the most observant person, but she was thorough where it counted.

At least that was what she thought until she got to the front of the line and the guy at the register asked, "What can I get you?"

With her mouth open to take in plenty of air, her own order was on the tip of her tongue. But, huh, what did Ice Pants Guy want?

"Okay," she said, showing the guy a hand. "See, I'm actually just keeping the place for the guy I sort of assaulted… It wasn't like a real assault, you know, not a deliberate assault… I didn't hurt him." She paused. "I don't think… I guess I might have caused some shrinkage, but that's not painful…" Her head tilted as she blinked at the register guy. "Is it?" When he didn't answer, she looked to the man behind her in the line. "You want to hold my place? I'll run and find out what

Ice Pants Guy wants." She grinned and bounced up to her tiptoes to kiss his cheek. "Thank you!"

The restrooms were off a little hallway in the back corner of the coffeehouse. Of the three doors back there, she figured the one with the picture of a skirt-less figure was the best bet. Tapping a knuckle against it, she waited for a response. When there wasn't one, she got closer, pushing her lips to the side as she leaned in to angle her ear nearer the wood.

"Hello," she chirped in a low, sing-song voice. "Are you in there, Ice Pants Guy?" What was he doing? She couldn't hear anything so got even closer. "Hello?" The snap of the lock jolted her back to nestle against the frame. When the door opened a few inches, she did her best to show contrition. "I'm sorry." He didn't say anything. His expression wasn't easy to read either. "The ice was worse than the coffee, right?" He nodded once. Filled with sorrow, she cringed. "I'm a noodlehead. I'm so sorry." Rainie took a shot at smiling. "I didn't get your order. There's a guy in the line holding our place... What do you want?" He didn't say anything. Was he mad? Like really super mad? "Do you want to call a cop? Have me arrested? I'll accept the charges; you just have to let me call my boss so I don't get fired. Girl has bills to pay, you know?"

Her awkward laugh didn't do much to ease his tension. What the hell else could she offer? Her mind was blank. She was still searching her brain and his brooding brown eyes when, all of a sudden, he thrust the door further open and snatched her hand.

"Oh, we're walking," she said, her arm stretching from her shoulder as she hurried to keep up. "Where are we going? Oh, Ice Pants Guy, you're fast." Grabbing her purse that was hanging across her body, swinging back and forth in the space between them, she didn't want it to smack him in the ass... that really would be assault...

One her hands might envy the accessory. "Where are we—"

Whoever he was stopped and swung her around in a wide arc, bringing her to a stop only when she dropped into the chair at a table near the edge of the room. Still trying to catch her breath, she recoiled when he slapped one hand to the table and bent down to get in her face.

"Mocha frappé?"

Her order. "No whip."

He nodded once and strode off toward the counter. With rounded eyes and her mouth still open, she wasn't sure what was going on. Her heart beat hard and fast, like she'd just run a couple of miles on the treadmill.

The guy was… whoever he was. Strong, sure, determined… and, unless he planned to buy her drink only to pour it over her, he was forgiving too. Her lunch break was finite, though Stacey wouldn't be surprised to hear she got waylaid after being a ditz.

If it wasn't her clumsiness getting her into trouble, it was her mouth. Her lack of spatial awareness was one thing; that was physical. She stood too close to people, leaned on things that shouldn't be leaned on, and tended to miss basic observations. The only time she wasn't falling all over the place was when she and her girlfriends went dancing. Somehow, her rhythm was just fine… most of the time.

Still, for all the occasions she'd said something stupid or been maybe just a little too blunt, someone could be forgiven for thinking she'd have learned just to keep her mouth shut. But, nope, that failsafe circuit most other people had between their mouth and brain didn't exist in her anatomy.

The line to the register was shorter. The guy who'd said he'd keep her place was nowhere in sight. Ice Pants Guy wouldn't have known who he was anyway.

She could go over there. Except IPG had put her in the seat for a reason, no doubt to save himself from anymore of her drinks being spilled over his clothes.

When everything was going wrong, the simplest, most comforting thing to do was sing. Music rose in her head, something fun always cheered her up. Cyndi Lauper was a good call, and her lips moved in silent recitation of the lyrics.

She was in that coffee shop at least once a workday and often at the weekend too. Her gym was close by and the apartment she shared with two roommates half a dozen blocks over. There were other coffee places between work and home, but she loved loyalty. And that was why she frequented so many of the same places rather than shop around.

Rolling her tongue side to side in her mouth, she sang in her head, passing the time. It was crazy just how bad she was at sitting doing nothing. The unexpected sound of a phone vibrating on a hard surface startled her. The device on the table. Ringing. There was a phone right there. A random phone. Did it belong to IPG or was it left there by a previous customer?

IPG put her in that seat, she shouldn't go anywhere. Knowing her luck, if she got up with the phone, she'd only drop it or find some other way to damage it. Figuring that she spent her days answering calls and taking messages, she picked up the phone and swiped to answer.

"Twice in five minutes, what's going on?" The abrupt male voice didn't land on angry or amused. How should she respond? "Hello?"

It took a second to kick herself from her stupor. "Uh… Hello?"

Silence. "You're a woman."

Glancing down at herself like she actually needed to check, she nodded at no one. "I am."

"That's not your phone."

"No, it isn't… But I can take a message."

"A message? Where is he?"

"Uh…"

"Who are you?"

"Who are *you*?" she asked in return, exhilarated by the quick-fire exchange.

"I'm the guy calling my guy's phone, you tell me who you are."

My guy. She smiled. Was IPG's boyfriend worried about his fidelity or his safety?

"You could be some crazy telemarketer trawling for personal information or an identity thief," she said. "Are you an identity thief? Hmm?"

"How do I know you're not a crazy mugger?" the guy asked. "You've got my guy's phone and no good explanation why… I'm calling the cops."

"I already offered your guy to call the cops. I think he's going to buy me coffee instead. I was pretty freaked, he's such a good guy." She smiled. "You should be proud of him. You found a good one."

"A good one," the guy said with a note of sly intrigue. "I found a good one."

"Yes," she said, nodding. "He's hot. He hasn't said much yet, but, you know, he didn't scream in my face, which is something that happens more than you might think… Your guy's a good guy."

"My guy's a…" When he cleared his throat, she thought there might have been a whisper of a laugh in there. "Yep," he declared. "Crazy in love with that guy, I am."

Oh, she loved people in love. Their openness and vulnerability were humbling. "You're very lucky. I promise not to corrupt him."

"I'd appreciate that." The lightness in his voice was reassuring, he must have been really worried.

Alleviating his concern was the least she could do. "He works hard, you know? Sometimes I just worry he's being taken advantage of."

"Well, not by me," she said. "I can promise you that. Do you want me to tell him you called?"

"No," the guy said. "I'll talk to him later. You enjoy the rest of your day now."

Polite *and* kind. How sweet! Both of them were lucky to have found each other. "You too."

There was a brief chuckle before the line went dead. She put the phone back on the table with a broad smile still stretched on her face. People in love were adorable. She envied them and their relationships.

The kind of security she wanted, the type of relationship she craved, didn't exist. Time and experience taught her that. Everyone she talked to about her romantic aspirations told her they were an impossibility. And despite her desire not to believe these others, it was becoming more and more difficult to refute the longer time went on.

FOUR

COFFEE APPEARED IN FRONT of her before she saw him coming. As he went around the table to sit perpendicular to her, she swept the cool plastic into her hand.

"Thanks," she said, righting her purse in her lap. "What do I owe you?"

"Don't worry about it," he said, putting his own coffee down.

Curious about his order, she smiled at his black coffee. "Americano?"

"Americano," he said. "Easy to please."

"You're very understanding."

For a few seconds, he was confused, then clarity hit. "The coffee," he said, leaning back to glance at his lap. "I have plenty of pants. Don't worry about it."

"You have to get home like that. I am so sorry."

He smiled. Wow, and that dazzle was a sucker punch.

"I live right across the street. I'll be fine."

Shaking off the shiver his smile sent across her

shoulders, she licked her lips. "I am in here every single day."

"And you're wondering why you've never seen me before?"

"No," she said, almost laughing. "I'm expecting kudos that it's taken until now for me to spill on you."

That earned her a laugh. "And I'd give you it, except I've just moved to the neighborhood."

"Damn," she said, sucking in a breath. She shrugged. "I guess I'm the welcoming committee. Couldn't get much worse, right?" She frowned. "Wait, forget I said that. I don't want to tempt fate."

"I think we can take fate if she comes for us," he said, watching her slip the straw between her lips. "So Viva Marketing, what is it you do there?"

Swallowing the coffee, she released the straw. "How come work is always the first thing people ask new people about?"

"Because it's safe. Neutral." The power of his subtle smile was enough to mesmerize her. "Not like you can walk up to a new person and ask, 'Am I the only one thinking about sex right now?'"

She laughed. "True! That would definitely give the wrong impression. Though…" She rolled her eyes at herself. "That's exactly the kind of thing I would say. My filter has been faulty since birth."

"You can't keep secrets?"

"Oh no, I can keep secrets. I just don't realize how awful something sounds until I see the reaction of the person I'm talking to… I'm not subtle."

"Being direct isn't always a bad thing," he said.

"It isn't my only flaw."

"Everyone is flawed."

Locking her fingers around her cup, that comment drew her closer. "What's your biggest flaw?"

Another flash of a smile. "Oh, I meant everyone

except me. I'm completely perfect."

The guy was hilarious. His suggestive wit gave him a shrewd, sly air that somehow made her skin sparkle. She didn't know how he did it or why her body reacted to a man who wasn't even attracted to her sex, but she wasn't surprised. If there was a way to sabotage herself, she'd find it.

"I talk to myself… and inanimate objects. Not just talk, but converse like I hear them respond," she said. "I think I should be a crazy cat lady, but my roommates won't let me get a pet."

"So you're a crazy cat lady without a cat."

"Exactly," she said. "I play music in my head sometimes… Rain is my favorite weather. Ironic given my name."

"Is it short for Lorraine?"

"No," she said, shaking her head. "Rainie is it. Maybe that's why I love to be outside in the rain… I've always wanted to make love in the rain, but never found a willing guy…" She frowned at herself. "Does that sound like I just go around asking guys to have sex with me when it's raining?" His lips curled, which was confirmation enough. "I don't… I really don't."

"What did your boyfriend say when you asked him?"

"Right now I don't have a boyfriend." His expression flattened. "Demetri and I broke up five months ago… He went to some island somewhere to shoot a movie."

"He's an actor?"

Pulling the straw up, she pushed it back down to stir it around in her drink. "Sort of," she said. "He was an underwear model, not like Times Square Calvin Klein, more catalog… He had big ideas, poor execution."

His smirk was telling. "A model dater, huh?"

"You're laughing at me."

"No! No, not at all."

Except his smile was even wider. Hooking an ankle around her chair leg, she shuffled closer. "You should laugh at me. Dem was the first model I ever dated. We met through work. A client brought him in for a specific campaign. We don't usually let clients cast ads, but it was a big client… Not my department exactly, definitely not my department to ask questions. It's my department to keep clients happy. I had to meet with Dem to report back to Mr. Donal… just to check he wasn't a freak."

"And you fell in love."

Her brows went up as her eyes rolled back. "Fell into something way faster than we should have…" She took a deep breath. "You know, I'm not the kind of woman who leaps into bed on a first date. I don't always have the best judgment, so I like to take my time… And I think that's okay. Foreplay doesn't have to be limited to the minutes before sex. Done right, it can last days… weeks even." His blink reminded her where they were and that they were strangers. "Oh my God, I'm talking about foreplay. Guess I was wrong when I said it couldn't get any worse."

"I'm enjoying myself," he said, relaxing against the back of his chair. His knee passed hers as he manspread her way. "Tell me more."

With her fingers curled, she rested her chin on the heel of her hand. "Why don't you tell me what you do?"

"Foreplay?"

Tease. "For a living," she asked, enjoying his playfulness.

"I'm a consultant."

The little line between her brows creased. "You ever hear some words and nod along while never quite understanding what they mean?"

"All the time."

"Who do you consult? And what do you consult them about?"

"I consult companies on the way they run themselves."

"To make them more profitable or more efficient?"

"Both," he said. "They go hand in hand." After another mouthful of coffee, he leaned in to rest his weight on his forearms on the edge of the table. "I want to hear more about your idea of foreplay."

Despite him being yummy attractive, some comfort came from knowing he had a partner. Straight away, she didn't have to worry about crossing any lines or being misconstrued. On top of that, they had something in common by virtue of who they'd been born to love.

"I don't know if it's different for men and women," she said, watching her straw smooshing in and out of the crushed ice in her coffee. "I like to talk... about everything. I can talk and talk and talk all day. It's important, I think, communication that is. How can I be upset by someone doing something I don't like or not doing something I want unless I tell them?"

"In bed?"

"In everywhere," she said, her chin moving on her hand so her eyes could find his. "We're friends now. Wouldn't it be easier if I was just straight with you rather than assuming you'll read my mind? We have to help each other. Human to human, we're all in the same race, trying to make it as fun and easy as possible before we get to the finish line."

He thought about it for a second before asking. "The finish line is death?"

"Who knows what comes next? Maybe death is worth it."

One side of his mouth rose. "You have a unique way of looking at things," he said on a whisper of a laugh.

"Am I wrong? Do you know what's next?"

"No, and maybe you're right… and it's a race, no doubt about that… Helping each other? That's not something everyone subscribes to."

Sitting up straight, she shook her head like her hair was free even though it was still in its messy bun. "People come into our orbits for a reason."

"You believe that?"

"I do." Popping the lid off her cup, she held it to the side while slouching to tip some of the slush into her mouth. The corner of the base stayed in contact with the table the whole time. "I love ice. Do you love ice?" She cringed. "Was that insensitive?"

"No," he said, snickering. "And I can't say I ever formed an opinion on ice."

"I focus on dumb little things sometimes," she said. "I love ice… I love water." She screwed up her face for a second. "I don't like it when they put lemon in water in restaurants… lime I like. I'd still drink it either way, it's not offensive or anything." She shrugged. "Just one of those things… Do you have siblings?"

To his credit, he didn't take long to adjust to the gear change. "No."

"Are your parents alive?"

"My father."

"Are you close?"

He shook his head. "No. He wasn't around when I was growing up. My mom died when I was fifteen and I became his problem. I'd only seen him a handful of times before then. Didn't see him much after either."

"My parents are divorced… I haven't seen my dad since I was twelve. They split up when I was eight. We saw him less and less and then he just disappeared."

"I'm sorry."

Wasn't his fault, but it was nice to have his sympathy, even if she didn't need it.

Pushing her shoulders back, she straightened her spine. "I'm not. We can't force people to care about us and if they can't, we're better off without them."

"Good attitude. Better off without them. How does that fit in with your 'people come into our orbits for a reason' theory?"

"Some people come into our orbits to teach us a lesson."

"That we're better off without them?"

"Exactly," she declared, happy he was following along.

"Damn, you're cute as a button," he murmured.

Suddenly, it struck her. "I don't know your name, Ice Pants Guy." The corner of his eye twitched. She couldn't blame him for hesitating given how they'd met and her revelations. "You don't have to—"

"Alex," he said. "Alex…" The pause was odd, but she figured something distracted him. Something distracted her all the time. "Payne. Alex Payne."

"This has been nice," she said, offering her hand. "Meeting new people can go either way for me. Usually they're offended, but you really bounced."

"It'll take more than a little coffee to put me off," he said.

"That's good. I never say no to new friends." Fixing the lid back onto her drink, she slid the cup onto the edge of the table. "I have to get back to work now, but it was really nice meeting you, Alex… Thank you for the coffee and sorry about the coffee."

Standing up, she intended to go around him and head for the door. He surprised her by shooting to his feet, blocking her way.

"Is your lunch at the same time every day?"

"Yes," she said. "Twelve thirty to one thirty.

Why?"

He just smiled. "No reason. Have a good day."

"You too."

And off she went. Sometimes life was surprising, and she didn't mind embracing that surprise when it came in packages like Alex Payne.

FIVE

"SO ETH AND I HAVE been brainstorming," Lance said on the video call Xander had just answered through his laptop.

"Brainstorming what?" he asked, sinking into his chair.

All day he'd been trying to set up his system and get to grips with the new apartment. So far, it hadn't been as easy as he'd hoped.

"Qualities the woman you're looking for needs to have," Ethan said.

They were at three different points on the globe, but it didn't matter. Technology allowed each of them a window into the others' environments. They may as well have been in the same room.

"She has to be smart," Lance said, waving something at the camera that might have been a pen.

Ethan got closer to his. "Yeah, because you'll want to be able to have a conversation. And you don't usually pick Mensa members when left to your own devices."

"Not that she has to be in Mensa," Lance said.

"'Cause you're not exactly Mr. Brainbox yourself."

"Yeah," Ethan said, enjoying Lance's jibe. "We don't want her to get bored explaining herself to you."

"You're wasting your time," he said, linking his fingers at the back of his head as he pushed back in his chair to recline. "I already met her."

"The woman you're committing yourself to for the next ninety days?"

Surprise shaded both his friends. Not only did Ethan's tone give it away, but Lance dropped whatever he'd been waving.

"Ninety days, ninety years," he said, swinging side to side. "Whatever."

"Jesus, for a second, I thought you were serious," Ethan said, clutching his chest.

"Yeah," Lance said, "you've never met a woman you wanted to marry in your life."

He stopped swinging to lunge forward, flattening his hands on the desk. "I love innovation, right? New, unique ways of doing things, thinking outside the box?"

Ethan was suspicious. "Yeah."

"This woman is as far outside the box as you can imagine. You were right. No more cookie cutter for me. All I want is Rainie."

"You've had her?" Lance asked. "Geez, did you break the deal and buy her diamonds already?"

"Where is she?" Ethan asked, his face coming up close to the camera like maybe he could manipulate the space and look around the room just by getting nearer the lens. "I want to see her. Is she sleeping? How late is it there?"

"No diamonds and she's not here... yet. She will be. We're just friends right now."

Because he hadn't told her he planned to show up at lunch the following day for another date. And the next day, and the day after that.

"Friends?"

"Yeah, the deal was I commit myself to her," he said. "And I am committed. Totally faithful. Nowhere said she had to commit herself to me."

"I think this is fucked up."

"He's not wrong," Ethan said, ever the epitome of fairness and impartiality. "We can't ask that he waits 'til they get to a point where they're talking exclusivity on both their parts. That could take ninety days by itself."

And as much as he didn't mind spending that time with Rainie, he couldn't wait that long to be honest with her.

"Okay," Lance said. "How did you meet?"

"In a coffee shop."

His friend and colleague scoffed. "You were on the phone telling me you didn't know how to pick up a woman—"

Ethan laughed.

"That's not what I was saying," he said.

"You wanted instructions. I told you she wouldn't just crash into you and introduce herself. You've gotta put the work in with women."

"So is she hot?" Ethan asked. "Did you just walk up and say hello…? What were you wearing?"

How was that relevant?

In contrast, Lance got it in a heartbeat. "Yeah, 'cause if you went strolling up in a hand-tailored fifty-thousand-dollar suit…"

"Women notice that shit," Ethan said.

"You think I snuck clothes out of the hotel?" he asked, amazed they'd believe him to be so conniving. "You were in the suite when I left."

"Didn't raid your luggage though," Lance said. "And you have a whole goddamn wardrobe on the jet."

"You really don't think a woman could just be interested in me?"

"She could, but coffee shop meetings aren't as common as you'd think," Ethan said. "Usually if you try talking to a woman there, she thinks you're a creep with one thing on your mind."

When Rainie was around, it was difficult to think of anything else. Especially when she kept talking about it. Sex. He'd never considered talking about it before. Once in a while, he'd be with a woman who appreciated a suggestive phone call, but he rarely had time to fully commit. And when Rainie talked about it, she wasn't doing it to arouse him. She was just that honest. Just that open.

"It didn't happen like that."

"So how did it happen?" Lance asked.

He'd been looking forward to telling that truth. "She crashed into me and introduced herself." Silence. "Honestly."

Ethan laughed while Lance was just dumbfounded, searching for something to say in the face of such an unlikely scenario.

Clarity struck Lance. "Wait, did you buy her coffee?"

"Did I—yeah, why?"

The slow smile that crept onto Lance's face was a prelude to his exhaled laugh. "Did she ask if you were involved?"

"No," he said. "We were just two people talking."

Though he had worked the question into conversation. A boyfriend wasn't prohibitive, just meant he'd have to work harder and maybe longer. Whatever it took, he wanted a fair shake with Rainie. For the first time in his life, he was anticipating a meeting that wasn't professional.

"Want us to do some digging?" Ethan asked. "Put our people on it? Find out what we can about her?"

"No," he said, scowling in disgust. "I'll learn about her as she tells me. Why should we suspect her of anything?"

"Just don't start sending her pics until we've vetted her," Ethan said, suddenly serious. "Just because you don't recognize her, doesn't mean she hasn't recognized you."

"I'm not famous."

Ordinarily, he understood the need for discretion. The women he'd been intimate with had their own careers and reputations to be concerned about.

"No, but you're rich," Ethan said. "Come on, man, I don't have to talk to you about blackmail or extortion."

"It would've been impossible for Rainie to be in the exact right place at the exact right time to run into me," he said. "I didn't even know there was a coffee place there, let alone know I'd go into it."

"Still, just humor me," Ethan said. "Maybe she's an opportunist."

Rich didn't mean instant recognition. The companies he owned, and yes, there were scores of them, weren't the type of companies that put him in front of the camera lens. Not in the mainstream media anyway. Sometimes he might do an interview for a college or some blog online, but they were niche markets. Once in a while, a request came up for him to go on television, but he much preferred his team sending a statement on his behalf than commenting on whatever current situation the media wanted his take on.

Someone on the street was more likely to know his name than his face. He'd never had a problem walking around. People didn't hound him. Sure, okay, so most of the time he was driving or being driven rather than wandering around. But if he had to get from A to B on foot, he wouldn't be chased down like some others who came to mind.

A few of his friends were notorious. Not Lance and Ethan. Zairn? Roxie? Yeah, being chased down was routine for them. Maybe Knox and Jane too. He didn't envy either couple that attention.

"You have to meet Rainie to know there's just no way," he said, smiling at the memory of her.

Even though she was clumsy, he couldn't imagine Rainie had a single bad or manipulative bone in her body. Maybe that was why he was so enraptured. Every other woman he'd dated had an agenda. They were driven in their careers or their personal aspirations. Of course he had the means to fund any kind of lifestyle a girlfriend or wife desired, and he'd have no problem doing that. But there had to be something more between him and a partner for him to consider tying the knot. Until he met Rainie, he hadn't known what that was. With her, everything just clicked.

A big believer in instinct, his gut had made him a very rich man when it came to figures on paper. His intuition had never reacted to a woman the way it reacted to Rainie. Sure, it could be his libido screaming at him, but it was more than that. He'd wanted women before. Been mad with lust, eager to the point of desperate to sink himself into a date. He knew lust. Recognized it. Whatever was going on with Rainie was something else. Something new.

"I'd love to meet her," Ethan said. "We'll make space in the schedule. Lance?"

"Yeah," Lance replied. "I need about ten days here, maybe twelve, and then we're good."

"I wasn't inviting you to meet her," he said, struck by something he'd never had to consider before. "I don't have anywhere to put you."

Both of his friends enjoyed that truth. "Topher made sure the couch pulled out," Lance said. "Worst comes to worst, we'll buy the building."

He shook his head at his amused friends. "Real estate? Our latest venture?"

"There's a lot of money in property development."

"A lot of red tape too."

"Zairn has a place in Chicago, doesn't he?"

Yes, he did. Though he didn't know where exactly.

His friends would have to meet Rainie eventually. Ten days might not be enough time to get their relationship to the point of her meeting the people in his life. He'd also have to find a way to explain why Lance, Ethan, and every other friend of his, were in an affluent, and arrogant, sphere. He didn't want to lie to her anymore than was absolutely necessary.

"Leave it with me," he said. "I have to get my bearings first."

"I can't believe you're really seeing this through," Ethan said.

"Our guy can't yield in the face of a challenge," Lance said. "Have you ever seen him blink first?"

No, no one had seen it because it had never happened. He set his sights on something and did everything in his power to achieve his goal. In business, it was so routine, it was almost rote. Rainie, his personal, she was no routine, and he doubted she ever would be.

SIX

RAINIE WAS BUSY THINKING about her client's latest request when she glided into the coffee shop. Something in her subconscious must've taken her attention to the table she'd shared with Alex the previous day. He hadn't been in her thoughts until she saw him sitting there looking at her. She stopped, her head angling in question.

He smiled and gave a deliberate two fingered salute. That could've been the sum total of their interaction if he hadn't stood up and opened an arm toward the table containing more than just his coffee. Heading over to the spread, two cups stood with three plates containing different foods. A salad, a sandwich, and the third held a muffin.

"I didn't know what you'd like," he said, going around to stand at the back of the chair she'd sat in last time. "Will you join me?"

"Uh… okay," she said because at least there was coffee. The lunch line always took valuable time to get through. As she sat, he pushed the chair in under her.

"You just happened to be here today?"

He swung himself around into his own seat. "I came to see you. To have lunch with you."

Surprising. Flattering. Sweet. Being new in town, he probably didn't have a lot of friends. She didn't mind being a comfort.

"Don't you have any consulting to do today?" she asked, accepting the coffee when he offered it to her hand.

"I work from home at the moment. So I need to take breaks too."

"And you're just across the street?" she asked, enjoying the cool liquid. "It was smart to come in before I got here." His brows rose in question. "You got through the line with clean clothes. Smart move."

He laughed. "That was the plan." He pushed one plate toward her and then the next. "What would you like to eat? I can go back up and get whatever you want. I almost got one of everything but thought that might be cheating."

"And expensive," she said, pointing to the muffin on the other side of the table. "I don't like the statement salad makes, so I'll choose number three, please."

At lunch, she didn't usually bother eating, but since it was there…

"Good choice," he said, picking up the plate to put it in front of her. "Do you have any allergies? I wasn't sure about dairy or nuts… But I figured the frap is dairy, so you should be good there."

"No," she said, peeling away the muffin paper. "I'm not allergic to anything… nothing I've found yet anyway. I'm lucky that way. It must be a horrible way to live, worried about something as fundamental as food. Are you allergic to anything?"

"Idiocy."

Smiling, she glanced up at him quick. "Then I'm surprised you want to be friends with me." Picking up the knife from the side of the plate, she cut the muffin in two. "Share it with me."

"No, I'm good. I got it for you."

"And I'm a woman in my twenties. If I eat a whole muffin by myself, the guilt will eat me alive."

"The guilt?"

"Sure," she said, putting the knife down. "Why do you think I rejected the salad? I'm only a leaf eater in private. Everywhere we look women are told to diet. Told we're not good enough. Told we have to be desirable at all times, just in case we happen to walk into a man's eye line. It doesn't matter what we want, or how we feel, so long as we're not an embarrassment to the men in our lives."

"You're in my life and I'm not embarrassed," he said. "And I think you're beautiful, Button."

It was sweet of him to say. "Thank you… But you're not exactly our target audience." Reaching across the table, she was pleased that he'd got napkins. "I always get napkins. For someone like me, it makes sense. There's always a good chance of spillage. If I don't use them, they just get stuffed all the way down to the bottom of my purse. I pull out half a tree once a month, it's such a waste." Putting one half of the muffin on a napkin for herself, she pushed the plate toward him. "This food is a waste too. You should wrap it up to go… Save you cooking later. Do you cook?"

"Uh, no, not really."

"That's a shame," she said, licking her fingertips. "There's something strangely satisfying about the sight of a man in the kitchen. Don't ask me what it is. Cooking is a sign of self-sufficiency, that's what my roommate, Gwenie, says. A man shouldn't wait for a woman to take care of him, he should do it for himself." Inhaling, she took her attention from the muffin to pick up her coffee. "Sorry, I'm waffling… again."

"I like it when you waffle," he said, always being so kind. "How many roommates do you have?"

"Two," she said, tearing off part of her muffin. "Gwendolyn and Tia." She popped the sweet treat between her lips to let it fall apart on her tongue. "Mm…" A moan, which was probably far too loud, escaped her throat. "I can't remember the last time I had any kind of cake or dessert."

"You don't like dessert?"

"I love dessert. We just can't have it around the apartment. Tia has a real thing about temptation. She has zero willpower and a boyfriend who's all about her figure."

"Her figure?"

"Mm," she said, eating some more cake. "He buys her all these clothes, super revealing, so, *so* tight. He asks her to wear them when they're going out with his friends." She shook in an exaggerated shudder. "So creepy."

"He wants his friends to check her out?"

She held up a halting hand. "You don't want to know what he wants his friends to do to her. He's turned her into such a paranoid, anxious mess… He's a jerk and she's so beautiful. Really beautiful."

"Why does she put herself through it?"

She shrugged. "Why do any of us put ourselves through anything? Whether it's our partners, our jobs, our family or friends, we strive to be better. To impress, not disappoint. We tie ourselves in knots because society makes us believe we're not good enough."

"You don't seem like a paranoid, anxious mess."

She tipped her head his way. "I don't have a boyfriend putting me on the scale every morning he stays over."

"You or Gwendolyn didn't think to tell her he's a jerk?"

"We tell her she's gorgeous all the time because she is. When it's just us, she's happy and vibrant. Bryan is just an asshole. And she won't see it until she wants to see it. Haven't you ever noticed that it's easier to see something when you're on the outside of it? She deserves such love and happiness. Until she realizes Bryan is toxic, she won't find either."

"Have they been together long?"

"A year almost. She's convinced he's always just a day away from giving her a ring." She swayed closer. "Spoiler alert: if he tried to give her a ring, I'd tell her to stuff it down his throat."

"You don't believe in marriage?"

"I don't believe in marriage for the sake of it," she said and shrugged, licking her fingertip to gather up some stray crumbs. "I would rather a guy love me and be loyal than demand a piece of paper. Wouldn't you? Isn't love and loyalty more important?"

"Absolutely."

"Thank you. Geez, who cares about a piece of paper?"

"A lot of people do."

"I suppose it matters more if you have kids," she said. Was she talking to herself or him? "Then you can all have the same last name… And I guess I'd want my partner to be my next of kin. I wouldn't want tough choices to be on my mom."

"The hope would be you'd go after your mom."

If the world played by expected rules, which it didn't. "Yeah, but you have to think about these things. You wouldn't want your dad to make medical decisions for you, would you?"

A careful frown faded up on his expression. "Why have I never thought about that before?"

"I don't know. I guess no one thinks they'll need to think about it."

"I have a will. I wrote it about ten years ago, but… shit." His fingers went into his hair for a second before he shifted to retrieve a phone from his back pocket. "Excuse me. I'm sorry."

His fingers moved fast across the screen.

"No time like the present," she said. He'd be reaching out to his partner to address the subject. "Glad I can help."

"Nothing is certain in life," he said, finishing up his message.

"Just death and taxes."

He put his phone back into his rear pocket and rested his forearms on the table again. "And that I'll be here every day to meet you for lunch."

She laughed. "Every day? You must have a really nice boss." From what she'd gleaned, he worked for himself. They shared a smile. "You know my gym is right around the corner. I'm here on Saturdays too."

"Then I'll be here on Saturday as well."

"Wow, you must really need a friend."

"A woman with such amazing insights, no chance I'm letting you go, Button."

"Oh, you'll regret saying that. Loyalty means a lot to me. Once you're in, it won't be easy to get out."

"I'll take my chances."

SEVEN

AFTER HER WORKOUT that Saturday, she went to the coffee shop out of courtesy. Alex was already at their table, just as he had been nearly every day for over two weeks.

She went closer, but stopped short, choosing to maintain a meter of distance. "Psst, Alex." She got his attention. "I can't stay. I'm sorry." He twisted around to rise out of his chair, but she just waved. "Really, I'm sorry, I just didn't want to stand you up."

"What's wrong?" he asked, wearing genuine concern. "What happened?"

He could probably tell just from looking at her that something was up. At least she had the hoodie to cover her torso and ass in her yoga pants and tank. Rather, her soaking wet yoga pants and tank.

"Oh, some pipe burst at the gym and they evacuated everyone. There was water pouring out of the ceiling." She smoothed a hand over her damp hair. "I have to go home and shower, I'm a mess."

His concern ebbed to give way to a smile. "Good

thing it's the weekend and I live right across the street."

"What?" she asked as he put an arm around her to take the lead in maneuvering them toward the door. "What do you mean?"

"Use my shower, take your time, and then I'll take you to lunch. Anywhere you want to go."

Stunned, she was in a daze as he led her across the street. "Anywhere I want to go?" she asked.

"Well, anywhere in town. Unless you're packing your passport."

His joke grounded her. Passport? That was funny. They weren't the kind of people who went jetting off around the world at a second's notice. Not for something like lunch anyway.

They went into his building, and he took her hand to guide her up to the third floor and along to his apartment.

"Wow," she said as they went inside. "This place is great."

Light streamed through the sliding glass doors on the opposite wall. The kitchen to the right of the front door was small, gleaming, and way more modern than the one in her apartment.

"Bathroom's to the left," he said, gesturing past a closed closet. "There are towels in the closet by the door in there."

"You…" she said, throwing her bag into the bathroom. "Are a star." Kicking off her shoes, she was quick to drag down the zipper of her hoodie to yank it off. "Bryan stayed with Tia last night. They're doing something in the apartment. I don't want to think what… or interrupt not knowing what I'd see."

"You're welcome to get naked here anytime."

Appreciating his humor, she took her hoodie into the bathroom and stripped off. She had a complete change of clothes in her gym bag. No blow dryer, but she'd make do.

In the shower, there wasn't much in the way of toiletries. A same sex relationship had bonuses. The couple shared soap and shampoo. The single bottle of shaving gel betrayed they shared that too. Only one razor sat on the corner shelf. The level of intimacy was beyond anything she'd experienced with a partner.

If she was with a woman, they could share everything. Product. Clothes. Secrets. That was the type of relationship she wanted. One with complete truth and honesty. One with faith and loyalty and love. One with absolute openness. Where she could tell any truth and be accepted. Do anything and still be loved. Know that her heart was as safe as the one she'd be given in return. Why couldn't she be attracted to women? Shame.

She took her time shampooing her hair. What gift could she give Alex in gratitude for saving her? Alex didn't share much. He responded to direct questions most of the time. Sometimes his answers were brief and vague, sometimes he changed the subject. She didn't push. It wasn't her place to force anyone into sharing anything. Maybe that was why she was doomed to never have the relationship she wanted. While she had no problem telling people what she wanted, she had no interest in manipulating or cajoling anyone. The whole point of what she wanted was that her partner would want it too.

Getting out of the shower, she dried off with a towel she found in the closet, just like he'd said. How long had she been monopolizing the bathroom? Quite a while. She got dressed fast.

Would Alex or his boyfriend have a blow dryer? She opened the bathroom door and went out to the living room. Empty. The bedroom door was open, showing that it was too.

On the kitchen counter was a piece of paper with

her name written in thick black letters at the top.

Beneath it read: "*Went to get takeout instead. Make yourself at home.*"

"Takeout," she murmured, putting the paper back on the counter.

Figuring she'd be there a while, and because she didn't want to go snooping or just lounge in front of the TV, she sought the washer and found it in the closet by the bathroom. She'd just pressed the button to start the load when there was a knock on the door.

She laughed and headed over to open it. Had Alex done something more like her than him? "Did you forget your own key?" The smile fell from her lips. It wasn't Alex; a stranger stood at the threshold. "I'm sorry. Can I help you?"

"Can I help you?" the stranger asked, his confused and concerned attention descending her body.

Obviously, he hadn't expected her. If he was looking for Alex, it would make sense to invite the guy in. Except she didn't know if the stranger was a friend or enemy.

"Are you looking for Alex?"

"Alex…?" he said, still perusing her. "Yes, I am looking for Alex."

Something about his voice was familiar. What was it?

"He's not here," she said, "but he'll be back soon… Do you want me to tell him you stopped by?"

The harsh look on his face relaxed until a smile had taken its place. "You're Rainie."

At least one of them knew what was going on. "Should it flatter me you know that?"

"I should say so," he said, raising a hand. "Lance Payne."

Lance… Oh, shit! Alex's boyfriend, of course.

Her smile was quick. "Oh my God," she said on

a joyous laugh. Bypassing his hand, she threw both arms around him to hug him tight. "I'm so pleased to meet you." After kissing his cheek, she drew him inside. "Come in. Come in. Well, sorry, I don't have to tell you that. This is your apartment too." She closed the door and pulled him over to the couch. "Did you take his last name or did he take yours?"

"I'm sorry?"

She bounced onto the couch next to him. "You're both Payne, right? How did you make that choice?"

"Oh, yeah, he took my name," Lance said, relaxing into the corner of the couch. "I'm the top and he's the bottom."

She smiled. "Huh, I would've thought it was the other way around." He frowned. "Alex went to get food. He should be back any minute." And he wouldn't want her hanging around when he saw who'd come to surprise him. "That's a snappy suit. You know, Alex never told me what you do." She went to grab her bag from the bathroom, calling out to continue the conversation. "He's private, I guess, and wants to protect you! It's sweet!"

"I work away a lot!" he called back.

Lance was still on the couch when she returned to the living room.

"I guess that's why he needed a friend," she said. "He probably gets lonely, especially being new around here. He's a good man. You chose well."

That smirk on his face was all pride. It warmed her heart. Tossing the strap of her bag over her head, sound from the washer reminded her it was on.

"I'm a lucky guy," Lance said.

"I still have stuff in the washer, nothing important. I can get it whenever."

He twisted further toward her. "Don't run out of

here on my account. I'd love to get to know you."

"I don't want to ruin the surprise," she said.

His knocking on the door was a good sign he'd wanted to surprise his partner with his arrival. That Alex hadn't mentioned a clock or other plans made the truth obvious: he hadn't known Lance was coming.

Quick stepping it to the door, she grabbed the handle, intending to say goodbye one last time. Except before she could, the handle jerked from her grip and the door opened, sending her stumbling back a few steps.

Alex looked as startled to find her there as she was to have been caught on her way out.

"Where are you going?" he asked, a box resting on his forearm. "I got us food. No salad, I promise."

"I have to go," she said as he pushed the door further open. "You have a visitor."

"I have a…"

The rest of the apartment came into view and Lance stood up from the couch.

As Alex slid the food box onto the small kitchen island, she grabbed his opposite forearm to bounce up and kiss his cheek.

"Have fun," she whispered.

He grabbed her wrist before she could retreat. "You don't have to leave."

That was funny. "Are you kidding?" She grinned. "If the man I loved surprised me by coming home from his business trip early, I wouldn't want some third wheel gooseberry friend cutting into our reunion time." Giving his arm a squeeze, she liberated hers from his grip and retreated to the door. "Enjoy each other, lovebirds."

Although part of her envied their love, another part was over the moon for them. Love had to be celebrated. The more those in it could rejoice, the better.

EIGHT

"WHAT ARE YOU DOING here?" Xander asked Lance after Rainie closed the door behind her. "And what the hell is she talking about? Why did she call us lovebirds?" His friend's smile was both contrite and ashamed enough to be concerning. "Lance?"

"I don't think you could get a woman so different from your usual type. She's something."

His avoidance of the question wasn't a good sign.

Giving the food box another push, he strode toward his friend. If he could still be called that.

"What…" he growled, "did you say to her?"

"You used my last name. I didn't know that."

Restraining his anger wasn't easy. It was necessary. The longer he could stay calm, the more he'd get out of Lance.

"You were the last person I spoke to before she asked for my name. I was on the spot," he said. "You told her your name and she thought we were married? Why not brothers?"

"Maybe 'cause I'm so much more handsome—"

He lunged and Lance leaped back. "Okay! Okay!" He took a breath. "We talked the day you met. She answered your phone, said you were getting coffee."

"So?"

Shaking his head, Lance seemed to search his recollection. "I don't know. I made some comment about her answering my guy's phone and she took it to mean..."

The anger faded as he absorbed the gravity of what his friend was actually telling him. "The day we met..." he murmured.

"Look, I'm sorry. I didn't know that she was... that you liked her. I mean, honestly, what was the chance of you meeting a woman you'd want to date in the first minute you were out in the world? I was just messing around. She said it and I just didn't... correct her."

Sealing his lips tight, his breathing grew so shallow that it came out in harsh pants.

All the time he'd known her... Since they'd met, nineteen days ago, every time he'd thought he was flirting, when he believed they were growing closer, she'd believed he was...

"Oh my God," he exhaled, backing off. "She doesn't have a damn clue."

The only reason he'd gone out to pick up lunch, as opposed to taking her somewhere, was he'd planned to make his move while they were alone in his place. Not that he'd expected they'd get naked, but he had the chance to ask her out properly... to kiss her. Yet, all the time, she'd believed he didn't... that they couldn't...

"Doesn't have a damn clue who you are? No, she doesn't, but she was never supposed to," Lance said, coming to lay a hand on his shoulder. "This was a game from the very beginning."

Throwing Lance's hand off, he wasn't amused or interested in platitudes. "Not with Rainie. She doesn't like games. You fucked up the first real relationship I ever had."

"She knows nothing about you." Lance opened up his arms, appealing to the ether. "She thinks you're what? A consultant living in a basic apartment that goes for less than twenty-five hundred a month. In your actual life, your real life, you spend that on…" He paused, probably trying to come up with something ridiculous. "Air freshener for the jet in a week… She thinks you're gay, man. That you're in a committed relationship. She doesn't even know your real name. What the hell does she know about you that's real?"

The facts, about his folks, his opinions on things they'd discussed. She knew how he took his coffee and that he preferred the chocolate muffins to the lemon ones she favored. But Lance was right. Whatever he'd thought they were building, whatever the foundation, it was an illusion built on a lie.

"I have to tell her the truth," he said, spinning around, the door in his sights.

"Whoa," Lance said, rushing around to get between him and the exit. "You tell her now, she'll be mad. She'll think we're some kind of weird, warped perverts."

"She'll think *you* are, and I don't give a damn."

"Think about it," Lance said, trying to calm him. "These past couple of weeks, she's believed you're gay."

Why should that prevent him from being truthful with her? "And?"

"You've been no threat," Lance said, putting a hand on his shoulder again. "Women are weird with their gay friends. Remember in the office when we were doing the deal with Nyholm? When Geoffrey was our point guy?" Xander nodded. "The women in the office flocked around him. How many times did we hear them talking about waxing or dating or laughing about some sex thing?"

"All the time."

"And Geoff said they went quiet when we came in because he was just another one of the girls. We weren't allowed in that safe circle. Rainie has believed, all this time, that you are completely safe. She can talk to you about anything. You're like another one of her girlfriends because you have so many things in common."

"Not the target audience," he muttered, replaying the odd things Rainie had said in many of their conversations. So much became clear. "Goddamnit."

"She'll feel violated if you tell her. Like you lied to manipulate her."

"I didn't lie. *You* lied."

"You've got to let it go," he said. "Trust me, you don't want any of that. If you tell her, she'll be sad at first, but then she'll get angry. Angry women want revenge. If she finds out who you really are and exposes this to the press…"

That would be a big story. Billionaire mogul gets his kicks duping beautiful women in coffee shops. Posing as gay to get them to reveal their secrets.

"Rainie isn't like that," he said, though he'd never been on her bad side.

"All women are like that, trust me. It doesn't have to be her; she tells one girlfriend who tells another. They have their own network, believe me, it never works out well for us."

"So that's it? Just… over?"

"I'll give you credit for nineteen days because I'm partially responsible."

"Partially? No. You're completely responsible," he said, a solid weight growing in his chest. "I can't just give her up. Rainie isn't the sort of woman a guy can drop cold turkey."

"There's no other way," Lance said. "I suppose you could still meet her for coffee once in a while, but…"

"But what?"

"You still have to find your real woman for the deal."

He exhaled. "Who gives a damn about the deal?"

"We can forget about it if you want," Lance said, nodding. "We can get on a plane today and get back to work." And never see Rainie again. "But you'd owe me a million for BlueGold."

He didn't care about the million. He wouldn't put time into BlueGold; Lance would be responsible for nurturing the budding firm.

A million dollars? It was laughable. Rainie was worth so much more than that. No amount of money could replace her. Riches wouldn't compel him to willingly hurt her. No figure would be worth her pain.

A desire to tell her the truth, the whole truth, and nothing but the truth, burned within him. But they'd known each other for nineteen days and didn't have a strong standing to fall back on. If she got mad or felt used, which she would because truth and loyalty were so important to her, he'd have done her job for her. Revealing himself and the deception all at once would give her valuable information to sell to the press right when she was at her most vulnerable.

Whatever he did, one thing was evident, the optimism of the relationship he'd hoped to have with her was gone. For good. They'd never have a future. The adage was true, money definitely could not buy happiness.

NINE

AT LUNCH IN THE coffee shop on Monday, she was eager to see Alex to find out all about his weekend. Well, not *all* about it. Couples were entitled to some secrets.

He didn't notice her hurrying toward their table. Usually, he'd get to his feet, ready to pull out her chair. His mind must still be on his weekend, on his love. Lance hadn't been explicit about how long he was in town. If he'd gone away again, maybe Alex wasn't feeling so great.

Putting a hand on his shoulder, she got his attention, but kept going, running her fingertips across the width of him.

"Hey," she said, swooping around into her usual seat. The coffee was there, but so were two huge hunks of indulgence cake. "Oh, sweetie." Rainie reached across to take his hand. "Did he leave already? It must be so difficult living apart."

He cleared his throat, his focus locked on the table between the two plates of cake. Worry welled; she'd never seen him so dejected.

"We broke up."

That was the last thing she expected to hear. "Oh my God!" she said, clutching his hand tighter while dragging her chair closer. "Oh no, baby, I'm so sorry."

Throwing both arms around him, she pulled him close until his head rested on hers. They sat there in silence. He'd need time to reflect, her embrace was the only strength she could hope to give.

Sitting back, she took his hand in both of hers and stayed close. "Okay, talk to me," she said. "What happened? Did you have a fight?"

After inhaling, he breathed out an ironic laugh. "Yeah, we did."

"I'm so sorry. Don't worry. I'm sure you can fix it." When his eyes sprang to hers, she smiled and touched his cheek. "Talk to him. I'm sure he still loves you. One fight doesn't—"

"It's over," he said, examining her face. "You're not like any other woman I've ever met, Rainie Tait."

"I'm here for you, Alex. For whatever you need. You'll get through this and when you're ready, we'll get you back into the game." She laid a hand on his chest. "Whatever you feel in here now, the pain that's there. It won't last forever. I know it's cliché, and it doesn't help right now, but you'll see... You'll get through this." Leaning back, she picked up a fork to scoop up a piece of the chocolate cake and offered it to his lips. "Chocolate helps."

Conceding a subtle smile, he parted his lips to accept the cake. After he swallowed, he gathered her hand into his again.

"Thanks."

"Do you want to talk about it? What went wrong? Were you fighting for a while? Was it sudden? No one really knows what goes on inside any relationship except the people in it, I know... Was it him traveling? The business trips?" She smiled. "I ask if you want to talk about it, then don't shut up and give you a chance. Sorry. You go."

Instead of saying anything, he took the fork from her fingers and stabbed it into the cake, taking off another chunk.

When he offered it to her, she was quick to accept. Tit for tat. He needed someone to accept him. Someone on his side and she'd be it.

"It's been a long couple of days," he said. "Do you think we could just... talk about anything else?"

"I can tell you about Stacey being chewed out in front of the whole office."

"Perfect," he said, forking up another piece of cake to feed it to her.

"Mr. Donal came down from up on high all stressed out about something. He went into Stacey's office, the back wall of it is all glazed and isn't exactly soundproof. They were arguing... Well, I guess you could say he was yelling. Something about expenses on the Northberg account... They did really well with Viva a few years back then went to a cheaper agency." Alex fed her another piece of cake. "Viva tempted them back, I don't know how, that's above my pay grade. Anyway..." Another taste of indulgence, then she leaned closer and lowered her volume. "Word is, they've racked up this huge bill with Viva and their payments aren't covering it. Some say they're about to go bust. If they do, Viva might not get paid... which could leave a lot of people, namely me and my department, jobless."

"Do you think Donal is worried? It can't be Stacey's fault the higher-ups extended their line of credit too far."

When he tried to feed her more cake, she stole the fork from him to place the tasty treat in his mouth instead. The chocolate was supposed to make him feel better. It wouldn't do that if he wouldn't eat it.

"I guess that's the catch twenty-two with marketing," she said.

"Speculate to accumulate."

"Exactly. I don't know," she said, selecting another hunk of cake. "Like I said, it's not my department. But if they downsize because they can't keep their numbers in line, relations will be the first for the chop. Especially if the yelling was because Stacey authorized a big chunk of change to keep Northberg happy. Viva absorbs some of those costs for clients, but if Northberg is already in the red with us and Stacey did it anyway..."

Teasing him with the fork, she offered it to his lips only to steal it back the moment he opened them. Smiling, she tried it again, but he caught her hand and guided the food into his mouth.

As he consumed the bite, the light of his smile reached his eyes. Oh, it was a pleasure. Such a relief to be helping, to have lightened some of his burden.

He swallowed and reached over to tuck a loose wisp of hair away from her face. "You like to tease, don't you?"

"Nothing wrong with having some fun once in a while," she said. "You said you didn't want to talk about it, but if—"

"I don't," he said, easing away to pick up his coffee. "I want to talk about you having fun."

If he wasn't what she knew he was, she may have taken those words and the light in his eyes as a different kind of mischief.

"Talking about having fun," she said, eating a piece of cake herself. "You will never believe who I got an email from yesterday. Well, he actually sent it like two weeks ago, but I just dragged it out my junk folder when I was looking for something else." She rested her chin on her shoulder to add, "I forgot I spammed his ass after we broke up."

"Demetri?" he asked, straightening up.

"Demetri," she said, cutting another chunk of cake with the side of the fork. They were fast running out of cake. "Can you believe it? Months of radio silence and then just out of the blue…"

"What did he want?"

She put down the fork to have a drink instead. "Just checking in, or so he said."

"Did you reply?"

"Sure." Alex seemed surprised. "When my relationships end, I get mad or sad, stay that way for a while and then…" She shrugged. "I don't hold grudges. I'm friends with every guy I dated."

"Every guy?"

His astonishment wasn't an unusual reaction. "Gwenie makes it a point not to be friendly with her exes. Tia doesn't really get the chance since most of her break ups are so messy. But I don't know, I guess in my case, in the long run, I realize the breakups were for the best."

"For the best?"

Acutely aware that he'd just separated from his partner, she had to be careful. Her horrible habit of saying the wrong thing in the wrong moment could hurt him more than he'd already been hurt.

"Have you done any work today?" she asked. "I don't know much about consulting, but I can do paperwork if you need help to keep up with things?"

Sometimes when grieving a relationship, it was impossible to focus, even on tasks that were important.

"Don't change the subject," Alex said, catching her in the act. "I want to know. Why were your breakups for the best?"

The conversation was one she'd had many times with Gwen and Tia. "Because they couldn't give me what

I wanted… I'd never have been happy, so I'd never have been able to make them happy."

"That's important to you."

"Of course it is," she said, bowing over the table as she popped the lid of her cup to tip some slush into her mouth. "Happiness is what life's all about. It shouldn't come at the detriment of others' happiness, but, yeah, that should be everyone's aspiration. Happiness."

He leaned closer. "And what is it that would make you happy? What do you want, Button?"

"We need more cake," she said, pushing out her chair. "Wait here and I'll get it."

Alex needed a friend. One who didn't rabbit on about relationships while he was still raw. She could do it; she could be a friend. It wasn't in her blood to abandon someone in need. Right then, and maybe for a while, Alex needed her.

TEN

THAT NIGHT, AFTER GOING home to change and pack some supplies, she stopped to pick up way more food than they'd ever need. Her destination? Alex's apartment. Friendship with her meant the good times and the bad. She'd be supportive, no matter what he needed.

Knocking on his front door, she waited. Was this overstepping? It could be too much. Too much was better than too little any day. In this circumstance anyway.

He answered wearing a frown, but she was already smiling, keeping her mood high.

She held up the bag of food. "I have Chinese food," she said. "Are you hungry?" He didn't say anything, and the frown was still there. A sign of overstepping? Maybe she should explain herself. "You need to know you're not alone right now…" Saying those words prompted a thought, "are you alone right now?"

"What?" he asked, apparently coming out of

some trance or hypnotic reflection. "Alone? Yes, I'm alone." Stepping back, he gestured inside. "Come on in."

"Thank you," she said, exaggerating her gratitude as she stepped inside. Putting the food on the counter, she toed off her shoes and dumped her gym bag on the island next to it. "I brought ice cream too." She unzipped the bag. "It's in there. Will you put it in the freezer, please?"

He came over to retrieve it and saw the DVDs underneath. "*Die Hard?*" he asked, putting the ice cream away.

"It's a box set. I have that…" she said, taking it out to put it by the food. "All the Lethal Weapons. The Terminator movies… I don't know, it's just something I do. When your heart is broken, you want to numb out." She removed her jacket and was grateful he took it because that left her free to deal with the food. "I never want to watch sappy films because I'm already all cried out. No one wants to watch chick flicks with the happy ever after when they've just broken up… or I sure don't." Opening drawers and cabinets, she found cutlery and plates. "And funny comes later, when I start to feel again." She took the plates over to the coffee table and came back to retrieve the food. "So I watch action movies. Shooting. Blood. Bad language. What's not to love?" She paused. "Is that okay?"

"That's okay."

Smiling again, she nodded at the bag. "There are also three bottles of wine in there, if drunk is your thing. If you want, instead of watching movies, we can get drunk and curse the evils of men and how we fall for their temptations."

"Food sounds good."

Satisfied, she went over to sit on the floor between the couch and the coffee table. "I didn't know what you liked, so I got a selection… This place, Chang's, it's my absolute favorite. They don't deliver to my apartment, so they definitely won't deliver here, but I picked it up. You deserve the best. In food and every other area of life."

Did he get that? Sometimes a breakup knocked someone's confidence. That was where she came in. Friendship was the support he'd need to get through the difficult time. She'd be high and happy or let him cry himself out, whatever he needed.

"Which of the wines do you want?"

"Anything will do," she said, gesturing at the island. "Pick a movie too. We better get started if we're going to get through more than one before we fall asleep."

"You're staying over?"

The surprise in his voice almost broke her heart. "Yes," she said, pausing in her searching through the food boxes to look over at him. "I'm staying right here until we mend your heart. Why do you think I brought so many clothes?"

Being alone was one of the hardest things about a breakup. The silence could be deafening. It would be worse for him because he lived alone. Just hours ago, before the relationship ended, he had a boyfriend he could call any time he needed someone. That safety net was gone. The security that came with belonging to someone was powerful. A breakup whipped that rug out from under a person. No matter how prepared they may believe themselves to be, it was always an adjustment.

Alex would need her. Whether it was for a day or a week or even a month, she'd be there. That's what friends were for.

ELEVEN

"SHE'S IN MY BED," Xander murmured into the phone as he reached his living room.

It was somewhere around three a.m.

Ethan was in Europe, where it would be morning already. "What?"

Rubbing his fingers back and forth across his brow, he kept his eyes closed. "Rainie. She's in my bed... I think she moved in."

"Wow, so maybe she's not all that different to your other girlfriends," Ethan said. "If you had sex, I guess you told her the truth. I'm not surprised she forgave you. Did your apology come before or after you authorized her personal expense account?"

"I didn't buy her, okay?" he hissed, keeping his volume low. In the tiny apartment, there weren't many places to hide. "And I didn't tell her the truth. How the hell do you know—"

"Lance called me as soon as he left yours. Figured you'd call when you wanted to vent about it. How pissed are you?"

"At him? I won't be answering his calls any time soon, put it that way."

"It's Lance. You know what he's like. He's always been like this. Pranking us is just the way he passes the time." For him, it wasn't so easy to brush aside his friend's actions as no big deal. "In his defense, we're used to you blowing through women. You've never really cared about one, not in any real, deep way. He couldn't have known he was breaking something important to you. You couldn't have known it that first day either."

Before meeting Rainie, he might have argued that he had cared about a woman. Plenty of them. But Rainie changed everything. What he felt for her was unlike anything else he'd ever felt.

"Every second that I'm with her, I'm getting deeper into the lie." He swallowed. "I've had to stop myself saying it more than once. Had to stop myself kissing her. Damnit, Eth, she came into my place tonight, taking off her shoes, making herself at home… I just wanted to go over and…"

He couldn't tell Ethan about his urges, not in detail. He'd thought about walking up behind her at the kitchen counter, sweeping her luscious hair away from her neck and teasing her with his tongue.

On the couch, after they'd eaten and consumed a bottle of wine, she'd snuggled against him. Wrapping both arms around his, she'd drawn it across the legs she draped over his thighs until he had a clear shot to squeeze her ass. Resisting wasn't easy, especially after she rested her head against him. Thank God they'd been watching in the dark and Topher had bought a bunch of pillows for the couch. Without them, she'd have noticed his boner for sure.

She smelled so good, and her hair was so soft. In the coffee shop during the day, she always wore it on the top of her head in a messy sort of bun with dozens of pieces of hair sticking out and falling loose. He'd thought that was endearing perfection until he'd seen it down. Untethered, it was pure tantalizing arousal.

He wanted to lose his fingers in it. To pull her to him any time she was close. The way they'd fed each other cake and touched each other… it felt real to him, powerful. That she didn't feel the same was its own brand of torture.

"Boss?"

He'd phased out. How long had he been standing there, losing himself in memories of her?

"She's in my bed, Eth."

"So go make a move."

His arm flopped down at his side. "I can't. I wouldn't do that to her… I told her to take the bed. She laughed at me and said we should share. Share, Eth, like it was nothing." Like he was no threat, just like Lance said. "You know what she's wearing right now?"

"What?"

"My shirt," he said, his stomach clenching as he relived the horror. "A tiny pair of thong panties and my shirt… She only did like two buttons over her chest…" His arm rose to straighten at his side. "There she is, the woman I want, in my bed…" He clenched his teeth. "In tiny thong panties and my shirt."

"If she didn't bring anything to sleep in, maybe she wants you to make a move. Seems like a signal to me."

He sank back against the wall. "You don't know her," he said and sighed. Being forgetful was just her way. "She doesn't play games like that."

"Did you get in bed with her?"

"Yeah," he said, his brows rising. "And she started talking about how horny she was and how that meant her period was right around the corner. How much is a guy supposed to take?" Ethan laughed. "I waited 'til she fell asleep and got up. I'm glad you think this is fucking funny."

"I'm sorry, boss, I am. But this is exactly the kind of luck you have in romance. In business, you shine, it's like you can't fail. But in love? You always meet the wrong woman or the wrong one gets her hooks in. Only you could meet the right woman and not be able to have her because of something like this."

"She wouldn't go to the press," he said, his hand on his heart, checking it was still in there. In any way that really counted, he'd already handed it over to the woman sleeping in his bed. "I don't know I'd care even if she did." But that wasn't it. Wasn't the reason he hadn't been honest. He faced the truth that was only just processing. "If I tell her the truth, it will hurt her. I can't do it. I can't win. The lying is wrong and hurting her, but if I tell her…"

"You might feel better, but it won't do her any good." His friend's sympathy was some consolation. "How did you get her into your bed anyway? Doesn't she think you live with Lance?"

"I told her we broke up."

"Another lie," Ethan said. "Is that a good plan?"

"I'm not dating him. It's less of a lie than telling her I am."

"Why did you break up?"

"I just keep telling her I don't want to talk about it," he said, knowing that wouldn't fly forever. "She asked me tonight if there was someone else involved. And, yes, there fucking is: her."

"Telling her that won't help," Ethan said, then sighed. "If you tell her, she'll hate you forever or you don't tell her and fake being gay for the rest of your life."

"I thought today would be the last time. I told myself to go to the coffee shop, see her one last time, and then draw a line under it."

"And somehow she ended up in your bed."

"She's being a friend. She thinks I'm going through a breakup."

Ethan sucked in a breath, which wasn't encouraging. "Which makes things worse. As she's being extra nice, you're getting deeper into the lie."

That was the point he'd already made. "What do I do?"

Silence lingered before Ethan stuttered. "I… I don't think you've ever asked me that. Of the three of us, you're the one who is always sure. The one who always comes up with a plan."

"I'm asking now."

Except his friend said nothing. Because there was no answer. Any way he looked at it, he was screwed. Rainie would get hurt if he told the truth or if he just abandoned her and disappeared. She valued loyalty, and he was proving himself to be a bad investment. He was spending her kindness with no way to return the favor, no way to soften the blow. And there was no way out.

TWELVE

MOVIES WERE NOT IN short supply. With streaming services at their disposal too, Rainie had lined up a whole host of definitely not sappy movies to get them through the nights.

All week, she'd only been three places: work, the coffee shop, and Alex's apartment. Some people might feel intruded upon. Not Alex. His willingness to have her around was a sure sign he needed a distraction from his breakup. Especially since he still met her every day at twelve thirty for lunch. They were temporarily living together and didn't need to meet in the middle of the day, but he was always there.

Breakups were never easy. Alex had to be struggling with the loss of Lance, yet he didn't talk about it. If he wanted to come out whole at the other end of this trauma, he'd need to work through his issues.

That Thursday, another movie night was in the cards. Mixed drinks waited, and the movie hung on pause, ready to play. Alex was in the shower and the pizza was on the kitchen counter getting cold. He'd been in there a while. She left the couch and went over to knock on the bathroom door.

"Pizza's here," she called through the wood.

Grazing her knuckle up and down, she worried for him. When she was in his shower, she didn't even close the door, much less lock it. Alex did both. That wouldn't be anything to do with her being heterosexual and everything to do with him needing some privacy. The shower spray could hide any multitude of shames. Not that he should be ashamed. If he needed a good cry, she'd embrace being a shoulder for him, but it didn't seem he was the type. Some people preferred to keep that kind of vulnerability to themselves. Still, she ached for the pain he must be going through.

No response. Had he heard her? Was he okay in there?

Her phone rang in the bedroom. She ran through and grabbed it up from Alex's charging dock, not surprised to read Gwenie's name.

"Hey, sweetie," she said, sitting on the edge of the bed.

"He did it again," Gwen growled, her anger right there on the surface. "The asshole."

She frowned. "Bryan?"

"Who else?"

She hadn't needed more than one guess. In her friendship group, there was only one person capable of making Gwen angry to such a degree. They'd lived through it so many times. If only there was a way to get Tia out of the destructive relationship. To make her see how bad Bryan was for her.

"He broke up with her?"

"Again. Yeah, and she's all over the place," Gwen said. "I don't know what to do. She won't stop crying."

"You need me to bring wine?" she asked, torn

between supporting Alex and the similar, more dramatic, need of Tia half a dozen blocks over. "Alex is in the shower."

"Bring him too. Maybe he can talk some sense into her."

Shaking her head, she looked toward the door. "He's going through his own stuff. I don't want him to be alone, but I don't want to break him either. Let me talk to him. If he's okay with being by himself tonight, I'll come home… I'm sure he'll say he will be, but to get a proper read, I need to look at him while I ask."

"Okay," Gwen said and exhaled. "I don't know how much more of this she can take. The guy just loves it, putting her through this shit. I'd love to just—"

"I know what you'd love to do; I'd love to do it too. She deserves much more. Much, much more. Being with him is just so damaging. We pick up the pieces every single time. Yet you know he'll come swanning back into her life in a couple of days, couple of weeks, and she'll take him back."

Gwen growled in frustration. "Someone needs to kick him in the 'nads. Hard… and often."

Breathing out a sort of laugh, she appreciated how much her friend cared. "I'll talk to Alex and call you back… or just be home. Soon."

"Thanks, Rainie. She needs you."

"I know, thanks for calling."

After hanging up, she sank back to lie on the bed, clutching the phone to her chest. Relationships were so difficult. They caused so much pain. Were they even worth it? Being with a guy, just for the sake of being with a guy, was a ridiculous notion. She was an optimist. Wasn't she? Happily ever after was possible. It was… right? Relationships could be built on trust and respect. Anything else just wouldn't stack up.

Life really was only for the strong.

The bathroom door opened. She sat up just in time to see Alex enter the bedroom, hair wet, small white towel wrapped around his hips.

"Whoa, boy," she said, grinning as she leaped up, leaving her phone behind.

"What's up?" he asked, heading for the closet.

"Wait up a second," she said, rushing over to grab his wrist to draw him back into the bedroom. "You are hot, baby."

His brows rose. "'Scuse me?"

She laughed, opening her hand to press it against his defined pec. "You're always on the phone, rushing over to your desk, dealing with paperwork. I thought that's what you did all day."

"That is what I do all day."

Tipping her head back, she showed her smile. "You sneak down to the gym to work out too though, don't you?" When his somber expression darkened, she laughed and squeezed his arm. "Don't worry, hottie, I'll keep your secret."

Still holding his arm in one hand, she stroked his side with the other. Inappropriate thoughts were difficult to chase away when faced with such a defined torso, such muscular arms… Shit, now she understood why he locked the bathroom door. Women could be sleazy too. It was nothing anyway. Just her subconscious fantasies reminding her conscious mind how long it had been since she got laid.

The back of his curled fingers brushed her jaw, tempting it higher. The exploration in his eyes examining her face was encouraging. Whatever she was doing there, whatever comfort she offered, it lightened the load of his heartache. For the first time, she really saw him considering the future. A compliment could go a long way with someone whose confidence had taken a knock.

"You will find it," she murmured, stepping a little

closer, resting her hands on his torso. "Sometimes life seems too hard, like maybe there's no point in facing a new tomorrow. But you will find someone to love you the way you deserve to be loved."

"Button—"

"I have to go," she said, inspired by the new aura around him. "I really wish I didn't, but Bryan's been an ass to Tia again and she's a mess." Backing away, she went to retrieve her phone from the bed. "The pizza is on the counter, and I left the bottle of tequila on the coffee table. Watch the movie and eat something." She went back to take his hand. "Call me before you go to sleep." Doubting herself, she squeezed her lips together. "I can stay if you need me to stay."

He didn't immediately answer. Was he worried? She fully expected him to say she could go but had to rely on instinct whether it was smart.

"I'll be fine," he said, curling his fingers around the ends of her hair. "You should go be with Tia."

"Promise?" she asked. He nodded and managed a smile. Typical of Alex to put on a brave face. "I told you Bryan was an asshole, didn't I? Now he's coming between us too."

"We shouldn't let him make a habit of that."

"I can come back, if she falls asleep."

"You have work tomorrow," he said. "And I don't want you running around the city too late."

"Okay," she said. "Promise you'll call me before you go to sleep."

"I promise."

"Okay," she said, glancing around.

Where was her purse?

"I hung it up by the door," Alex said, reading her mind. "Your shoes are on the floor underneath it."

She laid a hand on his cheek. "I'd be lost without you."

Tucking her hair back behind her ear, his fingers remained there. "You've been my rock this week, Button."

"That's what you do for friends," she said, turning her head to point at her cheek. "Kiss."

On a short laugh, he descended. "Okay."

Pressing his mouth to her cheek, the way he lingered closed her eyes. Something about his mouth there, the warmth of his breath, embedded a wonder deep inside her.

When he stood straight again, it took some effort to shake that awakening off. "Be good," she said. "I'll see you at lunch tomorrow."

"Yes, you will."

Since her gym was out of commission, Alex had signed her up as a guest to use the one in his building. Just like him to be so incredibly sweet. Learning he had a gym in his building was a real coup. Few people had that luxury. It also meant that after her workout, she could use the shower in his apartment… and check in on him.

"Still okay to use your gym on Saturday?"

"Definitely."

"Thanks."

Going to the front door, she ignored the chill in her fingers as they took her purse and jacket from the hook. Alex was a good man; that was a rare thing. Finding a friend like him was a win she wouldn't take for granted. As time went on, he'd eventually get over his breakup with Lance. Which of them would need the other more then?

THIRTEEN

IN THE TWO WEEKS following the breakup, she spent more nights at Alex's than she did in her own bed. Weekends especially meant sleepovers. But hanging out there on weeknights was now the norm as well.

The frequent interruption of his work also gave him the chance to educate her on consulting. He enjoyed mansplaining, but the humor in his condescending smirk confirmed he was only hamming it up… most of the time.

Still, they met for lunch every day too. Alex was a staple, a good friend she couldn't imagine her life without.

At some point, weaning them off the sheer volume of time they spent together would be necessary if either of them ever wanted an actual romantic relationship with anyone again. Though that probably wasn't on Alex's mind yet. Whatever was on his mind, he was keeping to himself. More than two weeks had passed since the breakup and Alex still hadn't talked about it.

She did her best to be sensitive with talk of love

or romance. Any time she tried to bring up Lance or the breakup, Alex would say he didn't want to talk about it. It couldn't be healthy to block off such an important part of himself.

Alex spent so much time working. His phone rang at regular intervals and every once in a while, he'd disappear to do things on his laptop. Keeping busy, dampening and ignoring his emotions wasn't necessarily healthy, but if that was how he processed…

On another note, Bryan and Tia were back together already. No big surprise. One night, Tia snuck out of the apartment and met up with him in secret. Figured. Gwen would've blasted right through Bryan if he tried that sweet talking thing while she was within earshot.

No ring resided on Tia's finger, but the woman claimed to be happy. Why did Tia put up with it? The stress had to be taking years off her life. But it wasn't her place to judge, not explicitly anyway, just to support.

Her phone buzzed on the kitchen counter and lit up to reveal a Huddle message notification.

HOTTFORME: I'M IN TOWN. WHEN CAN WE GET TOGETHER?

Shit.

Demetri's Huddle username might be stupid, but it suited him. In more ways than one.

Her phone logged into the social media app automatically. She hadn't used it for months.

"What's that?" Gwen asked, peeking over her shoulder. "Oh my God! No!"

"What?" she asked, putting the phone facedown on their kitchen island.

"You are not going out with him. You're not hooking up with him. Just no. No, Rainie."

Inhaling, she turned to hop up and sit on the counter. "What harm can it do to say hey?"

Gwen was filling her infuser, so it could do its thing in the fridge overnight before her friend took it to the office the next day.

It was a shame that on one of her rarer nights at home, Tia hadn't been around. Catching up with Gwen was nice, but her concern for their other roommate remained high.

"Haven't we just gone through this with Tia?"

"This is so not the same as that."

"It so is," Gwen said. "What do you plan to do? Go for dinner? Drinks? You just want sex?"

"It has been a while." Her friend peeked over her shoulder to glare. "What? What is wrong with getting laid?"

"Nothing," Gwen said, chopping her fruit again.

"Women are allowed to enjoy sex in this century."

"Yeah, in some circles. Sex is great, but why do you have to do it with your sleazy ex?"

"Dem might not be… cerebral—"

"Might not be conscious half the time you mean," Gwen said. As expected, Gwen did not apologize for her judgment. "You can do so much better than him. You need someone who excites you, but someone who's actually engaged. I doubt Dem could answer ten questions about you."

"Who cares about talking? I have you and Alex for talking."

"And if Dem wants to start things up again?"

Okay, that could be awkward.

"We'll invite him here."

"Then you won't have a choice. You'll have to have sex with him."

Sex sounded like a good idea in her head, but she

didn't want things to get messy. Could be she looked at him again and the spark just wasn't there. The guy was hot, no doubting that, was that enough?

"I don't *need* to have sex with him."

"Inviting your ex to your apartment is basically inviting him into your bed. You don't have kids or pets to discuss. You don't even share the same circle of friends. It's a booty call."

Turning over her phone, the message glowed up at her. Was that Dem's point? He just wanted to screw? If they did it once, did that obligate her to be his piece of ass on speed dial? Probably one of many a guy like Demetri could have lined up and waiting.

Sex was great, but not if it got in the way of time with her friends. Did she have time for a fuck buddy?

"You're safer going out," Gwen said. "Somewhere public. Take Alex."

She laughed. "I can't just take another guy on a date with us. How awkward would that be?" She sat straighter. "Unless you want to come too."

"Come with you?" Gwen went to wash her hands. "You, me, and Dem?"

She hopped off the counter to snag the towel and toss it to her friend. "And Alex."

"The four of us? Like a double date." Gwen grinned. "You know I've been desperate to meet Alex."

"And this is your chance. I'll tell Dem to meet us somewhere. At some bar. You and Alex can get a read on him. Is it just sex he wants? Does he want to start us up again? Do we have chemistry?"

"Okay, but don't expect me to be nice to the guy. I'll aim for civil, be grateful if I hit it."

"It's a good way to get Alex back out there too. No pressure of something romantic, just being out in a social setting, relaxing back into the rhythm of it."

"I'm in if Alex is," Gwen said, screwing on her

lid to put the bottle in the fridge. "What do you think he'll say?"

"He'll support me," she said.

Even if he was reluctant, she'd find a way to talk him into it. She wouldn't ever let anything bad happen to him. If they went out and he hated it or got upset, she'd call the whole thing off. Her friend's wellbeing would come first. Always.

FOURTEEN

ALEX HAD PUT UP with her strange ways thus far. There was a chance he'd play along. But with his recent breakup still looming large, it wouldn't be fair to push him. If they went out, one of two things would happen. Either he'd snap out of his denial, or the night out would send him into a downward spiral of self-destruction. High stakes. Would giving him an opportunity to face the truth help him out in the long run?

Hurrying over to their coffee shop table, she planted both hands on his shoulders from behind to bow and kiss his cheek before sitting down. "Okay, I need you to hear me out."

"That's an ominous start," he said.

She looped her purse strap off over her head to dump it on the table. "What are you doing this Saturday?"

"Uh…" he started, picking up his cup. "Working until you come in and steam up my bathroom."

She smiled. "How would you feel about a date?" His cup stopped before it got to his lips. Grabbing for his free hand, she didn't want him to jump to any conclusions. "Don't worry, it's not a real date, not really..." She frowned. "Not exactly."

"Babe—"

"It's Gwenie. She really, really wants to meet you and—"

"Your roommate?" he asked, the picture of shock. "You want to set me up on a date with your roommate?"

Nodding, she squeezed his forearm with both hands. "You don't have to worry about any awkward moments. She knows you're not interested in women, so—"

"Rainie—"

"Demetri is back in town," she explained. "He wants to go out. Gwenie isn't sure it's a good idea. We talked about inviting him to our place, but my ex in my apartment..." On a semi-groan, her head tilted side-to-side back and forth, weighing up the possibilities. "That's risky. If he thinks sex is guaranteed... I'm not ruling anything out, we might go to bed but—"

"Rainie!"

He'd learned a quick, sharp exclamation was the only way to interrupt the rhythm of an impending rant. Laying a hand on his cheek for a quick second, she appreciated him and put a finger to her own lips, showing she'd stay silent while he said his piece.

His eyes flicked back and forth between hers. What was he searching for? Permission? She smiled.

"Babe, I don't want to date your roommate and I don't think you should go out with Demetri."

"Well, not alone," she said. "That's the point of the date. We'll double date... I never thought about how great it was to have a guy friend. Now you and Gwenie can come with us and make your own assessment. At the end of the night—"

"My answer is already no," he said. "I don't need to meet the guy to know you shouldn't be opening that door again."

If they were a little further from his relationship with Lance, she might use him as an example.

Vague shouldn't open any raw wounds. "Isn't there anyone from your past? Anyone from your life, that if they called you up and asked you out, you wouldn't be in the least bit curious?"

Again, he stared into her. What was with the staring? A twitch in his jaw betrayed him. He was thinking of someone. Someone specific she'd bet.

"He didn't make you happy," Alex said. "You told me that and said we should all strive for happiness. This guy had his chance. Now it's time for the next guy to have a shot with you."

She snorted. "If you haven't noticed, they're not exactly lining up around the block. Plenty of guys ask me out, but I'm picky. Maybe too much."

And she was high maintenance. Expensive too. When was the last time she'd had to line up for a coffee or pay for one?

"Why do I have to say that?"

"You're one of my best friends," she said, raising her cup. "Should we start a kitty for this? I've been a complete freeloader in here."

"Why the change of heart?" he asked, ignoring her question. "You want him back? What? Did he sell you some line about changing?"

"I don't know that Demetri is capable of change. He's not the kind of guy interested in personal growth."

"But you want another chance at a future with him?"

"There's something nostalgic about spending time with former lovers, don't you think?"

"Nostalgic?"

"Yeah, you know how he'll touch you, what his kiss will feel like. There's comfort in that." Sliding her hand down his wrist, she parted his fingers with hers to link them together. "You know what it's like when you have that connection, when you feel the sparks, when you can just relax and feel. You don't have to worry or plan or be self-conscious… You can just trust and hand yourself over to someone else and be trusted with their pleasure… Time stops…" She breathed out as her eyes sank shut. "I need that. I need time to stop, Alex."

When her eyes opened, there was something intense in his probing expression.

A score of seconds passed before he spoke. "When and where," he grumbled, surrendering to her request.

A true friend, Alex was vital to her life. Honest and loyal. On the day they met, she trashed his pants, but she couldn't be sorry her clumsiness had brought them together.

***

ALEX WAS WAITING at the bar when she and Gwen arrived that Saturday. With her friend's hand in hers, she pulled her across the room to him. Like he sensed them, he turned to smile at her before they got anywhere close.

"Beautiful," Alex said, leaning in to kiss her cheek. "I got you both the rosé."

Her favorite. "Thank you," she said, pulling Gwen front and center. "Alex, this is Gwenie. Gwendolyn, Alex."

"Wow," her friend said, accepting his handshake. "You said he was hot. You didn't say he was GQ hot. Shit, are you sure you're gay?"

"Gwenie," Rainie hissed, putting an arm around her waist to direct her in close to the bar. "I told you not to do that."

Gwen picked up her glass. "For a woman so adept at not thinking before she speaks, you expect a lot from the rest of us."

She raised her glass to Alex and then Gwen. "Let's toast to friendship."

Her friends were polite enough to raise their glasses and drink. It didn't take long for Alex to lower his and prop an elbow on the bar to scan the space.

"So is the creep here yet?"

Gwen laughed. "The creep? That's what you call him? Demetri is never on time, Alex. Never, ever. I like this guy, Rainie." She thrust out her chest. "Look at my boobs. You feel nothing?"

"Stop," she said, pulling her friend aside to put herself between them. "Leave him alone; he's doing us a favor." Leaning against him, she laid a forearm on his chest to peek up at him. "I'm sorry. I promised this would be easy."

Alex tucked her hair behind her ear. "This was never going to be easy, Button."

"He's not that bad," Rainie said, turning on the spot to address Gwen. "Please tell Alex that Demetri is not that bad."

"The guy is hot as sin," Gwen said, enjoying her wine. "Not exactly a conversationalist, and completely shallow."

"Oh, he's not totally shallow," Rainie said, resting a hand on Alex's forearm when it curved around her torso to ease her back against him. "You were never a fan of Demetri's."

"Never a fan of the guy who made us sit and look through his portfolio ten times a week? He spent more time and money taking his own picture than anyone else ever did." Gwen twisted to face her. "How many times have we sat up late, drinking our wine…" She raised her glass. "Talking about what we want for our futures and from the guys we wish we could find?"

"A zillion," Rainie said like it was an accurate number.

"And Demetri's name never comes up. He is not your ideal man."

"I know. I never said he was," Rainie said, enjoying the texture of the fabric under her fingertips. "We disagree on just about everything and want different things from a relationship."

"So what are we doing here?"

"You don't have to be here," Rainie said. "You didn't want me to meet him alone."

"Because then you'd have sex with him and spend the next two weeks hating yourself."

"I am capable of spending time with a man and not sleeping with him," she said, pushing back against the friend behind her. "Ask Alex. We sleep in the same bed all the time." She raised her chin. "Have we had sex?"

"That's not the same," Gwen said. "So if it's not about sex, why are we here?"

"I didn't say it wasn't about sex," Rainie said. "I'm open to it. Maybe it's about sex. I'm horny… I've been horny for like a month straight. Dem wanted to meet, and we were a couple, why should I ignore his invitation just because we're not sleeping together every night? If it was about sex for him, he could've just drunk texted me at two a.m. He knows me well enough to know I don't play games. We were together. We didn't do the long romantic seduction thing every time we got down and dirty. He knows that. If he wanted sex from me, he could just ask. I could say yes or no and…" She smiled. "We would go from there."

"You need to get out more, Rainie. Next weekend, we're hitting the bars and clubs. We need to get back in the pool." Gwen looked over her head. "You can come with us, Alex. We'll show you the nightlife."

"No," Rainie said. "It's only been a couple of weeks; Alex isn't ready for a new relationship."

"He can get laid if he wants; he doesn't have to start a relationship. It's fun, Rainie! Stop worrying about him so much." Again, Gwen looked beyond her. "She worries about you all the time."

"Oh, stop," Rainie said, linking her fingers between Alex's, tightening his hold. "I don't worry about him all the time."

"She worries about everyone all the time," Gwen muttered.

Her mouth opened because she intended to refute that. Then she spotted Demetri in the crowd. "Oh, he's here."

"Time to give me my date," Gwen said, drawing her out of Alex's embrace to take her place. "And we need more drinks."

"Order whatever you like," Alex said. "I've got it."

Breaking away, Rainie went to meet Demetri. "Hey," she said, getting his attention.

The moment his eyes landed on hers, they warmed. Still that lazy smile and those drowsy eyes. Mmm. Gwen was right, Demetri was hotter than sin.

"Shiny," Demetri said, his slow arm slithering around her shoulders to pull her close. "Goddamn, you look good."

He descended to join their mouths before she'd thought of what to say next. It wasn't about sex… or was it? Demetri was a straightforward guy; in that they'd been the same.

Seconds into seeing each other again, he was kissing her. What did she want? Did she want him to kiss her? Alex and Gwen were just across the room, she'd expected a fun evening. Standing there, experiencing his kiss, time didn't stop. Oblivion was nowhere near.

She missed Alex's arm around her waist. How could she be fixating on that? It was nuts. Demetri was giving her something Alex never could. So why was she thinking about that arm? About how her friend was there before her and Gwen. How he'd bought their drinks and offered more. Alex took care of them. He was something different, something she was getting used to. That could be dangerous. If she ever wanted to have anything resembling a stable relationship again, maybe it wouldn't be so bad to lean a little less on her coffee shop buddy.

FIFTEEN

JUST A COUPLE OF HOURS into the evening, Demetri suggested they take the party somewhere private. It was possible he meant her bedroom; she chose not to interpret it that way.

Her ex only had a hotel room. If she invited them back to her apartment, Demetri would stay the night for sure.

As though he somehow divined her dilemma, Alex gave them the option of his apartment. It was smaller than her and Gwen's, but at least it didn't come with a carnal guarantee to Demetri.

Alex poured everyone drinks while Rainie gave Gwen and Demetri the brief tour. She left them on the small balcony with their drinks and went back inside to get her own.

Their host was pouring wine into her glass, concentrating on the task much more intently than necessary.

"Are you mad?" she asked when he put down the bottle and handed over the glass without looking at her.

"I'm sorry. I didn't know he'd want to socialize in private."

"He wants to socialize in private with you. What the hell was that kiss when you went to meet him?"

Her friend had been frosty most of the night. At least now he'd admitted why.

"I didn't know he was going to do that," she stated.

"You didn't seem to mind," he said, surprising her with his sarcastic anger. "I'd say you've already decided what you want to do with him. Why drag Gwen and me along? Why do we need to see it?"

Glancing back over her shoulder, Gwen was frowning their way from the balcony. The sliding glass doors were still open a crack, and Alex's volume wasn't all that discreet.

"Would you...?" Putting down the glass, she went around to snag his wrist and trailed him into the bedroom, closing the door behind them. "I didn't decide, okay?" she hissed. "In fact, if you really want to know, tonight has been absolutely excruciating. The second he touched me I knew he wasn't what I wanted. If I could've turned around and walked out of there in that minute, I would have."

"You could have. Gwen and I would've supported you."

"That's not the point," she said, combing her fingers through her hair. "It's a mess. Everything's a mess."

"What's a mess? What are you talking about?"

Anxiety grew to a heavy, agitated ball in the pit of her stomach. It had been there all night, churning her up.

Pacing across the room and back, the quickening of her heart only made it worse. "I'm stuck in this rut, in this ridiculous place of nothingness. I guess I thought if

I spent some time with Demetri, I could go back to how I felt when we were together. You know, happy and just… I don't know. I think I made it all up." She kept on pacing. "Demetri and I weren't happy. I was never happy with him or his lifestyle or what we were. He kissed me tonight and I felt nothing. Less than nothing.

"I literally stood there to be polite. Who does that? Let's someone kiss them just to be polite? I was standing there, wishing I could be anywhere else. No—" An ironic snicker vibrated her throat. "Not anywhere else. Back at the bar, with you. I wanted to be at the bar with your arm around me. That's where I was happy. Where everything felt normal… natural." Stopping in the center of the room, she groaned and tipped her head all the way back. "Why do I always sabotage myself like this? In my head, I made me and Demetri into something we weren't. All I want is something simple. Why can't I just meet a nice guy? A guy I can be comfortable with? A guy who wants what I want? It shouldn't be difficult. I'm not that high maintenance, am I? I'm happy with you. Why can't I find a guy like you who listens when I talk? Who makes me feel safe and appreciated and valued?

"You're the first man who ever made me feel unique without making me feel like a freak. I just want this. You touch me and hold my hand or put an arm around me and everything feels okay, but it still touches me, you know? Deep down inside." Groaning again, her head descended so she could look at him. "I'm sorry. I'm being ridiculous and inappropriate. Please don't think I'm suggesting anything. I'm just trying to say… everything between us has always been so easy and you mean so much to me. I don't have to be polite or worried with you. You accept me. And you make me feel… I don't know…" Her hands splayed on her belly. "Something… I feel you and that's what I want in love. I want to feel it, like I feel you."

Judging from the deep crease between his brows, her friend not only didn't understand what she was saying, he might actually be mad too.

Words. She needed words. To apologize. Something to…

He strode across the room and scooped both hands around her face, angling it upward. He'd been kissing her for more than a second when—shit, he was kissing her. The sudden explosion of delight in her gut was the first real wake-up call. Holding her head in a sure grip, he pushed harder, heating her lips with his certainty as his tongue sought refuge in her. Something completely involuntary overcame her. Her lips relaxed, granting him the sanctuary he needed. She gave herself to the sweet, arousing satisfaction of pure belonging.

That moan in his mouth—it came from her throat. From her. Oh, he felt so good that her vocal cords were announcing her involuntary approval.

It was good. Too good. Too exciting and yet too natural.

He was kissing her. Would he keep on kissing her, then and forever?

Mm, the bed was right there. His bed. His. Him. Alex. She couldn't sleep with Alex. Her friend. Her gay friend. What the fuck was she doing?

She pushed him away, frowning in question at the cautious conviction looking back at her. "That was about Lance," she whispered, searching for a reason, but Alex was already shaking his head. "You miss him, and you think maybe if—"

"No, Rainie," he murmured, turning his hand to caress her cheek with the back of his fingers. "It's about you, baby. It's about us."

She shook her head, clinging to his shirt. "You can't wish your sexuality away, despite what certain groups in society will tell you. You know that. You hurt now because you just lost Lance—would you stop shaking your head at me and why are you smiling? This is so sad! I'm ranting, putting my shit on you. I don't know who kissing me was supposed to comfort, me or you, but you're gay and you can't—"

"I'm straight."

Say what? She'd sort of steamrollered over him. He couldn't have said… "Excuse me?"

Alex was still smiling, stroking her face. "I'm straight, baby. Always have been."

Her confused frown joined the alarm building in her gut. "You're… what? But Lance—"

"Is an idiot friend who took a prank too far," he said. "I'm hetero, Button, all the way… and I'm in love with you."

Her eyes flared. Straight. Alex was… She couldn't process it. Her mind, her body just wouldn't accept… Their friendship flashed through her mind's eye in one blink. The things she'd said to him. The things they'd done… snuggling on the couch, sharing the bed. She didn't even close the door when she showered anymore.

Alex was straight. Anger flashed hot. The lying, manipulative… He was a sick fuck who'd been playing with her for weeks!

Shoving out of his arms, she didn't recognize the vigilant guy, showing her his palms like he wanted to calm her.

"Baby… Hear me out…" She couldn't hear it. Not more lies. She'd never be able to trust him again. "I'll explain everything, just—"

Storming straight past him, out of the bedroom, they were done whether he knew it or not. Nothing else needed to be said.

"Gwenie!" she called to her friend as she grabbed the wineglass to guzzle its contents.

"Rainie," Alex said from behind her.

She only looked at her roommate as the duo came in from outside.

"What's wrong?" Gwen asked, obviously sensing something.

Not that her mood was subtle. The lying piece of…

"We're leaving," Rainie said without looking at either male.

She went out into the hall; Gwen would follow. Her friend wouldn't loiter. Her real friend would support her. Not like…

Alex. Straight. The world was upside down.

SIXTEEN

ALL WEEKEND, SHE'D flip-flopped on whether to ever go back to the coffee shop where they'd met. Anger took her to it on the Monday. The guy might be lying scum, but she wouldn't let anyone run her out of a place she loved.

Ignore the urge to look at their table. He didn't exist. It didn't exist. Like their friendship had never happened, she joined the line. Oh, they had a new sweet treat. Would she eat that before or after the cinnamon bun in her fantasy feast?

"Rainie." His voice speared her with pain. Block him out. Focus on the cakes. "Babe, we need to talk about this." He'd called her babe a dozen times. In the past, it hadn't stung, not like it did in that moment. "Please, give me a chance to explain."

Explain. It was almost laughable. He'd lied to her. Let her believe the lie. Taken advantage of her trust. The list of grievances just went on and on.

"Hey, guy, there's a line," the guy behind them said.

"Do I look like I'm waiting for coffee?" Alex

sneered at the stranger. "I'm talking to my girl."

Which she wasn't and never would be.

Getting to the front of the line, she smiled at the server. "Hey, Chuck. Skinny mocha frap, no whip, please."

"Skinny?" Chuck said. "Guilty weekend?"

Conceding a laugh, it was easier to ignore the guy in her periphery when she had someone else to talk to. "You could say that."

"Rainie," Alex beseeched her again.

Her smile flattened. Restraining her anger wasn't easy. What she really wanted to do was spin around and release a tirade of truth that he definitely wouldn't appreciate.

"Is this guy bothering you?" the guy behind in the line asked.

"What the hell is it to you?" Alex snapped. "You're bothering her."

"Rainie," Chuck asked. "You okay?"

Community wasn't as dead as the media might have society believe.

"I'm fine," she said. "I just ignore it."

"I think you should leave her alone," the line guy said.

"I think *you* should leave *me* alone," Alex replied to him.

"You're harassing her."

Rainie showed Chuck another smile and left the men in the line to go to the end of the counter and wait for her coffee. At the milk cart, she snagged a few napkins. When she turned back to put them in her purse, Alex was right there in front of her.

"We have to talk," Alex said. "Please, just give me a chance to explain."

With emotion bubbling so close to the surface, it was difficult to restrain herself. Hence why it wouldn't be a good idea to look him in the eye. Except she did. His contrition was right there, as potent as her rage. It would be too easy to give in. Too easy to give him what he wanted. Since they'd met, he hadn't cared about her wants. If he had, he wouldn't have lied to her every minute they were together.

She wanted to slap him. To scream at him. To punish him for hurting her. Damn, she hated that he'd hurt her. Almost as much as she hated the tears gathering on her lashes. The moment he saw them, he inhaled, his whole body growing as he filled his lungs.

"Baby," he murmured, raising his curled fingers to her cheek. She recoiled before he could make contact. "I won't give up on this. I'll keep showing up until you hear me. You don't know how determined I can be, but you will…" She didn't reply. "What happened to the Rainie who doesn't hold grudges?"

Yes, she'd said that. But she'd also told him she was angry and sad before getting over whatever had happened. And that was in romantic relationships. She'd never had a male friend devastate her so completely. Even processing what had happened was near impossible. What would the long-term impact of his actions be? Would she be able to trust any new man who came into her life? She'd be more suspicious of new people now for sure.

"I don't want to lose you," he said, edging even closer. "I can't lose you, Rainie Tait. Please. Whatever it takes… You want me to beg?" Taking a long step back, he swallowed and opened his arms. "I'll drop to my goddamn knees right here if that's what it takes."

When his knee bent and it looked like he really might, she leaped forward, laying a hand on his chest. "Don't." Damn. Why had she touched him? Seeing her hand there against him, she squirmed and took it away. "What do you want?"

"A chance," he said. "To talk. There are things you have to know before you decide to hate me… I know you hate me now—"

"I don't hate you," she admitted. "I should. I want to. But I can't give you that power. You're not the man I thought you were."

"Talk," he said, his fingers grazing hers. "Please. I just want to talk."

They could go to their table and she could listen. But in that public place, she wouldn't be able to react, not how she wanted to react. She couldn't trust herself to keep a lid on her emotions.

Seeing him again had been a possibility, but she hadn't figured out what she wanted to say or how she really felt about what had happened. How she felt about the truth.

"Rainie!" the barista called out, putting her drink on the counter for her.

"I'll come over after work," she said, her tone flat.

Surprise became shaded with hope. "My place?" She nodded. "Okay." He breathed. "Thank you, baby. Shit… thank you."

"I'm making no promises," she said. "I'll come over, listen, and if I tell you we're done… I get ownership of the coffee shop twelve thirty to one thirty."

His smile twisted her up inside. "Okay. That's fair. Thank you, Button."

He tried to touch her again, but she pulled back, showing him a glare before retrieving her coffee. After work. That gave her just a few short hours to come up with something to say.

SEVENTEEN

GETTING TO HIS FRONT DOOR? Easy peasy. Knocking? Not so easy. She didn't want to be a liar and had agreed to be there… But she couldn't do it. How could she go in there, to a happy and safe place, and face his deception?

Alex wasn't Alex.

Never in all of their association had she experienced hurt like he'd caused her on Saturday night. What was he going to say? How could he explain away his betrayal? What would make it right?

Standing in the hallway wasn't achieving anything. The quicker she knocked, the quicker she could leave.

She knocked.

That was it. Done.

A flash later, the door opened, and he was there. Phone to his ear. "I've gotta go." Without giving whoever was on the other end time to respond, he hung up. "Hi."

"I can go," she said, gesturing back down the

hall. "If you're busy—"

"When the other option is you, I'm never busy," he said, stepping backward, opening the door further. "Come in."

Despite being exactly the same, the apartment felt different. Like a new place, not familiar or comforting, but neither was the man closing the door behind her. More starched than usual, his tension was obvious. Did he think she'd go nuts?

If she did, he'd deserve it. But that wasn't the point.

"So…" she said, taking the strap of her purse off over her head to dump the bag on the counter. "What do you want to say?"

"For starters, thank you for coming," he said, going to the fridge. "Do you want a drink?"

Yes, like an entire bottle of wine in the next three seconds. "No. I want to get through this and go home."

"Rainie," he said, softening. "Baby, I'm sorry. I'll keep on saying it. I'm sorrier than… I'm sorry."

"Is that it?" she asked. "You already said that." Purse in hand, she went for the front door. "I didn't need to come all the way over here to—"

He intercepted her fingers before they got to the handle. The moment his skin touched hers, she stopped talking. That warmth, that touch, she'd had that for six weeks, had the man she thought he was so close to her and never once considered doubting him.

"Why did you do it?" she asked, blinking her attention from his fingers as they tried to link themselves with hers. "Why me? Why would you lie—"

"I didn't know," he said, surprising her. "I didn't know about the phone call the day we met. I didn't find out you thought that… I didn't know until the day Lance showed up here." She frowned. "When I came back, and you were here with him… I didn't know until after you walked out."

"You didn't know?" she asked. He shook his head. "Who is Lance?"

"A friend. We've known each other for years. He's an idiot. But… he didn't mean to hurt you. I'm not making excuses for him, but he didn't know how I felt about you. How could he have known?"

When he took her hand, she was too immersed in trying to figure things out to object. "So he just goes around lying to random women about you and you're okay with that?"

"No, I'm not okay with it. I haven't spoken to him since he left here. I can't stand to hear his voice. I want to fucking tear him apart."

One of his oldest friends, and he'd cut him out. What should she do? What should she say? What did it all mean?

At a careful pace, Alex drew her away from the door, over to the couch. She dumped her purse on the kitchen island as they passed. If they were going to talk, really talk, it made sense for them to sit down and figure it out.

"You hurt me," she said once they were both seated, facing each other.

"I know, and I won't forgive myself for that."

"Do you understand?" she asked. "I thought you were my friend."

"I am," he said. When he took her hand to his lap, she pulled it away. "Rainie, please, we have to figure this out… I can't lose you."

She shook her head. "I don't know who you are. I know nothing about you. We weren't friends. We were… I don't know. You took advantage of me. Of my trust."

"I didn't know," he said.

"You just told me that you knew the day Lance

showed up here. You could've told me then; you could've told me that week. Instead…" Exhaling a laugh, she pushed the hair from her face. "Instead, you let me come over here and climb into your bed."

"I didn't…" Sealing his lips, he took a few breaths. "I know it's bad. I didn't want to hurt you. I thought if I told you…"

"At least now I understand why you didn't want to talk about the breakup. Because it didn't really happen. All this time I've been worried about your wellbeing. Worried that you were hurt or upset and bottling up how you felt, but it was a lie. You were snickering at me behind my back."

"No," he asserted, his shoulders straightening. "I struggled with this every minute. It was impossible. I didn't want to lie to you, not for a second, but I knew the minute I told you that you'd… you'd pull away from me. And I know why. I hurt you, and that was the last thing I wanted." Scooching closer, he scooped a careful hand onto her cheek. "Every minute I've spent with you, I've fallen deeper… Baby, Rainie, it's been agony to want you so bad and think that… to never have a chance with you."

"Is that why you told me?" she asked, toeing off her shoes to pull her legs up onto the seat at her side. "For sex? You thought you'd tell me, and I'd just shrug it off and fall into bed with you? You'd sacrifice everything I thought we had for a potential orgasm or two?"

"No," he said, shaking his head. His eyes narrowed. "You know me, Rainie. You know I would never treat you that way."

She pushed his hand away from her face. "I thought you would never lie to me. No, I thought my Alex would never lie to me. You, whoever you are, I don't know you at all."

"Everything between us was real. What you felt, you told me on Saturday that you felt something for me. That was real."

"I felt something for my friend," she said, enunciating the words. "That was about security and care. That was about the love I had for my friend, for the security I felt because I trusted you. I won't ever be able to trust you again."

"You will," he said. "Because I will never lie to you, about anything, never again. You have my word, and that's not something I give lightly."

"Last week I didn't think you'd lie to me, and it turned out everything was a lie."

"No," he said. "One thing you thought about me was a lie. Just one…"

Except his tone sort of trailed off and his focus drifted toward the television. Not exactly the most confidence inspiring move.

But no way, nu-uh. She wasn't letting him get away with that.

Getting closer, she put a hand on his cheek to bring his attention back around. "Alex?"

There was a brief moment of nothing, then his jaw moved to grind his teeth and the set of his brow changed.

"Xander," he said, widening her eyes in question. "Most people call me Xander… And it's not Payne either, it's Gauge. Xander Gauge."

Shock relaxed her arm as her fingers slipped from his jaw. "Oh my God."

"Lance and I made a deal… I broke up with the woman I was seeing, which led to a discussion about my relationships… About the kind of relationships I had and the women I had them with." What the hell was this? When would the hits stop coming? She couldn't believe it, couldn't take it all in. "What I do prevents me from dedicating myself to a woman in the way she deserves… I say that but it's an excuse. Work gave me the excuse to put romance and my personal life on the back burner. Have you ever heard of Venture International Incorporated?" Her response was a loose shake of her head. "That's not a surprise, most people haven't. We're an umbrella corporation, basically the parent company to a vast number of other companies and brands."

"Venture…" she breathed out the word.

"Yeah," he said. "Seven, is what we call it colloquially. V-I-I. Investments and acquisitions are what we do. We buy smaller companies and turn them into bigger ones or merge them with current operations. We also buy ailing larger companies, those who have lucrative assets or valuable intellectual property."

It was like her head was underwater. "You're not a consultant… You work for this Venture?"

"I own this Venture," he said, another shot of contrition in his gaze. "When I was a teenager, a friend and I created some software… basically an algorithm that read metadata and organized it efficiently… It was more sensitive than anything on the market. Boring. Uninteresting… Until the big leagues got wind of it… There was a bidding war and they eventually bought it."

"They bought your software."

"For twenty-four million dollars."

"Oh, wow," she said, the impact of that truth blowing some of her stupor away. "You're a millionaire?"

As his mouth opened, the flick of his gaze to hers was suspicious. "The following year, the company who bought it updated their products with my tweaked software… Their turnover was in the billions. Money like most people can't imagine… It pissed me off. I understood I didn't have their reach or their development facilities. I couldn't have used the software to the same effect, but I decided then I wasn't going to be the guy bought out… I was going to be the buyer."

Curling her arm, she rested her head on it against the back of the couch. "So you started Venture?"

"Used my millions to buy a school supplies company. They were in serious trouble. I got Ethan to work the numbers with me… Everyone thought I was crazy… Maybe I was, but I knew I could do it. I read the books; read everything I could get my hands on… This was long before I got my MBA. I turned it around."

"You did?"

"Provistock."

Wait… her head rose from her arm. "We use Provistock. Everyone uses their stationary… They make… everything. You own Provistock?"

"We created it. Pulled it out of near bankruptcy, turned it around, rebranded, gave it new life… That's what I do. We turn companies around and merge them with other assets or sell them on."

"My God," she said, relaxing her head again. "You own Provistock."

He smiled, catching a loose section of her hair from her temple to tuck it back into her locks. "I own a lot of things."

"So…" she said on a sigh, curious about the smile in his eyes. "You're a heterosexual millionaire who buys up companies to increase your empire."

His brows went up. "Billionaire, but that's not important. We invest too, give start-up money to budding companies." He seemed happy to just gloss over that shocking first revelation. "And we set up the Summit Sponsorship. The scheme allows companies who wouldn't usually have access to vast sums and elite professional expertise to get up and running."

"And you take a cut?"

"Sometimes… And sometimes we take a hit."

"If they don't make money?"

"That doesn't often happen. Usually, it's caused by something unforeseen."

"Unforeseen like what?" she asked.

"Fraud. Death."

"Wow. People have the audacity to die before they make money for you?"

One side of his mouth rose higher than the other. "It's inconsiderate, but I don't blame them for it," he said, tilting closer. "In fact, in cases like that, Venture will either buy out remaining partners or settle the losses, depending on the situation."

Out of her comfort zone, she cringed at her own ignorance. "I don't know if that's generous or you're duping me into thinking you're nicer than you are."

"No more lies, Button."

His fingertips slid up and down her leg. Their eyes locked; she couldn't move or look away.

"I don't know Xander Gauge."

"Xander Gauge is an idiot. He got drawn into a stupid agreement without thinking about how it could hurt the other people involved."

"What is this agreement?" she asked, recalling the deal with Lance he'd mentioned.

"It stemmed from his belief that women only date me for money. I travel a lot and I haven't always been the most attentive guy in relationships, but women don't complain… Usually, within a few months, they're talking commitment and marriage and… It was Lance's theory that no real woman would put up with me, that they wouldn't want me for me if I couldn't butter them up with diamonds and charge accounts."

"Do you date teenagers?"

He laughed. "No… But he wasn't wrong. What I had with the women in my past wasn't real. I knew that the minute I met you. I've cared about women before, but this… Rainie, you're a part of me. You're in my head all the time. I can't stop thinking about you… The day I found out what Lance had done, here in my apartment, before he arrived, I'd decided that I was going to… I wanted to tell you how I felt. When I learned you thought I was… In business, I know how to fix things. I know how to make decisions. I'm quick and decisive… but this, with you, I didn't have a damn clue how to fix things. When it really mattered, I couldn't decide what was right. The only person I wanted to ask, was you. What should I have done, Rainie?"

EIGHTEEN

"YOU SHOULD'VE TOLD me the truth," she said, resting her hand on his chest. "You should've walked into the coffee shop that Monday and told me it was a lie."

"You would've been hurt."

"I would've been shocked, yes, it changes the way I look at you. Changes how open I can be."

"I don't want it to," he said with a slight shake of his head, his hand traveling higher. "I want you to be honest with me, and I want you to trust me."

"Because you want to sleep with me," she said. "I can't sleep with you, Alex. I just don't..." Alex wasn't even his name. "Xander... It feels weird to say it."

"I don't mind Alex. You can call me whatever you want."

"This isn't that easy," she said, pushing his hand from her leg to get up and head into the kitchen. "In the agreement you had with Lance, you were supposed to be gay? I don't understand what that achieves."

"No," he said, twisting around to watch as she

went to retrieve wine from the fridge. "I was supposed to live as a regular Joe for ninety days. To commit myself to someone without them knowing about Venture and the money."

Frowning, she filled a glass. "You were supposed to fall in love?"

"No, it was never about love," he said, surging to his feet to join her. "They wanted me to understand what a real connection was, I guess."

"And whoever she was, you were supposed to lie to her," she said, handing him the bottle when he picked up the stopper. "You made an agreement to lie to an innocent person."

His shoulders dropped. "When you put it like that…"

"Did you ever think about her? About how she might feel after ninety days? Or did you just assume that 'surprise! I'm a billionaire' would erase all your sins? Did you plan to sleep with her? That's sexual fraud, Alex. You could get into serious trouble for that."

He put the wine in the fridge and went to his Scotch bottle in the corner. "Lance also brought up how what he'd led you to believe could be bad press."

"Is that why you didn't tell me the truth?"

"I knew you wouldn't go to the press," he said, pouring his own drink. He paused while putting the cap back on the bottle. "I didn't care if you did. If exposing the truth will ease any of your hurt, I want you to do it."

"I don't want to hurt you back, Alex. That's not the way I work."

"I know." She propped a hip on the counter as he sank into the corner. "Can you forgive me?"

Could she? It seemed so big right then, him, his life, the lie, all of it. "I don't know… I don't know how I feel about any of this… Was I her? Was I the one you planned to commit to for ninety days? Is that why Lance led me to believe you were gay? To screw with you? Make it harder for you to get laid?" He inhaled like he planned to say something but stalled, pinging her radar. "Tell me the truth. It's the only way there's even a chance of our friendship surviving this."

"I was attracted to you. From the very beginning, I was attracted to you. I'd just arrived in the city and was going to the apartment when I stopped for coffee. That's when I met you."

"You hadn't even been here yet?"

"No," he said. "We met and… I wanted to see you again. Yes, I suppose the honest answer is yes, because I intended to pursue you. That was why I asked about your lunch break. Your conversation with Lance happened while I was at the counter after we'd known each other ten minutes. Leading you to believe I was gay was his way of… messing with me. He didn't know anything about you. None of us did. None of us knew we would turn into… us."

"You didn't ask me out," she said. "There were two weeks between our meeting and the day I met Lance."

"I was enjoying getting to know you and didn't want to spook you… Maybe I wasn't honest with myself about how uncomfortable I was lying to you."

"About Venture?"

"Right. I wasn't completely honest with you… But this is all new to me, Rainie. I haven't had a genuine, organic relationship with anyone for a long time. With dating, my people get a call from some manager or PR company, or I have my people reach out to a woman I might be interested in… I don't just sit and talk with anyone… except Lance and Ethan and business dominates those conversations."

That name again. "Ethan?"

"Ethan Atwell, my CFO. Guy's a genius with

numbers… This whole thing's been a mindfuck since day one. I wanted you like I'd never wanted another woman, but Lance and Ethan were in my head. I wanted it to be real, us to be real. I didn't want it to be about the money. I didn't want you to see me as that guy; I wanted to just be myself."

"Except you didn't show me your real self," she said. "You didn't trust me or give me a chance to develop anything genuine with you because you lied the whole time."

Coming over, he put his glass on the counter and laid his hand beside it, looming over her. "Every moment between us was genuine. I didn't give you all the information, I won't deny that. But I was there, every second, with you because I wanted to be. I asked questions about you because I want to know everything about you… I waited until you were asleep in my bed then left you alone because I wanted you to have safety and comfort. I did want you those nights, every second I did, but it goes against every atom of my being to ever willingly hurt you… which is exactly why it took me so long to tell you the truth. I'm sorry I hurt you, Button. So sorry."

"Why did you tell me the truth?" she asked, replaying their kiss as she searched him for an answer. "Demetri?"

"I couldn't stand that scumbag anywhere near you, but… Seeing you in my room, scared and frustrated… You've talked so many times about what you want from a relationship, about how it's not out there, or it doesn't exist. I couldn't stand by and watch you upset, knowing there was a chance I could give it to you."

"Give what to me?"

"Everything you want."

"You mean like a private island and the Hope

Diamond?"

Despite the amused curve of his lips, his tone stayed low and slow. "If you want… Anything material you want is yours, no question. But that wasn't what I thought when imagining giving you what you wanted."

"Sex?" she asked. "You thought about sleeping with me?"

The light of satisfaction in his gaze grew. "More than you probably want to hear about right now. But it wasn't that either."

"Then what was it?"

"Truth. I got myself so tied up about the corner I was in because all I wanted to do was give you truth. Honesty. Intimacy."

Sweeping a hand up over her loose scraps of hair, the breeze tickled her neck. Aware of him everywhere, of how close he stood and the heat of his body, those parts she'd quieted around him so many times were awakening again. Instead of shutting them down, should she embrace them? The tingle between her thighs and the knots in her stomach were nothing to the tight yearning in her heavy breasts and the ache of her lips. In so many ways, it was too much. How could she trust herself?

Alex was her friend. She hadn't switched on the part of herself allowed to experience attraction to him. Even when it tried to rear up, she'd quashed it, demanding it stay dormant.

He'd hurt her. Lied. Trusting him might be impossible, no matter how many truths he told. But at least she could admit her attraction now, even if it was only to herself.

"In conning me, you took too much. You learned the secret part of me I wouldn't ever share with a partner."

"That's just it, Rainie. I don't want there to be anything you won't share with me. I'm an all in risk taker, baby. You want an absolute, complete consuming love. One that begs your surrender and gives you no less in return. I surrender myself to you, Rainie Tait. There's no part of me you can't have. No part you can't access. All of me is yours."

She shook her head. "We can't... I mean, I can't."

"That's okay," he said, his touch descending to her jaw. "I'm only telling you a truth. I don't make any demands. Whatever you decide, I'm yours. Whatever you choose."

"Xander Gauge," she whispered, testing the name on her lips. "I have to get to know him."

His nod was slow. "We can do that."

"I don't want any money. Ever."

His smile seemed to come closer. "Whatever you want, Button. Whatever you want me to approve or deny, you call the shots."

She licked her lips, sliding her hand up to his shoulder as he descended further. "Who was on the phone when I arrived?"

"Ethan."

No hesitation. He just answered the question. "Did you tell him?"

"That I kissed you. That I told you I was straight."

"Did you tell him you intended to tell me the whole truth? About Venture and Xander?"

He shook his head. "I've been thinking so much about you, been so worried, I didn't think about what I was going to tell you."

"So how do I know you mean any of this? If it's just a spontaneous impulse."

"How I feel about you... What I want from you, for us, that's not spontaneous. I've wanted that for weeks. I spent that time getting to know you because I didn't want to rush. I savored every second with you because I planned to have a lifetime of them."

"You want me."

"More than you can possibly know."

In a swift swoop, his mouth captured hers. Inhaling through her nose to catch her breath, she resisted her urge to yield and pushed him back.

"I'll be your friend, Xander… But I need some time to process all of this."

"You don't want me to kiss you?"

The answer was complicated. More complicated when he rose to full height without moving away, so the truth of what he wanted was pressing into her belly. It was strange. So strange that she smiled. Alex, who she had no idea could react to women, was hard for her.

"What's funny?" he asked.

"Nothing," she said, shaking her head and dropping her chin to hide her amusement. He caught it on a curled forefinger to raise it up and crooked a questioning brow. "You want me…" Widening her eyes, she dipped them down. "Like really want me." His expression betrayed he didn't follow. "It's strange. Last week I thought you were checking out the hot guys in the coffee shop, the same way I was."

"Only one I've been checking out is you."

Curious. "Has there been anyone?"

"No. Not since Courtney…" He inhaled as he pondered. "Maybe two months ago, I can't remember the last time we slept together… I can check my calendar if it's important for you to know."

Which was a sad statement of the former relationship or a revealing red flag about him. She couldn't get caught up in whatever chemistry there was between them. He'd had all his strikes. If he duped her again while she was on notice, it would be on her.

"You write in your calendar when you have sex?"

His countenance loosened. "No, but it will tell me when she and I were last in the same city. It would've happened then. We didn't spend the night together without sleeping together… I was usually only in the city with her for a day or two."

The intimacies of his previous relationship were his business. "I only wanted to know if in all this time I thought you were gay, you were actually out there seducing women."

"I'm not a player," he said. "It's not like that. I'm not like that. I wouldn't have the time even if I wanted to be. Not that I do."

She couldn't fault him for clarifying more than once. "Will you meet me at the coffee shop tomorrow?"

His simple accepting nod was encouraging. She eased him away and reached around to grab her purse.

"Wait, you're not leaving… You haven't drunk your wine."

And it wouldn't be a good idea for them to drink alcohol together for a while. Yes, she was still mad and hurt, but he was attractive, and the rules were different. He'd held off from seducing her before because he hadn't had a choice. She wouldn't let herself get that close to him, couldn't just give in to the physical. Forging a friendship was going to be difficult, and that was all they should ever really have.

"I'll see you tomorrow," she said, slinging the strap of her purse across her body and grabbing his shoulder to pull him down for a cheek kiss. When she stepped past him, he caught her wrist, holding her there. She exhaled. "You made progress. Take the win for what it is."

"I do and I'm grateful you're giving me a chance… It's never been easy for me to watch you walk out and now…"

"Tomorrow," she said, brushing her fingertips

across his stubble. "I'll see you at lunch."

Leading him on would be unfair. If she couldn't forgive and move on, she would have to be honest. If his feelings for her were real, and she couldn't reciprocate them, staying in his life would be cruel.

She had a lot to think about. Alex wasn't the man she thought he was, but Xander? She didn't know him at all.

NINETEEN

"SO HE'S NOT GAY," Gwen said, clarifying what she'd known since the kiss on Saturday night. "And now you find out he's not a consultant either?"

The Venture bombshell would wait for another time. The hits just kept on coming, it wasn't easy to absorb them all at once.

"He was proving a point to a friend," Rainie said. "About relationships."

Gwen was propped against her pillows while she leaned on the footboard. Wine and solidarity, it never hurt to have company.

"And you were his victim?"

"No," she said, sipping her wine, then holding the glass a little more away. "Maybe... I don't know."

"How do you feel?"

Her best friend had a way of coaxing answers out of her. "I have no idea." Her elbow found her knee as her fingers sank into her hair. "Alex was... my friend. I trusted him. I don't want to let men get away with bullshit like this."

"You think getting with this guy or not will teach all of them a lesson? It won't. Don't focus on the world, focus on this guy. No matter what you do with him, the next guy isn't going to know it."

"That's just it," she said. "I don't want there to be a next one."

Stunned, Gwen lurched forward. "You want to marry him?"

"No! I didn't mean… I mean, I don't want to go into a relationship thinking that it won't last. If I'm going to give anything a shot with Alex, I have to believe it will stick or there's no point."

"This just days after saying you'd hook up with your ex for sex."

Rainie groaned. "That's… if it's a hook up, at least I know it's a hook up and nothing serious. A relationship is a completely different thing, and you know that. You were with Steve for two years, and you still go back for a hook up now and then."

"Yeah, but I don't have your idealism. Men fuck up with me all the time and I let it roll off. Relationships with you are a zero-sum game. If he fucks up, then it's done."

"I'm not like that. I can be tolerant."

"It's not a bad thing, it's actually healthy. You know yourself, Rainie. You know what you can get over and what you can't. If you can't, then you end it, which makes sense. You're not dragging it out, wasting everyone's time."

And a man like Xander Gauge couldn't be frivolous with his time.

"Gwenie," she whimpered, hiding her mouth in her glass.

"Okay," Gwen said, wriggling closer to slap a hand onto her leg. "Pros and cons. Con: he misled you. Pro: he copped to it. He didn't feed you excuses or try to snivel out of it." True. "Pro: he's hot. Con: he's hot."

They laughed.

If he was who he made himself out to be, Xander was a serious man. Deliberate. Screwing around didn't seem like his style. Though it wasn't like she hadn't made errors in judgment over guys on that front before.

"He's smart and considerate," she said. "Attentive." Squeezing her eyes closed, she shook her head. "What am I doing? We can't just run down his qualities and make some quantitative choice."

"No, because you don't know what else might be different." That same question again. Who was Xander Gauge? "You have to decide if you can get over this… He wasn't the one who came up with the lie… if you believe him."

She did. Didn't she? She'd believed in Alex… then he turned out not to be Alex at all.

"I don't want to walk away from something that could be everything I've ever wanted," she said. "But I don't want to believe it could be because…" One thing was for sure. "If it goes wrong with him, it will destroy me."

Softly, softly seemed to be the best approach. Xander was right about one thing, whatever they were, for better or worse, it wasn't typical. But was he the man she'd been waiting for all her life, or the one sent to destroy her?

TWENTY

BY THE NEXT DAY, optimism was on high. Throughout her sleepless night, she'd swung back and forth on what to do. Reaching a decision sent her into slumber. This was it. She'd figured it out.

Work had whizzed by that morning, which was great. Lunch couldn't come quick enough.

Xander was at their table in the coffee shop. She went over, smiling at him as he rose to pull out her chair.

Before sitting down, she curved a hand around the back of his neck and drew him down to kiss the corner of his mouth.

"Feeling good, Button?" he asked, seating himself.

Their chairs were closer than normal, she had noticed, but wasn't objecting.

Linking her fingers together, she pulled her forearms close to her chest. "Mr. Gauge."

Her formal address raised his brows. "Miss Tait."

"You're a businessman."

"Yes."

"You understand contracts. Arrangements. Consideration."

"Yes."

Squeezing her fingers tighter together, she leaned closer, admiring his earnest gaze. "I have a proposition for you, businessman."

He adopted a similar pose, listing her way. "I'm listening, Miss Tait."

"It's important that you let me finish and don't give me your answer right now. Can I borrow your phone?"

Lifting his hips, he retrieved it from his back pocket, unlocked it, and handed it over. Under the moniker "*Button*," she entered her phone number.

"Did you sleep well last night?"

"Not really," she said, returning his phone to the lock screen and handing it back. "Not until I made my decision."

"And what's your decision?"

Examining his face, his features took on new light now the truth was out. How had she missed so many details? The flecks of gold in his chocolate brown eyes. The angle of his strong jaw, the inviting bow of his lips.

"You have a choice," she murmured, resisting the urge to touch his arm.

"Between?"

"My number is in your phone. I don't have your number."

"Baby, you can have—"

"You have a choice, businessman," she said, her hand going to his on impulse. "If you want, you can choose to call me."

"I choose to call you," he said, flipping his phone over.

She laid her hand over his to stall him. "I said it

was important you hear me out."

"Sorry," he said, turning his hand in hers, threading their fingers together. "I'm listening."

"I'll come over whenever you're ready, and we'll…" It felt weird to anticipate saying something explicit. Usually explicit sentiments tumbled out of her without forethought. "We'll have sex. I'll let you do anything and everything you want to me. I'll do anything you ask. I will be completely at your sexual beck and call until your ninety days in the real world are up…"

His breathing grew shallower, and his throat bobbed before he asked, "Or?"

She filled her lungs. "Or we try to rebuild our friendship. Spend some time getting to know each other, the real each other, and see where it goes. Option two comes with no guarantees."

"Does it come with a time limit, like option one?"

"No," she said with a shake of her head. "But it also doesn't come with a minimum term either. Option one, you get me the whole of the rest of your ninety days, no matter what. Option two, I can choose to walk away any time and you have to respect that choice… You can't switch from one to the other either. Once your decision is made, that's it."

"What's the point of this?" he asked. "To find out if I'm just about the sex?"

"No, it's not a trick, I promise. I can't say if I want to be in a relationship with you until I know the real you, until we've rebuilt trust. And who knows? That may never happen. Maybe we won't get there, and this will just fade away… If you don't want to take that risk or you want to make best use of your time, I'll go to bed with you."

"And we'll have forty-seven days together."

With a shrug, she nodded. "So that's your choice.

Forty-seven days of guaranteed physical intimacy or the potential for a lifetime of intimacy in its every form." She put a finger on his lips. "Don't answer me. You have my number. I want you to really think about this. Call or text me later when you're sure of your choice… I suppose option three would be we go our separate ways and—"

"There's no option three," he said, capturing her hand in both of his. "How long do I have to wait before I give you my decision?"

"I want to be confident that you made the right choice for you. Xander…" she murmured, sliding their linked hands to her chest. "We can't tell each other only what we think the other wants to hear. You promised honesty. You have to trust me to hear you, to consider you. I'm not trying to trick you. I swear…" Opening her fingers, she slid them up his jaw to the hair at his temple. "You are attracted to me, right? You said that you'd thought about sleeping with me." She smiled and pushed closer, moistening her lips. "If that's what you want, you can have it, baby. No judgment. I won't reject you for being honest."

"Sex wasn't the only thing on my mind," he said, his hand skimming over hers. "I thought about waking up with you. Coming home to you. Asking your opinion on issues… Pouring wine for you after a hard day. Joining you in a bubble bath… Lifting your veil to kiss you."

Laughing, she drew back, putting some space between them. Falling into him would be so easy.

"We need some coffee," she said, sweeping up her cup. And some perspective. It had been an intense few days. After a long drink, she put the cup down again. "I suppose now we're being honest, I can ask about Lance. You didn't want to talk about him before. Can we talk about him now?"

"What do you want to know?" he asked.

"Unfortunately, I can't fire him for a personal dispute."

She showed both hands in surrender. "Your personal issues are your own, I won't get involved. But I am curious how he got you to make the agreement. Did he just goad you into it or were there stakes?"

He hesitated for a second. "I mentioned the Summit Sponsorship?" She nodded. "We disagreed over a potential investment opportunity. If I stuck it out here, we'd never talk about it again. If I didn't, he gets the investment."

"That's huge," she said with concern. "What if it fails? You could lose a fortune."

"My time is worth more than my money and he didn't ask for that. Losing only costs me a million dollars—"

"A million dollars?" she asked, stunned. "Oh my God!"

His warm smile didn't settle her hammering heart. "No amount of money could replace you. Ethan is in Sydney dealing with a complicated negotiation. It's not even four a.m. there yet. I'll call him in a couple of hours, tell him to release the million for Lance's BlueGold investment. He can run point on it." He winked. "And deal with the paperwork."

"I thought you had ninety days. Why are you conceding now?"

Might he just vanish overnight? The prospect was unsettling.

"The deal was I commit myself for ninety days. He gave me credit for nineteen days 'cause he fucked my chances with you."

"So for seventy-one days, you have to commit yourself to a woman who doesn't know you're a billionaire playboy?"

"I'm not much of a playboy, Button. And yeah, that was the point."

"Was there a time limit? He couldn't have expected you to meet a woman on day one." Although he had. Clarity switched her thoughts. "Hold on, back it up and forget I said that."

"Yeah?"

"Yes," she said, lacing their fingers together. "You're handsome, and smart, and charismatic. If a woman knew you were straight, she'd go out with you in a heartbeat."

"I'm straight," he said, coming over all serious for a second before conceding a smile. "Just making sure you know."

"You shouldn't give up," she said, squeezing his hand. "According to what you've said, I've been the main woman in your life since we met and that was…"

"Forty-three days ago," he said before she worked it out.

Astounded, she recovered by liberating a short laugh. "Was that quick math or have you been keeping track?"

"Both."

"Gwenie still wants to go out this weekend," she said, distracted by their linked hands. "You can come with us. We know plenty of bars that would be target rich… Does your lady have to be committed to you for the full term?"

"No, we talked about that. I can't bring up commitment on day one."

"No, or you'd be the same as the women trying to race you down the aisle… You don't want a woman who gets serious from day one either. She'll be harder to shake in seventy-one days."

He raised her chin with a finger. "None of that matters anymore. I'm done with that. I only want you."

The notion was seductive in itself. "You've been committed to me for forty-three days."

"Yes, I have."

Mischief came to mind. "He doesn't have to know that I know." Her smile was slow. "I know you haven't made your choice and I'm not suggesting you don't ultimately make the investment…"

"But we can keep him in the dark for a while, let him think he lost."

"I don't condone lying," she said with wide, innocent eyes.

"If there's even a chance we can't salvage this because of his fuck up… Baby, I don't even want to think about what I'll do to him."

"He's one of your closest friends," she said. "You don't throw that away for the sake of a woman."

He nodded, though his conviction told another story. "I wouldn't. Not for the sake of a woman. But for the sake of *the* woman…"

It didn't matter how much rope she gave, he didn't seem to be going anywhere.

"Xander," she murmured his name, angling her head to look deeper into him. "Xander."

"Yes?"

He drew out the word like he didn't have a clue what was going on.

"Xander Gauge… are you a third? Sounds like a regal sort of name."

"No," he said, humoring her. "Everything I told you about my past is true."

"Where did you learn to write software?"

"School."

"Fancy school."

"I went to boarding school with a couple of geniuses," he said and lowered to whisper, "not that I'd call them that to their faces. Another couple of guys there had the gift of the gab too. It's amazing what you pick up if you listen to the right people at the right time."

"Friendship means a lot to you?" He answered in the affirmative with a brow raise because his mouth was busy with his coffee. "Have you thought about my mouth on your cock?"

He spat his drink across the table, hit by a sudden coughing fit. Tables around them glanced and gawked at her sputtering friend.

"I'm sorry," she said, grabbing for the napkins on the table to offer them to him. "I'm sorry. My mouth worked faster than my brain." Though given what she'd said, in such a non-seductive way, that may not be the right way to put it. "I'm sorry."

He wiped his mouth. "Would you like to walk me through the thought process behind the question?"

"Depending on what you choose, this could be the last time we ever talk." She turned over his hand on the table to trace the lines on his palm with a fingernail. "I didn't just want facts you'd share with anyone. I want to know something personal… and I was thinking about our hands… how often we hold hands and… My hands might touch you… in places I haven't seen." Pressing her palm flat on his, she met his eye. "One day I might have your dick right here in my hand." His glazed look accompanied his lips parting. "And your fingers…" Drawing around his digits with a fingertip, she smiled. "One day you might be inside me. Everywhere…" She exhaled her disbelief. "It's crazy, right? We're sitting here talking like normal adults, drinking coffee in public because that's what people do. But if you decide you want it… the next time we're alone—"

"Rainie, baby," he said, holding onto his calm with fraying resolve. "I love the train of thought. But if you finish that sentence…"

"It's okay. I know I said too much."

"Not too much," he disagreed. "You never have to apologize for what you say, and I want you to have those thoughts about us. About me. Just… Have mercy on a man who's been jonesing after you for weeks."

Before he'd made his choice, it wouldn't be a good idea to climb in too deep. There was so much about him she wanted to know, but if he chose to keep their association strictly sexual, she wouldn't ask any more personal questions. Her body would be his for a limited time, but every other part of her, she'd keep locked up safe.

TWENTY-ONE

"My place. Tonight. x"

THAT WAS WHAT his text said.

It was nuts to be disappointed. Not in him. Judging his choice wasn't her place. But that text, accepting his choice in those words… man, she'd wanted it to go the other way. She'd said she didn't mind which road he chose. Apparently, her subconscious had.

Still, she'd put the offer on the table and was going to follow through.

Her lingerie collection wasn't paltry, yet it seemed that way when she tried to find something suitable. Especially for a billionaire's viewing. Going with a shiny gray balconette and thong set, she grabbed her thigh-long trench, slipped some condoms in her pocket, and left her apartment.

If it was going to be sex, she'd be strict with herself. No lounging around after, no long seduction. Get there, satisfy him, and leave again. Her heart wasn't in play. Nope. No hearts. Just bodies. They couldn't be friends. Lunch together might not be a good idea either.

By the time she got to his apartment, that choice was still in the air. Maybe she could just not show up for lunch. Her routine would be scuttled. Better that than breaking her own heart by being an idiot. Xander was leaving in forty-seven days. That was the maximum time they could have. Their expiration date. And he wanted physical. It would be fun.

Fun.

She could do fun.

At his door, she tossed her hair one more time. Ignoring the pinch of her ridiculous platform heels, she knocked.

A few seconds went by. Nothing. Maybe he wasn't in.

The door suddenly opened, startling her. Once again, he had a phone to his ear.

"…yeah, but I don't give a damn," he was saying into the phone as he slipped an arm around her to draw her inside. "You know how I feel about eleventh-hour haggling, Eth."

He closed the door, and she took his other hand to guide him deeper into the room. With him distracted, she had the chance to make a few choices. Easing him back against the side of the kitchen counter, she slid both hands up his torso. He was so solid beneath the cotton of his tee-shirt. How was it that she'd never thought about his body in this way? Fun would be easy with a body like his as a playground.

"We pull out, I lose nothing but face," Xander said, an unfamiliar stern note in his voice. "Yeah, well, your time doesn't mean that much to me, buddy." That teasing was more familiar. She cast a smile upward, but his focus remained straight ahead, a frown emerging on his face. "You told me you covered that… Eth—"

Whatever was going on, it was probably important. So important that he didn't react as she unbuckled his belt. "I know exactly what it is. How often do we deal with this?" She popped the top button of his jeans, then inched back just enough to loosen the belt of her coat. "It's on my radar. This kind of cheap tactic doesn't bring positive attention, I'll tell you that." Picking up his hand, she watched the nuances of his expression as she brought it up to kiss his fingertips. "No, that'll reinforce this shit…" His mind was somewhere else. She had two choices: either leave or take control. If the physical was what he wanted, it was what he was going to get. "Eth, there's no way I alter the terms. I don't care what is on the table." Lowering his hand, she slipped it into her coat to press it against her breast, squeezing him hard against her sensitive flesh. It only took a flicker of a second for his expression to change and his attention to drop. She smiled and yanked his fly, opening the rest of his buttons. "I've gotta go, Rainie's here. Everything else just became a distant second."

Again, he didn't give his compatriot a chance to respond. He hung up and tossed his phone aside. His fondling hand stayed busy, while the other rose to cradle her face, tipping her chin up with the pad of his thumb as he descended to kiss her.

Yes. That sweet touch of his mouth was the gateway to her pleasure. Their pleasure. For the first time, she could relax and savor the urgency of that press, the warmth of his breath, the glorious desire of his tongue.

Making love wasn't in the cards. The rocket fast escalation of the tender kiss exploded. Their mouths battled, demanding more, devouring each other. Need became command. Want, addiction.

Snagging his neck, she pulled him closer, alight with a fire burning strong. She fought to cast off her trench and caught his neck again just as he hooked a hand under her thigh to pick her up. It was right. Being with him was more than just coming home. It was what they should've been doing from the minute they met. Her being had been crafted to join with his. This was it. The true course.

The cold counter met her ass, but the shock only jolted her body closer to his. Opening her mouth wider, she begged for more of him. Their hands worked on instinct, tracing and exploring their newest mate. Quakes of electricity seemed to follow his fingertips as they trailed up her sides, over her shoulders and down to her breasts.

There would be time for slow and careful later. In that moment, she only wanted one thing; she wanted it there and then. Slipping her hand into his pants, she didn't need to do anything to get him ready; he was already there. Squeezing him through the cotton of his underwear, she caressed him, earning herself a groan of satisfaction.

She'd never been so pleased to please a lover. Throwing a forearm up around his neck, she pulled herself higher, demanding more from his kiss while her hand worked faster.

He pulled back. "Wait…" he panted. "Wait, wait a second."

"There are rubbers in my coat pocket," she purred, kissing his jaw and throat.

"How did you get naked so fast?" he asked, discombobulated.

"I arrived like this," she said, still kissing.

"She arrived like this," he whispered. "Jesus Christ."

"You think only your fancy supermodels know how to make an entrance?" she asked, dragging her teeth across his flesh. "Let's do it here. Right here."

Maybe not the most romantic of settings, but that was sort of the point.

Sweeping her hair away from her face, he used the pressure to push her head back and make eye contact. "Is this what you want?"

She wasn't sure she liked his discernment. It suggested he wasn't as blinded by lust as she felt.

"I respect your choice," she said, squeezing his cock again. "Do you want me to do something for you? Take control. Tell me what you need."

Bowing, he pressed his lips to hers. The excruciating way they lingered conveyed such tenderness, such need, such ownership. She wanted all of it. He seemed ready to give it when his fingertips slid the length of her arms until he could take hold of her wrists. She smiled when he looped her arms around his neck and picked her up. As he appreciated her admiration, he accepted the brief kiss she boosted up to give him.

They weren't going to the bedroom. The balcony maybe? Was it big enough for them to do it safely? If he thought so, she'd trust him. And, yes, someone would probably call the cops, but Xander could afford the fine.

Except rather than go outside, he dipped down to seat her on the couch. "Wait here," he murmured and left her there.

He picked up her coat with the condoms in the pocket. Rather than go for them, he took it into his bedroom.

Pushing her hands against the back of the couch, she straightened up. "Alex?"

"One second," he called back.

Hmm… Uh, what was going on? She'd said he could do anything to her. Maybe giving him such broad scope was a mistake. Although she'd been joking about the supermodel thing, it wasn't exactly outside the realm of possibility. A guy like him probably had access to fulfill any fantasy or curiosity. He'd have experience in areas of proclivity she'd never even heard of.

Releasing her elbows, she grabbed for a throw pillow, holding it against her stomach. Suddenly, sitting there in her underwear seemed rather conspicuous.

Xander emerged without her coat, though he was carrying fabric. "Breaks my heart."

"What?" she asked as he took the pillow away from her to scan her figure. "What are you doing?"

"If you stay like that, I won't be able to concentrate," he said, offering her the material.

A shirt. One of his. "You want me to put this on?" she asked. He nodded, so she took it and sat forward to do as he asked. "Are we recreating a night I stayed over?"

"Remember how I asked you to have mercy on me?" he said, opening the fridge to retrieve her wine. "That's what we're doing."

Sucking on her lower lip, she bided her time. He poured them drinks, switched on the TV and grabbed the remote to put it in her hand.

"What are we doing?" she asked, looking from the remote to him on his return to the kitchen. "Do you wanna watch porn or something?" Sex with Xander wasn't going at all like she'd thought it would. "I don't know how to get porn on a television without cable... Do you have cable? Of course you do. What billionaire would be without it?"

"How about Netflix?"

"I don't think they have an adult section." She frowned, turning her attention to him. "Do they? Let me check."

There was another knock on the door, but she was too interested in her task to check who'd arrived. The only person she knew in Xander's life was Lance. If it was anyone else, she'd probably have to leave.

"Thanks," Xander said at the door, and then it closed.

No luck with the adult section. And no one else seemed to be with them. No person, but, from the smell, there was food in those bags he held while grabbing plates and flatware.

"What's that?" she asked, flicking down the list without looking at the screen. "Are you hungry?"

"I thought we would be."

After sex? "Uh, no, that's not allowed. No socializing. Just sex."

With the bag hooked on a finger, he brought everything over and sat next to her.

Leaning in to kiss her cheek, he put everything down. "I didn't choose sex," he breathed in her ear. "I pick option two."

Confused, she was only half paying attention as he unpacked the food and checked in the boxes.

"But you invited me over," she said, her hand with the remote-control loosening. "You kissed me… You touched my boobs."

"Both of which I promise to do again. If not today, another day, whenever you're ready."

Still, she didn't get it. "Huh?"

Freeing his hands and hers, he drew her around until they faced each other. "I pick option two," he said, pushing her hair from her blinking gaze. "No guarantees, but the potential for the biggest reward." He smiled, linking their fingers. "I make calculated risks every second of every day, babe. I'm not afraid of failure, I'm always confident of success."

"You want to be friends," she said, aware again of her apparel. "Then I am definitely not dressed right."

When she tried to take her hand back, he tightened his grip. "Yes, I pick option two, but I have conditions of my own."

Oh, well, fair was fair. "Okay, hit me."

"I won't say no."

Why did this guy insist on never making sense? "Uh…" her gaze drifted. "That doesn't sound like a condition."

"Whatever you want, you'll get. Sex, money, whatever I can give you, I will. I told you nothing but honesty, so that's what I'm giving you. I'm warning you in advance."

"Use my power wisely?" she teased, raising their joined hands to her cheek for a second.

"Right. Your only condition is no guarantee?"

"Friendship," she said. "No guarantee. No time limit."

"No other guys," he said. "Until we agree there's no chance for us. No other guys."

"So we're exclusive friends," she said. "What if we never agree? How about, no other guys until one of us decides there's no chance for us, but…" with one caveat. "We have to tell the other first. No blindsiding each other or moving on without talking about it."

"Okay," he said, studying her mouth.

"Any more conditions?"

"Do I get to add physical conditions?"

"Like?" she asked.

His lips twisted into a smirk. "I like your outfit."

Meaning if he got to add physical conditions, he'd pick lingerie?

She laughed, tugging her hands free of his. "Don't flirt with me."

"That's not a condition I can agree to, I'll definitely be doing that."

"Xander, you better play nice."

As she sank against the back of the couch, he came around to lean over her, using a fingertip to push aside the edge of her shirt, revealing more of her breast. Arching into his arousing scrutiny was automatic.

"Last condition," he said, his finger going deeper into the fabric until it touched her trembling flesh.

"Mm hmm?"

"You asked for honesty, I want it in return. We answer each other's questions with the truth. Always. We tell each other the truth, baby. I don't want there to be anything you don't tell me."

"Okay," she said, pressing her hand to his pec. "I really thought you chose option one."

"Disappointed?"

"Mm mm," she said, rejecting the notion as her hand slunk higher and her fingertips crept into the neck of his tee-shirt. "We have to tell each other everything?"

"Everything."

"Then you should know I'm really stupid."

"You are, huh? Watch it, that's my friend you're talking about."

"Yeah, but she somehow missed just how much her friend was into her... and managed to convince herself that she wasn't insanely attracted to him."

"It's the money," he said at the same time his phone rang on the kitchen counter. "Does it every time."

He got up to go over and grab the phone, leaving her there stupefied. Money? The goddamn money? Either he was right, and she was disgusting and shallow, or he was wrong and had basically just called her a hooker. That's what prostitutes did, they slept with men who paid them.

Standing, she got moving, knowing exactly where she was going: home.

She sailed straight on past him, opened the front door, and walked out.

Prick.

"Rainie?" he called after her, his voice echoing

down the hallway.

Without slowing, she raised her hand above her head to show him the finger.

Money?

Asshole.

At the top of the stairs, she yanked her shoes off one after the other. With the crazy heels on, and being wound up, she'd fall down them for sure if she didn't lose the platforms. She got down one flight before he caught up with her.

"Baby?" he said, trying to get hold of her. She whipped her arm out of his reach. "What happened? Where are you going?"

"Turns out there was an option three after all," she said, focusing on the stairs. "I'm going home, and you can go fuck yourself."

"What? What did I…? Shit."

Smart man. Yeah, he figured it out just a little too late. When he stopped descending with her, she put a flight between them. Then his footsteps started again overhead.

"Button," he said, catching up. "I'm sorry. It just came out. With Lance in my head, I—"

"You can't blame him for this. You did this one all on your own. Congratulations! You just learned the fastest way to fuck up a relationship. You managed to end it before it even began. Well done."

b"Stop," he said, pulling her to a halt when they reached the foyer. "Rainie, I'm sorry."

With the stairs in her past, she bent to put on one shoe, then the other. "You know what, Xander?" she asked, slapping a much less aware hand to his chest. "You can have women far more beautiful and glamorous than me use you for money. Go find yourself a woman with nothing better to do than spend all day at a spa in anticipation of spending a night with you. Find one of those perfect Vogue models. Give her access to credit, buy her a big house, and knock her up so she's guaranteed hefty child support after the divorce. Really, you'll be much happier if we all descend to meet your expectations."

"Rainie," he said, catching her arm before she could walk away. "I'm sorry."

Once again, he was contrite, and she was mad. It was becoming habit. In his defense, he could only base assumptions on experience. Their worlds were polar opposite.

She sighed, conceding a little. "Don't be. You have experience, I guess you can spot a gold digger on sight. I'm new to this; maybe the money does matter to me. Maybe it did make a difference. I never thought cash mattered to me... maybe what you see in me is right. Whatever it is, it's too complicated. I don't want complicated. I promised myself I'd tell you if it became something I can't get over. It's too much. I didn't want it to be, but it is." She licked her drying lips, grabbing for her resolve. "Stay away from me, Xander Gauge."

His hand drifted from her arm as she strode away. Damn complications. The relationship she wanted wasn't supposed to be difficult. It was supposed to be smooth. Easy. Natural.

For a hot second there, she'd wanted Xander to be it. Shame nothing with him was simple. Maybe he was right to suspect her because she wasn't the woman for him. One way or the other, there was no denying that anymore.

TWENTY-TWO

THE COFFEE SHOP was a blip in her past. Over and done with. She got through an entire week without going anywhere near it or Xander's place.

Yeah, okay, maybe it wasn't a major achievement. He'd called about fifteen times in the hours after she left his apartment, so she'd blocked his number. Making him a blip too. Cutting ties was the easiest way to forget about him.

That was all she had to do.

Forget.

Every step counted.

Her cellphone rang as she hurried along the corridor toward a conference room at work. Stacey had sent her an email requesting her presence. No meeting was scheduled, not in her calendar or mentioned at the morning briefing. Not much went by unscheduled these days.

The phone. Right. The phone.

"Yeah?" she asked, the weight of her thoughts stalling her as she answered.

"Shiny?"

"Dem," she said, closing her eyes. "Sorry, I missed your call."

More than one of them. He'd left a few messages over the weekend, and she hadn't returned any of them.

"Yeah, I'm getting a complex over here since you ran out on me the other night."

Ran out on him at Xander's almost two weeks ago.

"I'm sorry. I had my reasons. Long, complicated reasons. I can't get into it right now."

"You hate complicated."

Thank you! At least one man understood her needs without her having to explain herself. "Thank you, Dem. Yes, I hate complicated."

"You busy tonight? We could start over… over again. Just us this time."

Without her tagalong friends. Should she? Probably not. Being around him hadn't felt great the last time they'd met up. Though Xander had his own role to play in that hot mess.

"What do you want to do?" she asked. "Dinner? Drinks?"

"The Grand. Room two thirty-four," he said. "We can get room service."

And there it was. Just like she'd said, Dem wanted it and was direct about it.

Getting down and dirty with any man was about the furthest thing from her mind. While she was conscious anyway. Her subconscious kept R-rated dreams running all night, but Demetri wasn't the star of those.

Even considering being with Demetri felt like a betrayal. Damn, she needed to get over it. Xander wasn't the one putting that guilt on her, she'd told him they were over. She didn't owe him anything.

It was a betrayal of whatever was going on inside her.

A betrayal of what her body craved. Giving herself to anyone else would be a bad substitute. She couldn't con her body into thinking Demetri would be enough. Even in the dark, and despite never being intimate with Xander, her libido would know he wasn't the one devouring her if she got it on with Demetri. A ringer would never satisfy it.

"Let me think about it," she said. "I'll call you later?"

"Sure."

They hung up and she stayed there, leaning on the wall, her phone resting on her jaw. Sex with Demetri. She could do it. He was good in bed. Present. Though he didn't spend a lot of time staring into her. Even if it did feel awkward or weird, Demetri probably wouldn't notice.

Xander.

Why couldn't she get him out of her mind?

Closing her eyes, she lowered her chin, bouncing the corner of her phone off the center of her forehead. Was she a gold-digging whore? Had she turned out to be one of those people? Xander was used to people like that, probably had a sensitive radar for it. She didn't have any concise idea how she felt about the money. Did it matter to her or not? With that uncertainty, she couldn't argue the point with him.

Though he was the one who wouldn't get out of her head, not his money. She didn't obsess over how the money kissed. How its hands felt on her. How it put a smile on her face and teased her with gentle touches.

"Stop it," she hissed at herself.

The guy had made one comment. She, being her, jumped on it as a major insult only to then conclude he was possibly correct. She should apologize. That would be the decent, human thing to do.

But whatever they weren't, she looped back to his condition. No other guys. And the caveat… That would only matter if they were still friends. If they were still…

Why had she bolted so fast? Because Xander touched a raw nerve? Because she was terrified he could be her everything? Her mind was all screwed up. The same thoughts had been floating around, intruding on her every moment for the last eight days.

Damnit, something had to change. She stood up straight and went into her contacts. Text would just memorialize her muddle. Voicemail? What was the chance she would get through to his voicemail?

With the conference room just a few meters away, at least she had an excuse for getting off a call quickly if he picked up.

Clearing her throat, she scrolled through and found his number, saved as X. Nothing more. It was supposed to be just his initial but seemed prophetic.

Quick. Come on. She didn't have all day. Fuck it. She pressed call. No going back.

Raising the device to her ear, her whole body was tingling. Her stomach flipped over and over. Why was she nervous? Could adrenaline be responsible for numbing her fingertips, or was she having a stroke?

It rang and…

Another tone echoed from further down the corridor. Frowning, she peeked left and right. There was no one there. And that ringtone. It wasn't typical. In fact, she'd only heard it one other place.

Creeping along the corridor toward the suspicious sound, trepidation seeped in. Her boss wanted her in that conference room.

Lowering the phone from her ear, she rounded the door and…

Xander.

Several people occupied the conference room, but she only saw one. Him. Standing there behind a trio of Northberg associates. Viva's own top-tier team stood near Eric Donal and her supervisor, Stacey. Everyone was fawning over the older guy surrounded by the Northberg people. Everyone except Xander.

This was a nightmare. Had to be a nightmare. Oh, God, she better not be naked.

Xander slipped his hand into his inner pocket. For his phone? Maybe.

Without looking, she pressed the disconnect button on hers.

What was he doing there?

Why was he loitering in the background? Not that he looked suspicious. No, despite being closest to the corner, he was still the most intimidating. Maybe the brooding, unimpressed thing was a tactic.

Although his phone stopped ringing, Xander retrieved it anyway. It took him just a second to read her name on the screen. Like he sensed her, his attention pounced to hers.

She wasn't a bad person. Being clumsy, and sometimes saying the wrong thing, didn't make her evil. Xander had told her if going to the press and outing him would make her happy she should do it. It hadn't even occurred to her. Never would she do something so callous and intrusive. Why open a can of worms she'd be powerless to close?

Except, he was doing the equivalent.

Alex, the man she thought her friend to be, would never intrude on her livelihood. Her job was her life. Not because she wanted it to be exactly, but she wasn't like him. Her savings were meager. If she lost her job, she wouldn't make rent.

And she hated games. He knew she hated games.

Why would he invade her workplace? What could be his reason?

They just stood there. Eyes locked. The contrition she'd seen in him in the past wasn't gleaming like she expected it might. Xander wasn't sorry to be there. He was determined.

The setup didn't seem right if his aim was to get her fired. Ruining her would take nothing more than a single phone call for a guy of his influence.

Her mind wasn't as shrewd as his. How conniving might he be? To reach his stratosphere of success, Xander must have a ruthless streak. Something she was learning in real time.

"Rainie." That happy voice belonged to Stacey, her boss. "Come over here and meet Hal Crean, Northberg's CEO."

So that was the older guy surrounded by his cronies? Ignoring the menacing figure in the corner, she pasted on a smile as she crossed to join Stacey and Eric Donal.

"It's a pleasure," she said, shaking his hand and the hands of the three people around him.

The Northberg trio were Viva's usual contacts. Having their CEO in the room, with Xander in attendance too, couldn't be a coincidence.

"We were just discussing what's next for Northberg," Stacey said. "Won't you please sit down?"

The top-tier team took their places around a central Donal at the closest side of the table while she sat at the edge of the room at their backs, like always. Xander didn't take a prominent position. Quite the opposite. He sat at the other side of the room, behind the Northberg delegation.

Like an underling.

It didn't make sense.

If he was such a bigshot, why was he seated there

like a lowly assistant?

Hal Crean, the Northberg CEO, started going on about a renewed relationship and a bright future. Taking notes on her phone was normal; no one batted an eye. Sometimes they had tablets, but there was a finite number in their department and the others were in use.

Notes on Hal's monologue weren't required, giving her the opportunity to text the interloper.

"What are you doing here?"

Xander's phone chimed in the same moment she hit send, reminding her to put her own on silent. She tried to focus on Hal's talking. Northberg was moving into a new era, stronger than ever. They needed a dynamic team to rise with them. Her phone quaked in her hand.

"I miss you, Button. x"

That was his reason? It didn't make it right. Hal was still going on about synergy and diving deep, so she responded.

"That's not an answer. This is my workplace.
I don't like games."

His reply was quick.

"No games. I'm here to stay, baby. Meet Xander Gauge."

Listening was getting more difficult as her thoughts got louder. She'd said she didn't know Xander Gauge and wanted to get to know him. This. In her work, surrounded by colleagues, was not what she'd meant. She texted back.

"What does that mean? Is that a threat? I have bills to pay, I didn't think you were this guy."

Threatening her was beyond what she'd expect. But she wouldn't have expected him to show up at her work either.

Her phone vibrated again.

"I am your guy, Rainie. I don't give up. You have to know how serious I am about you. About us being together. I'd give you anything I have, anything in my power to give is yours. We agreed to communicate, Button. Lay that honesty on me. Don't block me out. x"

Honesty. How could she be honest with him when she couldn't figure herself out? Doubting him was secondary to her doubting herself, that much was obvious.

In the interests of honesty, she could only tell him what she knew for sure.

"Dem wants to have sex in his suite tonight."

That was the truth. She read it back. Oh, God, was that callous? Hurting him wasn't her goal. She'd been calling to tell him that. Her heart raced. Peeking up, past the people at the table engaged in discussing promoting their products, her eyes met his.

Those weren't happy eyes. Weren't amused or even reasonable. It was rage. Cold, disgusted, almost challenged anger burned across the width of the room, losing none of its potency on the journey.

Slowly, his head shook. Not for long, but she got it. He was saying it wasn't allowed.

He shouldn't be able to say no if they'd put their relationship behind them. No person should have the right to tell another what they could and couldn't do if all parties were single, legal, and consenting. Yet, she wasn't mad or even offended by his nerve.

Whoever Xander was, however much of Alex was in him, if he'd said the same to her about Courtney, she'd not only be mad, she'd be devastated too.

Exhaling, Xander said he'd craved her advice after learning Lance lied to her. She got it. She wanted to talk to her friend and ask for his advice right then. Maybe that was the key. Whether they could work out the romantic part of their relationship or not, their friendship was real… or it once had been. Maybe she cut that part off too quickly. She missed her Alex.

TWENTY-THREE

EVERYONE AROUND THE CONFERENCE table stood up, startling her.

"Yes, we'll show you around and then get to work," Donal said. "Dinner at your hotel tonight will give us a chance to hammer out the specifics."

As the conversation kept going and everyone drifted toward the door, Stacey came rushing over. She leaped to her feet to meet her boss.

"We need to pull their files and figure out everything there is to know about Hal Crean," Stacey whispered, resting a hand on her forearm. "He's taking the lead here because of the guy sitting back there…" Stacey's eyes got wide and she tipped her head back a tiny increment. "That's Xander Gauge. He owns half the companies on the planet. If we impress with Northberg, who knows how much of his business we can attract?"

"Okay," she said, resisting her urge to seek him out.

"Find out what Gauge likes too and where he's staying. Send gifts to his suite and his family. Find out if he's married, if he's got kids, we need to use every detail to our advantage. We're having dinner with him and Crean tonight." We? Please don't say that included her. "Hang back and do the research. We have to show them around the place and then we'll do a Q and A."

Stacey patted her arm and spun around. She paused when she noticed Xander was still present. Standing on the other side of the table, on the phone. The supervisor glanced back, like she was maybe unsure if she should leave him or not.

"Stacey!" Donal called from outside the conference room.

Stacey jumped and sped out.

Hang back. Okay. So she could sneak to her desk to do the required research? Should she just—her hesitation gave Xander a chance to walk to the door. Good. Go follow the others. Instead, he closed the door, trapping both of them in the conference room.

Shit. No. This wasn't the place to talk about… anything.

The phone was still to his ear, but she went over, shaking her head. "No," she mouthed.

When she tried to walk out, he hooked an arm around her torso, drawing her into the room again.

"A dozen? No. Make it two," he said into the phone before he offered it to her. "Give Topher your address."

"Who's Topher?" she whispered, taking the phone.

"My assistant. We have a direct account with the best florists in the world."

Oh, well, if that was what it was.

She took the phone and broadened a glossy smile on her lips. "Topher?"

"Uh… yes, ma'am."

First thing she learned about the assistant? He

was smart because he sounded worried.

"My name is Rainie Tait."

"Yes, ma'am."

She closed her eyes and opened them again when they'd ascended to Xander's.

"If your boss ever instructs you to send anything to me for any reason, you have my permission to tell him to go to hell." Slapping the phone onto Xander's chest, she glared. "Don't ever assign me to your assistant again."

He hung up the phone and put it back in his inside pocket. She'd never seen him in a suit before. Strange as it was, he definitely pulled it off.

She heard him inhale as his mouth opened. "I'm lost without you, Button. I don't know how to make this work with you working against me."

"It's okay," she said, folding her arms to ensure she'd keep her hands to herself. "I owe you an apology."

That not only silenced him, he frowned too. "You do?" Something seemed to occur to him. "You already slept with Demetri?"

"No," she said, shaking her head. "I walked away, and I shut down. This is new to me too. You're new to me. I was offended by what you said, but like I said, maybe you're right. Maybe I was considering a relationship because you can offer security. That's seductive… especially for someone used to living paycheck to paycheck."

"You didn't like me trying to spend money on you just now with Topher."

"Flowers?" she asked. "I wasn't mad about the money; I've had boyfriends send me flowers before. I am upset you'd delegate me. Don't ever delegate me. If I'm not worth a few minutes and a little effort, we shouldn't even think about being friends, let alone anything else."

"Hmm," he said, wrapping his arms around her.

"I see your point."

Her forearms relaxed against him. "And if anyone should send flowers, I should send them to you. I don't know what happened."

"You doubted yourself," he said. "I made a stupid joke in bad taste, and it hurt you. I hurt you. Again."

"No," she said, though the protest caught in her throat. "Maybe. All I've wanted to do this week is talk it through with you, but I wouldn't let myself talk to you."

"Why?"

"Because what if you're right? I don't want you anywhere near me if I'm a money hungry whore."

"You're definitely not."

"How do you know? I showed up to your apartment in my underwear."

"Baby…" Crouching, his hands slithered lower on her back until he rested his nose in her hair to inhale her scent. "The money has come between me and every woman I've been with… You're the first one I can't be without… Tell me how to fix this."

"Tell me why you're here," she said, tipping her head back to look up at him. "My work, Xander, really? You can't play with me here."

"You wanted to know Xander Gauge. This is what he knows. I know business. I needed an in and I know how to do this. Got your attention, didn't it? You shut me out and I'm not easily dissuaded. If you look me in the eye now and tell me you never want to see me again, I'll leave and never cross your path again. So… are we through, Button?"

The easiest thing would be to say yes. That would save both of them from riding the emotional rollercoaster.

"What are you doing here?"

"Northberg was in trouble," he said. "That's

what I do."

"You bought them?"

"I might," he said. "I paid their Viva bill. Secured your job, baby. I don't want to threaten your security, I want to ensure it."

"Crean was talking about a new beginning. Paying one bill doesn't save their company."

"No, it doesn't. They're a mess."

Her lips curled. "And you already have a dozen ideas how to fix them."

"Viva is my priority as long as you're a part of it. If you want me to acquire Northberg—"

"You do what's good for Seven." She sighed. "But thank you. This is difficult for me, but I understand a leopard can't change its spots."

"Am I the leopard?"

"A wild animal I have no hope of taming? Yes, you are. You wanted to reach me and, like you said, this is what you know."

"Anything to get me close to you, Button."

"Your friend," she said, reaching around to take his arms away from her body as she stepped back. "I've never been good at complicated. Simple is all I've ever wanted. I want to be friends, to get back to how we were. You being here at my work isn't simple."

"Okay."

"You can't have dinner with Viva people."

"Make me a better offer," he said, surprising her. At least it did until one corner of his mouth ascended. "I cancel on people all the time. I'll stay away… Though I'd love to have you over for dinner. I got your favorite the other night and it went to waste."

"My favorite is Chang's, and they don't deliver to you."

He bowed forward to whisper above her ear. "They do for a twenty-thousand-dollar tip."

His smug teasing tempted a smile to her lips, though she resisted and shoved him back. "You paid twenty thousand dollars for my dinner?" she asked, to which he shrugged like it was nothing. "And you didn't get laid?" She hissed in a pained breath. "That's got to sting."

He laughed. "That's nothing to what it'll cost me to have it flown to London or Rome when you're traveling to visit me there. Maybe I'll just hire their chef for you."

She couldn't restrain her smile anymore. "Man, you are arrogant."

"How do you think I got where I am?"

"Are you married?" she asked.

Still smirking, his brows rose in question. "Excuse me?"

"Stacey wants to know if you're married."

"Not married, but I'm taken," he said, touching a loose section of her hair at her temple. "Memory never does justice to your beauty."

"Stop it," she said, assaulted by bubbles of excited flattery. "I'm at work... Alex." Her friend. Nothing more. Though holding on to that truth was a struggle as she gazed up into him. "Tell me something no one else knows."

"You're the first thing I think of in the morning."

"Before Venture?"

"Oh, long before then," he said. "Venture doesn't come to mind until after we've been in the shower."

"We?" she asked, almost aroused by the thought. "You're flirting with me, Mr. Gauge."

"Let me buy you dinner and we'll flirt some more."

"I'll come over tonight if you let me handle dinner."

"You want to cook?"

Rolling her eyes to their top corners, she raised a shoulder. "Something like that. Will you trust me?"

"Will you come over in your underwear again?"

"If I say no, that implies I won't be wearing any."

"One way or the other, suits me."

"Do you have children?"

He exhaled a laugh. "Children?"

"Stacey wants to know."

"My personal life is none of Stacey's business. But if Rainie wants to ask me…"

"Okay, but you see, we've wasted a bunch of valuable time. I am supposed to be researching you so I can send gifts to the people you care about."

He frowned. "That's counterproductive. I'll buy you anything you want. Why would you use your company's credit card to buy it when you can have mine?"

"I don't want anyone's credit card," she said, prodding his chest. "And I don't think I can report back to Stacey that we should send me gifts. I don't think she'd like that… or believe me. And I've already cost you a fortune in coffee. No gifts for a while."

"I won't say no, I warned you," he said, leaning in. "What do you want, baby? What can I do to make you feel good?"

That question could go either way. Except the suggestive light in his drowsy eyes betrayed only one thing was on his mind. Peeking over her shoulder, the conference table was enticing. It might be fun to throw caution to the wind and get dirty right there.

Fantasy. Not reality. Risking her job would be insanity. Though maybe if her bosses saw that, they'd reward her for going to any lengths to please such an important client.

"I have work to do," she said, stroking the side

of his neck. "I'll come over tonight?"

He nodded. "You want me to send a car?"

"Stop that," she said, fighting her smile again. "We're regular Joes… Have you talked to Lance yet?"

"No, and I don't intend to any time soon."

"Forgive him sometime."

"I will just… not yet."

"Okay," she said, pulling him down to kiss his cheek. "You be scary boardroom guy and I'll go Google you."

"Don't believe everything you read," he called to her as she went to open the door.

She glanced back at him once more, appreciating his smile as she showed him her own. Friendship. They could be friends. That wasn't complicated… not exactly.

TWENTY-FOUR

"WHAT'S ALL THIS?" Xander asked as she entered his apartment later that evening.

Dumping the grocery bags on the counter, she began to unpack. "I didn't know what you'd have in your cabinets."

"These don't look like the fun kind of supplies," he said, peeking into the bags. "You got some toys hidden in here?"

"You really think if we were to have sex for the first time, I'd want toys in our bed?" she asked, gathering up the empty bags to dump them in his hands. "I know what you're packing in those pants. I can work with it even if you don't know what to do with it."

Walking past him, she hid her smile. Damn, hadn't she told him no flirting? She was bending her own rules.

"I know what to do with it," he said in her hair above her ear. "Anytime you want me to prove it…"

"And this…" she said, spinning around to present him with a chopping board, "is why we're cooking together. You deal with the knives, I'll only hurt myself."

"What are we making?"

"You don't like being out of control, do you?" she asked, stripping the onion.

"What gave me away?" he said, putting down the board and showing her the knife he'd chosen. "This is your plan to keep me busy."

"Dice, dice, dice," she said, searching the cabinets for what she needed.

"Yes, ma'am."

As she seasoned the chicken and heated the oil in the pan, she was aware of him there, slicing and dicing. There. Close. Breathing. Thinking. Her shoulders shivered as her gut lightened. Shit.

"Stop it," she whispered, the tickle of his attention tormenting the base of her neck.

"What?" he asked, his tone betraying his own awareness. "I'm chopping, like you said."

So why was she thinking about forgetting the meat in the pan in favor of spinning around and grabbing for his? Distractions. She needed a distraction. Reaching over to push one packet aside to line up some of their supplies, she did a mental check on everything.

"Garlic *and* onions," he said, wiping the onion from the knife with the side of his finger. "Won't put me off."

"How was work?" she asked, changing the subject. "Did you talk to Ethan about Northberg?"

"You know I'm the boss, right? I can spend my money any way I want. I don't need a green light from Ethan."

"There must be some oversight," she said, turning the chicken.

"Yeah, me."

"Do you monitor every decision every one of

your companies make every day?"

"No, then I wouldn't have time for anything else. We have a hierarchy. People I trust in vital positions."

She bounced on the spot. "So if we get trust back, I can work for you? What position would you give me?"

She didn't intend to actually work for him, but she'd never been averse to a game of make believe. Except he didn't say anything, so she lost her smile and glanced at him. A stillness complemented his serious concentration. He must have stood like that for twenty seconds before his smile faded up.

"I can't think of anything that won't sound disrespectful," he said, conceding a brief laugh. "You can have my job."

"Yes, I can," she said, returning her focus to the cooking. "I'd be better at it too."

"Bet you would," he said. "Can't imagine any guy playing hardball with you in the boardroom."

"I'm my own worst enemy. You haven't figured that out yet?"

He put the onion in a bowl, ready for her and moved onto the mushrooms.

"You don't have to worry now you have me in your corner."

His phone rang behind the supplies she'd lined up. With his hands dirtied by the vegetables, he couldn't answer. Not that he even looked at it. She reached over to answer and put it on speaker.

When they made eye contact, it was clear he wasn't happy. Uh huh, just like she'd thought, he hadn't intended to answer.

"What?" Xander barked. "Didn't I say no interruptions tonight, Atwell?"

"Can tell you're still not getting any. Shit, man, you better work that fist fast if you don't want your head to explode."

She'd be shocked if it wasn't for the smirk Xander landed on her.

"That's mine and Rainie's business, no one else's."

Still, Ethan wasn't deterred. "You know, I have to hope this relationship doesn't work out. The Rainie factor is not good for my equations."

"Worry less about your equations and more about what's in front of you," Xander said.

"She must be a looker. I've gotta say I was surprised Lance says she's got a playboy rack. That's never been your thing."

Her mouth opened in surprise and she glanced down before looking at him. Except the amusement gleaming from him put a smile on her face. The poor guy on the phone had no idea she was there.

"You fucks talking about my woman?" Xander asked with impressive severity given the mischief dancing across his expression. "Leave that rack to me, Eth. It's my concern, your concern is in Sydney. Tell me you've got ink on paper Down Under."

Ethan exhaled. "We've been in meetings all morning," he said, obviously at the end of his rope. "It's crunch time. It's not going to happen unless we give. Want us to walk away?"

"I want you to get it done. I sent backup. Are you telling me you and Payne can't get it done… together?"

"Only way this happens is if you show face. I told you. How many times—"

"It's a no go. How many times do I have to tell you that I won't join negotiations? Rainie is my only priority."

That was sweet and startling. She took the chicken from the pan to replace it with the garlic and onion.

"This is a billion-dollar deal, Xander," Ethan said with trepidation and caution. "We lose sixteen months if we—"

"As long as Rainie needs me, I'm here."

"I don't need you," she said, attracting his attention. "I don't."

There was a pause on the line. Xander lost some of his starch as he relished her revealing herself.

"R… Rainie?" Ethan asked.

"Yes, Rainie," she said. "I don't need him right now if you need him. I don't want him screwing up a billion-dollar deal… How will he send all our future babies to college and buy them Ferraris if he squanders deals like that?"

Xander laughed and sloped her way to kiss her head. "I'm not going anywhere."

"Are you in bed?" Ethan asked, suspicious.

"If we were in bed, I wouldn't have answered," Xander said.

"You didn't, I did," she said, reaching over to steal a mushroom. "And I want you to go. Your business is important."

"You're more important," Xander said. "I want to be here."

"And I want you to prove you can do both. You can be Xander Gauge and my Alex at the same time."

"This is getting complicated," Ethan muttered.

"No, not complicated. We don't use that word in front of the future Mrs. Gauge."

She laughed. "You're really on a roll tonight."

"Just wait until later. You'll love what I've got lined up for you."

"You won't be here later," she said. "Topher will already be warming up the jet."

"She knows," Ethan said in wonder.

Xander went to wash his hands. "Everything,"

he said. "We're doing honesty."

"All the way," she said, concentrating on her cooking until Xander's hands crept around her ribs to cradle her breasts.

"All the way?" he murmured into her hair.

"When do you need him, Mr. Atwell?"

"He's got enough of an ego," Xander said, continuing his progress until his arms were tight around her. "Don't encourage it."

"I've got an ego?"

She slipped out of his embrace, putting the spoon in his hand while she dealt with the stock. "How long is the flight between here and Sydney?"

"A day," Ethan said. "Topher still have the jet?"

"Yeah," Xander said. "No flight for me, sorry."

"Ethan, could you call Topher and arrange what needs to be arranged, please?"

"Babe, I'm not going," Xander said, watching her put ingredients in the pan.

She took the spoon out and put the lid on. "Yes, you are," she said, sidling close, raising her fingertips to his jaw. "I'll still be here waiting for you. I'm not going anywhere."

"Okay," he said, sweeping her hair from her face as his other arm encircled her again. "I'll go. On one condition."

"What condition?" Ethan asked.

"Not from you," Xander said, shuffling them closer to the phone. "Set it up."

He reached over to disconnect the line.

"What condition?"

"Stay the night with me."

That set off her alarms, and she tried to back off, but he tightened his embrace. "Xander," she whimpered.

"No, I'm not asking you to have sex with me. We slept together when we were just friends before."

"When I thought you were gay."

"I'll keep my hands to myself, promise."

"And your mouth? And your penis?"

"Unless you ask really, really nicely, yeah."

"I'll stay the night," she said, settling against him, surrendering to his hold. "So long as you promise to do your job right. Get the deal or walk away, whatever you decide, but you're there for as long as it takes… You can't hurry or cut things short just to get back to your friend."

"You call the shots," he said, licking his lips as he admired hers. "Tell me how to spoil you. I want to make you so happy."

"Spoil me with the truth," she said. "And if I'm staying, pour me some wine."

"You got it, babe."

The food had to be her focus. The man in the background dealing with drinks was her friend. Only her friend. And in the morning, he'd jet halfway across the globe. That would be the real test of their friendship, of their feelings, of what would come next.

TWENTY-FIVE

"THIS IS A BAD IDEA," she said.

Xander was standing at the end of the bed, stripping down to his underwear. When they'd slept together before, the underwear stayed in place.

Yet, he asked, "Should I take them off?"

"No!" she exclaimed, propping herself on her elbows in the middle of his bed. "Please don't make this hard, Xan."

"You always take care of that, baby," he said, diving on top of her, catching his weight on his straight arms.

Lying down, she kept her hands on his biceps. "Don't flirt with me when we're in bed."

He kissed her forehead then vaulted to his own side. "I like you talking as though this will happen a lot."

"This will not happen a lot," she said. Tucking her hands under the pillow, she rolled to her side to face him. "How often do you go to Australia?"

"Whenever it's necessary. It's beautiful. Have you ever been?"

"No," she said, almost laughing at him. "I've never left the lower forty-eight."

"Oh, we'll definitely be changing that." His hand slid onto her waist as the rest of him came closer. "Friend of mine has a place south of Hawaii… If we asked, he'd let us have it to ourselves for a few weeks."

"A place?" she asked, enamored with his gold flecks. "A condo? A time share?"

"An island."

It took her a second to really hear that. "He has an island? Like a whole island? Your friend owns an actual island?"

"He's spent a lot of time, money, and favors getting that place up to scratch. It's amazing now. Full infrastructure. Corporate complex… There are two private houses on the island… a resort building too. He can have it fully staffed for us or completely deserted… After tasting your cooking, I vote for the latter."

"So with a corporate complex, you could work all day and I'll just wait around to cook your dinner?"

"And put out, yeah," he teased, somehow sliding lower. "An island all to ourselves. And if the Pacific doesn't appeal, another friend has a Bahamian island."

She scoffed a laugh. "Of course, yeah. How many rich friends do you have? Let me guess, all your friends are rich."

"Depends what you define as rich. Most of my real friends do okay financially."

"Financially?"

"Rich doesn't have to mean money. Some of them are getting their lives together in other ways too. Meeting women, getting engaged. Planning a future beyond their businesses."

"And their women don't want their islands to themselves?"

"A bunch of them just got back from the

Bahamas about ten days ago. One girlfriend in particular ripped me a new one for this, our situation."

She grinned. "I like her already."

"We met up here in town when they got back. You and Roxie would get along great. She's a Chicago girl too."

Surprise sat her up. "Roxie?" She almost couldn't process. "You mean—you don't mean…?"

"Roxie Kyst? Yeah," he said and smiled. "Zairn and I were at school together."

"Oh my God," she said and socked his shoulder as she lay back down. "Are you going to their wedding?"

He shrugged. "That's up to Jane."

"Who's Jane?"

"Their wedding planner," he said, laying an arm across her. "Roxie's former roommate, now Knox's girl too."

"Knox…?" Her mouth opened and just hung loose for a second. "Collier? He and Zairn were—"

"In the Bahamas together, yeah." He laughed. "If I'd known name-dropping was your thing, I could've got in your good graces a lot faster."

"Is that what this is about?"

"This?"

"Us. You see your friends getting married and engaged, so you want what they have?"

"More of my friends are single than married. But I won't deny that since meeting you, I understand their relationships better. For the first time, I get why they went all in. What it is to care about a woman and be so sure of a relationship."

What was it like from the other side of that? From Roxie and Jane's points of view. From being a regular nobody to being catapulted into super stardom. It didn't matter that they weren't actresses or models, people in the street knew who they were. Roxie especially, the woman had become a star in her own right.

"I saw that stream, forever ago, when she was sick."

"Rox?"

"Yeah. It was like in a second Zairn Lomond went from this famous, aloof, playboy to… he was so gentle with her. I've gotta admit, I swooned."

"You and the rest of the planet."

"Was that setup?" she asked. "Was it fake?"

"A hundred percent real."

"But their relationship is tumultuous, right? He can't be that good for her if they're breaking up all the time."

The rumble of his laugh warmed the palm she laid against him. "Zairn and Roxie are solid. So solid that whenever any of us need a little misdirection, they're game to make a spectacle."

"The breakups were fake?" she asked, and he nodded. "They pretend to have dramas?"

"Roxanna Kyst is a fucking rock. And there's nothing Zairn wouldn't do for her. Nothing. She cares about her girls. It's becoming tradition when one of our guys gets with a new girl, Roxie acts as a kind of… ambassador. Unofficially." The smile on his face was proud, yet grateful too. "Getting with guys like us, guys who might be in the spotlight or have some microscope turned on us, isn't always easy. Roxie and Zairn make it easier by taking heat that might burn the rest of us."

"That's sweet."

"It is. We'll make sure you're protected."

"If this gets that far," she said, prodding his arm. "I don't need private islands and fancy jets. What's wrong with a hotel room and good old-fashioned room service?"

"My life is a hotel room and good old-fashioned

room service."

"Where do you live?" No response. "You don't have a home?"

"I have this place," he said. "For another few months anyway."

"This isn't your home, it's your cover." It didn't make much sense, but disappointment bloomed. "You don't have somewhere that's yours?"

"I've never been in one place long enough to settle," he said. "I go where the deal is."

What would happen to their friendship while he was hopping from continent to continent?

"Does that make it difficult to keep track of people?"

"Not with modern technology," he said, tucking her hair back from her face. "I keep the network tight, corporate and personal."

"I wasn't asking for me," she said. "I was asking for you. You don't have anyone to come home to, anything to look forward to."

Lance maneuvering Xander into the agreement was beginning to make more sense… if he was truly a good friend.

Brushing his thumb back and forth on her cheek, he wasn't worried. "Wherever I am, no matter how many miles are between us, I will always be coming home to you at the end of every day, Button."

Absorbing his sincerity, it was difficult not to be drawn in. He meant it. The words he'd said on the night he first kissed her came back. Love. He'd actually used that word. Lying in bed with him wasn't playing it cool or treading softly.

"You haven't forgotten that option two came with no guarantees, have you?"

"No," he said, combing his fingers through her hair. "You're an incredible woman, Rainie. The most beautiful I've ever seen."

"Stop that," she said, drawing his hand from her hair. "You can't turn on the charm when we're in bed… I'm not wearing a bra."

He grinned. "I know."

In his shirt and her panties, her apparel was the same as the other nights she'd stayed over, but the mood wasn't the same. Nothing was the same.

"Alex was respectful. Alex was sweet with me… and gentle."

"I can be gentle, Button. This isn't me pressuring you. Just appreciating you… I don't know how long we'll be apart."

"And you think you'll forget me?"

He laughed. "Guaranteed I won't. Seeing you on video, hearing your voice every day, it won't be the same as touching you." He leaned in to inhale the scent of her hair. "Breathing you in."

Man had a point, which was probably why she needed to run her hands up and down his chest and shoulders.

"Will you still be able to have lunch with me?" The way he hesitated raised her suspicions. "Honesty."

"Daylight savings screws us. It's a fifteen-hour difference instead of the usual seventeen hours."

"Alex?" she warned. "What time will it be for you when I start lunch?"

"Three thirty."

"That's not bad… Will it interrupt your meetings?"

"In the a.m.," he said. "Three thirty in the morning."

Her hands stopped mid-caress. "You can't call me at three thirty in the morning. You need sleep."

"I can start my day late. I won't have early meetings."

"Give me your phone."

Hers was in her purse somewhere, and he didn't have a problem rolling over to retrieve his from the nightstand to hand it over.

"What are you looking for?"

An app that helped with time zones at work. Sometimes their clients or vendors were based in other states, though none were as far away as Sydney. The more she read on the app, the more dismayed she became.

"When I get home from work, your workday will just be starting… I'll be in bed by the time you're on lunch."

"Don't worry about it."

Easy said. Sending him away was good for his business, but it would be a test on them.

Rainie swallowed. "Do you want my email?"

"Baby," he said, taking the phone to put it back on the nightstand. "We're good, right?" She nodded. "I will call you every day… probably more than once a day. And if you feel like sending any pictures…"

Though she shoved him, she wasn't really offended. "I'll get up early, like five or six… We can talk before I go to work."

"Any time you want to call me, I'll pick up. And if you want me to come home—"

"Don't," she said, touching his lips. "We're being honest. Don't promise me things you can't deliver."

His tongue met her fingertips as he moistened his lips. "Whatever you want, I will always deliver. I told you that. Use your power wisely."

His company was important. She wouldn't let him lose sight of all he'd built for a piece of ass. And, yes, she was the piece of ass.

"Why does this feel so different?" she whispered, tracing his collarbone.

"Every time I watched you fall asleep, I used to think about what it would be like to kiss you goodnight… to see your smile in the morning. I knew this had potential from our first conversation. You're going through what I went through those first couple of weeks."

"We're supposed to be rebuilding our friendship."

"We are… Before I forget, there are keys in your nightstand behind you."

Her nightstand. "Keys for what?"

"Here. The apartment. And you know half the closet is empty."

"You want me to move into your apartment?"

"Whatever you want. Keep using the gym downstairs, come up here after, change, hangout. It'll be empty anyway; I'll need you to keep an eye on the place."

Hmm, she wasn't dumb enough to buy that. "Like there's anything here you care about being stolen… You don't have any plants or a pet."

"It'll be empty," he said. "Use it, don't use it. It's your call, Button. And if you want to get a cat, get a cat."

"I'm not getting a cat," she said, wriggling closer to lay her head on him. "I haven't figured out how to tame you yet. A cat will have to wait." When he settled down, wrapping his arms around her, she smiled and closed her eyes. "Promise me you'll come back. Even if it's just to break my heart."

He swept her hair away to curl his fingers around her jaw, drawing it up so he could kiss her head. "Never, baby. Never."

Break her heart or come back?

His going away wasn't such a bad thing. Without space to breathe, she'd dive deep into him. If that happened, neither of them would ever come up for air again.

TWENTY-SIX

IN THE WARMTH and comfort of her dreams, she was invincible. Even as she breathed in deep to soak up all the happiness around her, the fingers of reality clawed her out of slumber. Stupid reality.

Her dream faded and the day crept in. Except when she opened her eyes, the room was still dark. Though not completely…

Light. Where was that light coming from? She rolled onto her back and spotted the vertical strip of it by the closet door.

Before she could think about sitting up, the sliver widened and Xander's silhouette appeared.

"What time is it?" she asked as a yawn overtook her.

"Just before five," he said. "Go back to sleep, Button."

"You were going to sneak out and leave me?" she asked, rolling onto her side, snagging his pillow to hug it to her face. "That's rude."

He came to sit on the edge of the bed and leaned

over her. "You look like an angel when you sleep. I couldn't wake an angel."

"You better because if this is how you plan to treat me in the mornings, I'll never sleep with you again."

He bowed to kiss her cheek. "Noted."

"Won't you be tired when you get there? Leaving this early?"

"I'll sleep on the jet."

Knowing a man of his means wasn't easy to get used to. "Do you want me to get up?"

His fingers kept moving in her hair, brushing it away from her face over and over. "To come with me? Abso-fucking-lutely."

"I don't have a passport." Though that wasn't what was holding her back. "I meant do you want me to leave with you, so I'm not alone in your apartment? In your bed. What if I steal stuff?"

"I told you, this is your apartment too." He kissed her temple. "And this is your bed. Our bed. I said you had all of me, I meant it… Do you want me to leave Topher here with you?"

She blinked in faux surprise. "In bed?"

"In town," he said, smiling, though not as much as her.

He was dressed dapper. Sophisticated and stylish, the buttoned-up businessman.

She stroked his lapel. "I don't need an assistant… You remember to be kind to Lance. Forgive him already. He's one of your closest friends."

"Okay," he said, sitting up to retrieve something from his inside pocket. "And this is when you try to remember how charming I am."

He held up a dark rectangle to show her, then put it on the nightstand. "What's that?"

"Anything you need. Keep it for emergencies, use it every day, whatever you want."

"It's a credit card?"

"A special one," he said. "I won't be here to cover your coffee."

"Yeah, and we know how that breaks the bank."

After they shared a smile, he grew solemn and curled his fingers around her jaw to angle her mouth to accept his.

It was just a brief kiss. A simple meeting of mouths and a too quick retreat.

"Call me anytime, okay?" he said. "Anything you need, it's yours."

"Call me when you get there."

He breathed out a laugh. "Baby, I'll call you from the plane before you start work... modern technology, remember?"

And he owned the plane, so no one would tell him to hang up.

"Okay, but be good."

"All yours, I promise."

"I didn't mean that kind of good. No more deals with Lance that break women's hearts, okay, please?"

"Okay." He tipped her head down and kissed her hair. "Bye, Button."

He lingered for just another second. Her heart pounded while watching him walk out of the bedroom. She sat up. Something screamed inside her that they weren't done.

Without even thinking, she leaped to her feet and scrambled across the bed to jump down and dart to the door.

"Baby!"

At the front door, seconds away from leaving, her exclamation brought his attention around. She was already moving, running to pounce up and wrap her arms and legs around him. Capturing his mouth without consent, she didn't want gentle or to say a simple goodbye.

There were so many variables. So many possibilities. So many things that could go wrong. Whatever they were, her body didn't care. Neither did her tongue as it raced to learn every millimeter of his.

Squeezing him tight, his passionate response spurred her on. They may not be together, but she wouldn't take the risk of letting him walk out without proving just how much headway they'd made.

Reluctantly, she broke the union, though she happily accepted his short farewell follow ups.

"That was a helluva goodbye," he said. "I already wanted to stay with you and now…"

"Take the win, businessman. Now go do your job. Faster you go, faster you're back with me."

Breathing out, he held her as long as he could as she slithered down his body.

"You're my light… I'll always do whatever it takes to get back to you."

She stroked his jaw and welcomed one more kiss as he opened the door at his back. "I'll see you soon."

"Soon," he said, kissing her head and taking her hand to hold on to it as he ebbed from the apartment.

She moved into the doorway, leaning against the frame to watch him walk away. He was leaving her alone, as she'd instructed. Already she was second-guessing that choice.

TWENTY-SEVEN

"IT TAKES AS LONG as it takes," Rainie said into the phone for what felt like the twentieth time in ten minutes.

"I told you last night, as soon as we touched down, I wanted to tell them to fuel up and take off again… I shouldn't be here."

Pressing a finger into her free ear, she leaned back against the restroom stall wall. "You sound grumpy. You can't go into your first meeting grumpy… Are you meeting the Sydney bigwigs now?"

"No, just Ethan and Lance for the updates," he said fast, then followed it with. "Why are you whispering?"

"I'm at work, remember?"

"It's Saturday," he said.

"For you it's Saturday. We're still on Friday over here." Getting used to the time zones would be difficult. Xander was supposed to be used to it. "And I don't know I'll be getting out of here any time soon. We're trying to impress some bigshot asshole, I don't know."

"Maybe I should throw some business Viva's way. Sign up a couple of my brands and tell them the only way I'll be a happy customer is if I get unlimited access to you."

She rolled her eyes. "People already think because I work in customer relations, I service clients, so thanks, but no thanks. No one would believe it was a coincidence anyway. We're a mid-level firm at best, and Seven is very not mid-level."

"Difference between mid-level and the big leagues is attitude, baby. It's all in the attitude."

"I'll remember that when I'm trying to make Fortune 500."

"We have the Summit Sponsorship. BlueGold will need representation. I'll sign them up with Viva."

She frowned. "Don't you need to like set up a company before you market it? What if you sign up BlueGold and our ads cause a million percent uptick in orders? How would you satisfy demand?"

"I'll always satisfy your demand."

Okay, she should chastise him for being suggestive. But sexy was better than sulky and he'd been that a lot since leaving her in the apartment.

"I have to go back to work now."

"Okay," he said on a laugh. "Call me when you finish up. You have another hour or two?"

"Depends how long it takes to get our work done."

"Okay."

"Okay."

"Bye."

He'd been gone less than two days and already saying goodbye was difficult. She wanted him back. There was security and comfort just in knowing he was nearby. Xander was literally a world away, but it was a distance that meant nothing to her heart.

***

BINGHAM BRIGHT WAS supposed to be a quick acquisition. A big one, but a quick one. That he'd been dragged halfway across the planet was already enough to piss him off. His best people were down there, and he didn't appreciate attention seekers. The fact that the demand took him away from Rainie, well, that was a new kind of pissed off he'd have to get used to if he planned to keep working.

Ascending in the elevator to the Bingham Bright top floor, a smile teased his lips. It hadn't occurred to him to think "if he planned to keep seeing Rainie." As far as he was concerned, she was the priority. Everything else would fit in around her.

He twisted a fraction toward Topher just behind his shoulder. "Send the number for the florist we like to my phone."

"Sir?" Topher asked with a note of surprise.

"Just send it to my phone. We have an account with them?"

"Yes, but I can do it. If you need me to call them—"

"I'll do it."

Rainie didn't want to be delegated; that wasn't a mistake he'd make again.

After a brief pause, Topher asked, "You got her address?"

No, he didn't. Though if he asked, she'd provide it. They were doing honesty after all. But the flowers should be a surprise.

"Viva it is," he said, choosing to ignore Topher's thread of amusement. "Roses are too generic for her… I'll need to do some research…" He was really talking to himself and didn't need an answer. "She deserves something special… unique."

The people waiting for the elevator moved for him. They always moved for him. He strode to the office Ethan had been using. He might not like being there, but he knew the building… more than he'd care to admit.

Without knocking or even hesitating, he went inside.

Ethan was already there, sitting in the guest seat at the desk. He wasn't alone either. To the left was an oval table with a baker's dozen seats around it. Lance was at the three o'clock position, swiveled to look at Ethan, who was facing his way too.

Obviously, they'd been talking, but that ceased the second he walked in with Topher at his back.

All of them took each other in.

Ethan was the first to leap up. "Damn, am I glad to see you," he said, rushing over to shake his hand and do the one arm hug thing. "I tried to call last night… thought you might want the update before coming in."

He'd landed late and stolen some time on video call with Rainie as she woke up and got ready for work. Being a part of her routine was amazing. Something so simple and yet it was intimate… and meant the world to him. She'd taken him out of the apartment and he'd joined her on her journey to work. After he amused her with his reluctance to hang up, he'd only been fit for sleep, though he'd set his alarm to join her at lunch.

"I read all the contract drafts and meeting minutes on the plane. I'm up to date."

"Xander…" Lance said.

Talking to Ethan was easy. When Lance spoke up, he tensed. Ethan backed away.

Rainie had told him to forgive. He'd planned to try his damndest. Lance was just stupid; the misdirection hadn't been malicious. Still, it wasn't easy to shrug it off when he'd come so close to losing the most important thing in his life. It wasn't even guaranteed they were out of the woods yet.

"You'll get your investment," he said without looking directly at his friend, though he could see Lance rise to creep over. "We'll deal with that after we sort out the crap here."

"You're still seeing her?"

The question was careful, yet his attention snapped around as anger heated his throat. "Is that your damn business?"

"Xander," Ethan said in defense of their friend. "He's a dick, but he had no reason to think she was… You always hooked up with women. It was never serious. How was he supposed to know that Rainie was going to be special to you?"

He exhaled. He'd used the same argument when trying to explain away Lance's actions. Seeing his friend in the flesh brought back memories of learning about the lie. If he didn't try to forgive and forget, their professional relationship would suffer, and their personal one would be over.

"Yes, I'm still seeing her," he said, trying his best to push past the rage.

"Then the investment isn't mine yet. You have another—"

"She knows," he said, making eye contact with Lance. "She knows everything." Lance frowned. "The arrangement. The investment stake. Seven. Me. Everything."

Lance's frown grew as he took in the news. Rainie had given him permission to string his friend along, and that might have been fun for a while. But, in truth, he was fighting the impulse to scream his love for her from the rooftops. He planned to call her often and would always pick up when she reached out, as promised. He didn't want to hide what he felt for her, or how important she was in his life, from anyone.

"What did you tell her about this? About coming here?"

Lance's questions were typical of how he'd be pre-Rainie. Those questions weren't benign. He was questioning Rainie, doubting her.

"I wouldn't be here if Rainie hadn't told me to come," he said, his jaw tight. "And don't fucking start doubting her. You know nothing about her."

"Do you?" Lance asked. "Honestly?"

Fucking asshole. If he kept this up, there wouldn't be a friendship to save. Fury took him a step closer. Ethan jumped in to grab his forearm before he could smack their friend in the face.

"Okay," Ethan said. "Maybe we cool off on the Rainie talk for a while. Just until everyone's back in the rhythm."

"I know he's pissed at me," Lance said. "That's fucking obvious, but who is this girl? Do we know? Have we checked?"

"Are you for real?" he asked, then looked at Ethan. "Is he for real?"

"Lance," Ethan said. "We're in uncharted territory here. I've never met Rainie, I can't speak to who she is or her intentions, but Xander is serious about her. We have to trust our friend. That's all we can do."

Lance met his eye. If his so-called buddy wanted to make something of it, he would. It was on him. If Lance accepted Rainie, Xander would keep the peace, only because his woman's directive was clear. She wanted him to get back on track with his cohorts.

Lance sighed. "I wouldn't get bent out of shape if I didn't care. I want you to be happy and if Rainie's it..." He offered his hand to shake. "Congratulations, man."

His friends were accepting his judgment. They

did it every day in business, yet the moment was profound. He put his hand in Lance's to shake. He'd convinced everyone important in his life that Rainie was his future. All he had to do was convince Rainie too.

TWENTY-EIGHT

SATURDAY. The weekend. She'd been to the gym, showered in Xander's apartment, now… what would she do with the rest of her weekend?

Coming out of the bathroom, she expected to be alone. But, huh, she wasn't.

A woman at the kitchen island had her back to her, which gave her a few seconds to scrutinize the petite brunette.

Who was this person and why did she—

The woman whirled around. Wearing a broad smile, with sparkle in her eye, she was immediately recognizable.

"Roxanna Kyst," she said in a rush of breath.

"Right first time. Casanova will like you," Roxie said and raised a wineglass. "Drink with me?"

"It's two thirty in the afternoon."

"It's always happy hour somewhere in the world," Roxie said and swept up a second glass. "No to the alcohol, got it." She glided over to the sink and poured out the liquid. "Coffee?"

"There's a coffee shop across the street," she said and squeezed her eyes closed. "But… what are you doing here? Are you looking for Xander? He isn't here."

"I know, he's Down Under. And my guy is in California. We're free!" With wide arms, Roxie whirled to face her, grabbing the counter at her back to support herself on tippy toes. "What do you say? Tokyo? London? Buenos Aires? Pick a continent!"

The woman's exuberance was contagious.

She laughed. "Thank you, Ms. Kyst, but I don't have a passport."

"New York it is then," Roxie said, boosting herself closer. "We'll get you a passport for next week. Not that it matters. Who cares about customs? I have the jet and Dennis works for me."

"Dennis?"

"Our pilot."

"You have your own pilot?"

"He's Zairn's pilot… or he was. Z trusts Dennis more than any other pilot, so now he's permanently assigned to me. I guess that means Z needs a new flyboy… or would he be a wingman?" Roxie laughed at her own joke and extended a hand to her while strolling to the door. "Show me this coffee shop. Did Gauge get you security yet? If he did, they suck, 'cause I haven't seen them once. A sniper doesn't count as standard security, I already asked about that one. Zairn thinks having my own personal sniper would be overkill." Her grin was instant and came with an eye roll. "Ha, overkill. I am on fire today. Can't beat Chicago air."

"Security?"

Roxie stopped. Her hand dropped. "Oh, if you go outside with me, you'll get your picture taken. You okay with that? Do your friends and family know about your boyfriend? Colleagues? Acquaintances? As soon as that first picture hits the internet, your phone will blow up. Every old boyfriend's next-door neighbor's great auntie will start calling you their BFF."

"I…"

Roxie exhaled. "Girl, you don't want to walk into this blind. Do your people know we know each other?"

"*I* didn't know we knew each other."

"Oh, Xander comes with a whole posse and we're the power behind the crown. One sec." She went over to open the front door and peek outside. "Yo, Trev! There's a coffee shop across the street. Will you go get supplies, please?"

"They sell booze?" a male on the hallway side of the door asked.

"No," Roxie said with exaggerated offense. "It's far too early for getting drunk, Trevor, don't be ridiculous. We want coffee. Mocha frappe for Rainie, hold the whip. And bring muffins."

"I'm not your valet," the male grumbled.

"Fine, make me go over there. See how quick you need to find yourself a new place to live. You want the lurker to know where we are?"

"You're being dramatic."

"And you like to complain."

"I'll send one of my guys."

"Whatever. I don't care who goes. Crack that whip. Run your own department." Roxie started to come in but swung back out. "You have no intention of leaving this door yourself because you don't trust I'd still be here when you get back, right?"

"Yeah," Trevor drawled.

"Okay, just clearing that up." Roxie came in, thrusting the door into the frame. "Let's go sit over there."

Roxie went to straighten the curtain then dropped onto the end of the couch.

She went to sit at the other end. "You came here

to check me out?"

"No," Roxie said, kicking off her shoes to bring her feet onto the couch. "I'm here for you."

"What did I do?"

On a laugh, Roxie leaned over to touch her shoulder. "Listen, honey, I heard 'Chicago' and was already on the plane. You're here, by yourself, and you're dealing with a lot. You're not alone. Whatever you need, we're here for you."

Someone acknowledging that gave her such a sense of relief. She hadn't considered it, but it had been an emotional few weeks.

The heavy ruby on Roxie's hand was incredible. She'd dub it awesome, in the original sense of the word.

"That's beautiful."

Roxie adjusted the angle of her hand. "Yeah, I don't have to workout this arm. Dragging this thing around all day is workout enough." She paused. "And let me guess, you're wondering if it changes things."

"It does change things," she said. "And to be honest, I don't know…"

"You're doubting yourself?"

"You don't come from money, do you?" she asked. Roxie shook her head. "I can't even imagine that much money. I'm no royal heiress, how would I fit in with that crowd?"

"On Xander's side, this is the crowd you have to fit in with," Roxie said, gesturing up and down at herself. "Your friends, the ones you have now, if they're real friends, there's no need to drop them. The people in Xander's life, the true, close ones who mean something to him, they don't care about society princesses or airs and graces. Have you talked about the future?"

"We're barely past the past."

"The bet."

"Xander calls it a deal, but yeah. We started in a

lie.”

"That doesn't have to be the foundation of your relationship. Lance might be an idiot, but he wasn't being callous. And Xander was in the dark, just like you."

"Until he 'broke up' with Lance," she said, putting the words in air quotes.

"And you should've seen him the weekend he told you the truth. He was a wreck. He ditched out on a friend intervention to be here with you."

"I know he was sorry." She exhaled and sank back. "I heard you stuck up for me," she said. "I appreciate that."

"Of course!"

Was it too late to ask for wine? "I wasn't mad. I mean I was—"

"Who wouldn't be?"

"But I was embarrassed too. And hurt and…"

"You lost someone close to you."

"I believed we were something we weren't."

"You were that something, just not quite in the way you thought. He does care about you."

"It's easy to believe a guy so gorgeous when he's seducing you," she said and licked her lips, adjusting to shift her weight to her shoulder against the back of the couch. "I don't have to tell you that. Is it possible to stay mad at your fiancé?"

"Oh, Zairn's had his share of the cold shoulder," Roxie said, mirroring her position. "But I get what you mean. When we want something, whether we're conscious of it or not, we make allowances."

"Is that what I'm doing? Am I making allowances because the idea of him is so seductive?"

"Let's get one thing straight, life with Xander will turn your world on its head."

"If I was smart, I'd walk away."

"The reality is, it's only seductive if the man is

right. Otherwise, it would get old fast. If I didn't love Zairn as much as I do, if I didn't know one hundred percent that I had a hundred percent of his support, I'd be over the nomadic lifestyle already. As it is, I love experiencing new things with him. But it's the man who makes the adventure. Without him…"

"Do you feel you've lost yourself to him? I don't want to throw myself into this and not recognize myself in six months."

"Things do change. Part of that is us. But we change them too. It's not the money and the lifestyle that changes us, it's the man. The love. The partnership." On an inhale, Roxie's chin rose. "Hmm…"

"What?"

"I'm trying to figure out if there's anything Zairn might say is too far, if there's any scenario where he wouldn't stand by me…"

The longer Roxie pondered, the higher her smile grew. "Okay, I get it."

"I almost lost him once."

Startled, she straightened a little. "You did?"

"Mm hmm," Roxie said, nodding. "Because I fooled myself into thinking I could live without him. That he wasn't my whole world."

"What happened?"

"He dumped me and left me."

"Oh, God," she said, leaning over to take Roxie's hand on the middle seat. "That's terrible."

"Nothing like watching the man you love turn his back and walk away."

"How did you get back together?"

"I kicked my ass into gear and went after him, but it could've gone the other way. Figuring out our relationship took effort on both our parts. You have to want it and recognize that you can be each other's greatest ally. But it can't be him and you. It has to be you both together. You both have to want it more than you've ever wanted anything your whole life. You have to hand yourself over to it and be ready to ride the rapids."

"Sounds terrifying."

Roxie laughed. "Sometimes it is. But it can also be the most epic adventure of your life."

In theory. Them together. Already Roxie had given her a lot to think about.

"Thank you," she said. "I didn't know you were coming, but I'm so grateful that you did."

"It's not my place to intrude," Roxie said, touching her clavicle. "Your relationship is your relationship. Please don't think I came here to push you one way or another. Xander left you alone, and he was worried. It's important to him that you have support."

"He called you?"

"He called Zairn. They talked. I might have been eavesdropping. They look at things from such a male perspective, which isn't always helpful. And if you're going to be a permanent feature, it doesn't hurt us to form our own posse."

"The power behind the crown?"

"Exactly!"

"You and Jane?"

"And Merci and Lilya." Roxie tilted to stage whisper. "Though Lilya's a secret right now, Kintyre's having issues."

"Issues?"

"With his ex-wife," Roxie said with a sigh. "Julietta's a handful."

"Julietta," she murmured. "Kintyre…" She straightened. "Julietta Ines-Kintyre. Oh my God, isn't she—"

"Yes," Roxie said, raising a flat palm. "But trust me, you don't want to wade into it. Toria and Astrid are part of our clan too, they're single right now. A relationship is optional in our group. You don't need a man to be whole, honey."

"But it sure helps?"

"Well, their bank balances do," Roxie said and laughed.

"You're lucky to have so many friends in your life."

Roxie took her hand and bounced to the front of the couch. "You have us too. Want to come meet some of our allies?"

The adventure starts here? "I should talk to Xander about—"

"Start as you mean to go on. We can ask his permission, or we can live our best lives."

Asking any man, or any person, permission wasn't her style. "Maybe I need a do-over."

"Yeah, you do. A fresh take and a refresh," Roxie said, surprising her with a clap of her hands. "Nowhere better for that than New York."

She raised her head. "New York?"

Roxie side-nodded and stood, offering her hand. "You need to get out of this apartment. Out of this city. Forget about your guy troubles and have some fun."

She took her hand and stood. "Fun? Where?"

Roxie waved her engagement ring in front of her. "The Ruby Room. Where else?" Her new friend drew her to her feet. "We'll stop by your place and grab what you need for your passport."

"My passport?"

"Never know what's right around the corner," Roxie said, guiding her over to the door just as it opened to a tall, broad guy holding a tray of cups. Her new friend just sailed on by. "Coffee? Geez, Trev, this woman needs a party. Where's all the alcohol?" She showed a teasing smile, tweaked the deadpan bodyguard's cheek, and linked their arms. "Don't worry, he loves me really."

TWENTY-NINE

ROXIE WAS FULL-ON. There was no other way to put it. The woman shimmered with confidence; every part of her was certain and straightforward. She teased and joked, yes, but she also listened and really cared about the people in her life.

After a stop at her apartment and a flight to New York, she was finding Roxie's rhythm was just her kind of tempo.

"Thanks, Dennis," Roxie said, kissing the cheek of the man who opened the plane door for them.

Roxie slipped on her shades as they descended toward red carpet on tarmac. A man over six feet tall stood by a spotless black town car. Whoever he was, he was broader and bulkier than the others she'd seen in Roxie's life.

"Wow," she said without thinking.

Roxie reached back from the bottom stair and linked their arms. "I know. He's always the guy we see second."

"Is he a billionaire too?"

"I don't know, I never asked," Roxie said,

hopping down to the red carpet. "Ballard, are you a billionaire?"

"One not enough for you, Little Rox?" the guy asked, opening the back door of the car.

"Miss me?"

"Not quite," he said, but caught Roxie when she launched up to hug him. "Can't keep you away, huh?"

"We came to town to party," Roxie said, leaping back to push her forward. "Ballard, this is Rainie Tait. Rainie, meet Sean Ballard. Zairn's Head of Security and Logistics. And his de facto best friend... don't tell Xander."

"You're Gauge's latest?"

"Not his latest," Roxie said, elbowing him. "She's his forever."

"What the hell have you started, Kyst?" Ballard drew a phone from his back pocket and pressed a button. "Here."

Roxie stepped back to gesture her into the car as Ballard held the phone out. "Who's this?"

"Your old man," Ballard said as Roxie took the phone.

She slid into the backseat, surprised by the younger woman seated opposite her. Roxie got in and the door closed.

"Astrid, honey," Roxie said, folding down a center armrest with a groove perfect for the cellphone. "I missed you!"

"Did you miss me?" from the phone a suave male voice stalled Roxie mid-almost-hug.

"Casanova," Roxie chirped and slid back in her seat to address the device. "You know that pussy you were balls deep in first thing this morning? I have it with me!"

"I wondered where it went. No harm."

"Easily replaced," Roxie said.

"Unlike your cellphone. You're testing my patience."

"Keeping you on your toes, my darling."

"As always. How was the flight?"

"Which one? I've flown clear across the country today. You better be looking after Jane."

"Jane's a sweetheart," he said. "You should learn from her."

"Aww, someone got fiancée envy? Too bad Knox got to her before you did."

"I don't know, I could send a few decoys into the New York club tonight. Take your pick, then I get out of this deal."

"A deal's a deal. And I'm keeping the ring."

"No problem, it doesn't fit me," the smooth operator drawled. "I know it goes against your every instinct, but please try not to ruin Rainie while you're there."

Her? How would she be ruined?

"Would I do that?" Roxie asked. "I didn't ruin Merci or Lilya, did I?"

"No, but you didn't have Toria with you for their orientation."

Roxie snorted. "Like we're employees beneath you. You boys better look out. When we women decide we're coming for you, you won't stand a chance. We're maneuvering you one by one. You don't even see it coming."

"Blowjobs are your secret weapon," he said. "Send that out in a memo."

"Assuming I haven't already?"

"Astrid," the male said.

The young woman jerked. "Uh, yes, sir."

"Charge her phone. Please. I don't want her slipping the net."

"Yes, sir."

"You know, you haven't even formally met Rainie," Roxie said, dipping closer to the phone. "You're making a terrible first impression."

"You're my first impression," he said. "People learn about me by looking at who shares my bed. You're an ambassador, remember?"

"Is Gauge really serious about this?" Roxie asked, throwing her a quick wink. "Is he serious about Rainie? Because he can't ask a woman to adjust to this kind of life if he'll get bored in a couple of weeks."

"Gauge's number will be in this phone, Lola. You want to grill someone, grill him. I'm serious about you, that's about as much as I have invested in this."

"Typical," Roxie said on a tsk. "You just can't see past the end of your own cock."

"Why would I need to? I know you're on the end of it most days."

"That where your world begins and ends?"

"With you?" he asked. "That's what you keep telling me."

"Aww, Casanova, you wouldn't have it any other way."

"You keep telling me that too."

"I am the sun which your world revolves around."

A short giggle came from the younger woman, who immediately tensed and touched her own lips.

"You're dampening panties over here, Casanova."

"It's a side effect of the sex appeal," he said. "Rainie, I apologize if my fiancée is inappropriate. We keep saying we'll get it checked out—"

"But he won't let me keep my clothes on that long when we're together," Roxie interjected. "He's smitten with me. Can't get enough. Rainie's offended by your implication that I'm faulty."

"Oh no, I'm not offended," Rainie said. "This is just… it's surreal. I only found out Xander and Zairn were close a few days ago. Now I'm in New York on my way to Crimson. We are going to Crimson, right?"

"Rouge HQ," Roxie said. "But, yes, everything under one roof. Including a lot of booze and our own personal nightclub. Get used to the high life, baby, it's on its way to a screen near you."

Except she was a little squirmy. "I don't want to take advantage of anyone. Xander and I haven't even…"

Did they know she and Xander hadn't slept together? Had sex was a more accurate descriptor. All of this would make sense if they'd committed to a life together, but they hadn't. Xander wanted it. He'd said he wanted her. She'd been the one to hold back. Then there she was, living it up as soon as he was out of the country.

"What did I tell you about men?" Roxie asked her. "You don't need one to be whole. Screw Xander, you're my friend. What happens in Crimson, stays in Crimson."

Except they only knew each other because of Xander.

"Does Xander frequent Crimson?"

When there was a pause, Roxie flattened the phone. "That one was for you, Casanova."

"When the moment calls for it."

"That's a politician's answer," Roxie said. "How about the truth, Mr. President?"

He exhaled. "Xander's about the job."

"All of you are about the job."

"It's different for Gauge," Zairn said. "The job is all he has." Okay, that was incredibly sad. "Everything he is, is tied up in work. He's put a lot of effort into reaching his level. He's never been one for shortcuts or cheats. He grafts, hard."

"It breaks my heart a little," Rainie said, her focus

tracking to New York passing by the side window. "He doesn't even have a home."

"He doesn't have a home?" Roxie asked. Rainie shook her head. "Where does he keep his stuff?"

"What stuff?" Zairn asked. "He moves from hotel to hotel. His life is Venture."

"Doesn't Venture have an HQ?"

"He has hubs across the world. Smaller satellite locations without a centralized HQ. Any operations he needs to position, he uses our HQs."

"Like Rouge?"

"Rouge, yes, Mosaic, Eclipse, Dyce, RCI," Zairn said. "He's not one for slowing down. He's always said if he stops, he stagnates."

"That's not true," Roxie said. "I guess it's on you, Rainie, to show him that."

"I wouldn't ask him to stop, to change. I just couldn't."

"Then what's your future?" Roxie asked. "How do you see yourselves in five years or ten?"

"How do you see us in five years or ten?" Zairn asked. "Let them find their own way, Lola. You know how it goes."

"I don't want them to obsess, but I do want them to be sure. Jane went through so much to get to where she is with Knox."

"And we didn't?"

"That's different."

Zairn laughed. "My perfect, beautiful Lola."

Roxie hitched her chin. "I'll follow you to the ends of the earth."

"You wouldn't have to because I'd already be on your tail."

"You love my caboose."

"I do," he said. "Want me to hop the red-eye?"

"I won't be long," Roxie said. "But you're on

phone sex duty. I will call from our New Year screw-room. Drunk calling probably."

"I expect nothing less," he said. "I have to go. Have a good time, Rainie. Roxie on her own is dangerous, but her and Toria together can be lethal. Please say no. Go with your gut." Roxie stuck her tongue out at the device. "Astrid, charge her phone."

"Yes, sir."

"Love you, Lo."

"I love you too, Scroogey," Roxie said with such sincerity it warmed her heart. The line cleared. "So that was my guy."

"He's…"

"Defies explanation, doesn't he?" Roxie asked and switched her focus. "Okay, Astrid, give it to me. What disasters do I have to clean up? What policies can we change to shake things up around here?"

New York, they said it was the city that never slept. In Roxie's wake, that had to apply tenfold. Getting to know each other was one thing, a crutch that she appreciated. But, more than that, she was getting a glimpse into the lifestyle. Maybe that was the plan. Without the sheen of her adoration for Xander, she got a more objective look. It was fun. Frenetic. Mind-bending in some ways. Except it wasn't the luxuries that were making their mark.

Roxie was happy.

So happy that her confidence echoed in waves in every space she occupied. That wasn't the lifestyle. No. The phone call gave her the clue. It was love. Roxie was happy and in love. Happy not because she was in love, but because she'd found the man. The One. He just also happened to be a billionaire.

That was it.

She couldn't blame or judge Xander for his success. It was a part of him. If he'd come to her dirt-poor living in a trailer or a slum, would she have cared? Love, if it was true, had to overcome the odds. She shouldn't be looking for obstacles or negatives. She wasn't excited to see Crimson. Okay, so maybe she was a little. But being a part of Xander's family, meeting the people he cared about, that was the real triumph.

THIRTY

"THOUGHT YOU WERE supposed to be hooking your single friends up, Rox," Toria said. "Since you locked Zairn down, it's his single friends who've been tying themselves down."

Rouge HQ was amazing. The building gleamed red, signaling sin like a siren calling people in. They'd driven around the back, down a gated alley to enter the building from behind. People were there to greet them. Greet Roxie. But the woman knew where she was going and didn't ask for help.

Just being there was a dream. One that got even more incredible when Roxie showed her to a gleaming guest room in her and Zairn's apartment, then took her to the closet and told her to help herself.

Had she really been in Chicago just that afternoon? It seemed like she'd been transported to Narnia, or some other mythical land of wonders.

After taking some time to get ready, though she didn't really know for what, Roxie came to retrieve her and introduced her to Toria and Merci, who were waiting in the living room with Astrid.

Well, not really waiting, they were already gorging on the tapas and cocktails spread out on the coffee table.

"You don't want to tie yourself down," Roxie said to Toria. "You're having too much fun living a New York life."

"I am," Toria said, wearing a grin without an ounce of shame. "But if he came along, I'd consider it. And what about Astrid?"

"Astrid has her own problem," Roxie said. "And it's called Sean Ballard."

"Who we met today?" she asked. "Your brother?"

"He's my cousin."

"Ah," she said, catching up. "So any guy who wants to get with you has to live with him breathing down their necks."

"She's a baby anyway," Roxie said. "She has to play the field, figure out what she likes, what she needs from a guy. Then when her perfect match comes along, she'll know it's right and she'll be done kissing toads."

"Frogs."

"Right," Roxie said, waving a dismissive hand over her shoulder. "In fact, Victoria Lovell, that is your mission, if you choose to accept it."

"My mission?" Toria asked, wriggling deeper into the couch. "Oh, you know I love a mission."

"Get Astrid laid," Roxie said. The young assistant gasped. "Okay, so laid is maybe too much too soon. You need to get out there, Ast. To date. Have drinks, dinner, flirt, just learn to relax and love."

"I don't have time for—"

"That excuse doesn't fly while Zairn and I are in LA. We're staying at Knox's house, and Jane is running after all of us. You can do your work in a nine to five here. At night, you can go out on the town with Toria.

Hell, we have 'town' right here in the building. You don't have to go far."

"Do you live nearby?"

"They live in the building," Roxie said, gesturing with her glass as she slid off the couch to sit between it and the coffee table. "They can get ready here, go down to the bar, restaurant, and the club, and come right back up when they're done."

"Doesn't solve the Ballard problem," Toria said. "If he wants to be a jerk…"

"I can take him to LA or just set him up with missions here."

"Why didn't you take Ballard to LA in the first place?" Toria asked.

"He's been non-stop since… well, forever. Before me anyway. Z said he needed some time off."

"Doesn't seem like he's taking much of a break."

"I don't think Ballard asked for time off, Z is just trying to be nice. In LA, we're treading established paths, from Knox's to CollCom to Crimson and that's about it. Ballard can run it from here. At least that was the idea, but I heard he's hiring."

"Yeah, a whole bunch of new hotties. I guess with you being Zairn's priority now, he wants as many security people on hand as possible."

"You can come and stay with us, Astrid," Merci said. "If you want to get away from Crimson."

Merci didn't say much. But that could be because Roxie and Toria's personalities were both larger than life. Listening to them was like watching a train shoot past at top speed, dizzying and fast. Picking a point of focus was a struggle.

"Astrid and Reid?" Roxie asked and snickered. "She'd probably pass out."

"They've met before."

"I always wonder what it's like to live with your

fiancé," Roxie asked, shifting onto her knees to begin mixing more drinks. "Does he talk?"

"Yes, he talks," Merci said, doing a bad job of hiding her automatic smile.

"Oh, hey, that says a lot," Toria said, digging an elbow into the pillow behind her to get closer to Merci. "That mean he talks in bed?"

"Sometimes," Merci said, her eyes slinking to the side.

"They have a semi-dom-sub thing going on over there," Roxie said. "Merci does what she's told."

"In some situations."

"What about Gauge?" Toria asked. All attention landed on her. "Is he a dirty talker? A dominant? He into anything kinky?"

"You can't ask her that," Astrid said, and she about exploded with relief. "It's private."

"We know Reid likes to dominate," Toria said. "Roxie and Zairn battle for power, and Knox falls to his knees for Jane."

"They're all so different," Merci said. "It's a wonder how they became friends in the first place."

"In situations like that, cooped up in a remote location, at school without family or much free time, they didn't have a choice who they spent time with."

"Do you know who I'm most interested in learning more about?" Toria asked, scanning the group, leaving some suspense time just hanging in the air.

"She's going to say Zane Dyce," Roxie said, picking up an olive with a toothpick.

"Because he's the richest?" Merci asked.

"He has his own island," Astrid said.

Hmm, Dyce must be the friend Xander mentioned.

"Not Dyce," Toria said. "Xavien Rourke."

Merci and Roxie both laughed. "He's an

asshole!"

"Yeah," Toria said unashamedly, scooting forward to peruse the food.

"And that does it for you?"

"He has something going on," Roxie said, bobbing her head side to side. "I don't know what exactly. Dyce said there's a woman involved somewhere."

"Wow, there you go," Toria said, "proving my point."

"What point?"

"That Zairn's single friends are tying themselves down."

"Tie yourself down if you want to, honey," Roxie said. "And if you want me to set you up with someone, take your pick. What do you want? Rich?"

"Oh, he'd have to be rich."

"Hot?"

"That goes without saying," Toria said. "I like muscles."

"You like personality," Roxie said. "If a guy can make you laugh, you're putty."

"Nothing wrong with that. It doesn't matter, I have to wait and see how your and Merci's weddings both go down first. I want to be single for those. And when I do pick a lucky winner, I'll have to make sure my wedding outdoes both of yours."

"Wait 'til I tell Jane that," Roxie said to be greeted by laughter.

"How great is it that Gauge fell for a Chicago girl though," Toria said, raising her almost empty glass in a silent toast before drinking the last of the alcohol in it. "What do you do?"

"I work for Viva Marketing," she said and noted how Roxie made eye contact with Toria.

"No kidding," Toria said, drawing her eyes away

from her friend. "I used to work at Hype."

"Wow? Really?" Hype was Viva's closest competitor in Chicago. "You quit to come here?"

"There was a… difference in style," Roxie said and leaned back while tipping her chin up to look at her. "Litigation pending."

"That sounds interesting," Merci said.

"Another couple of drinks and Toria will tell you everything you want to know," Roxie said. "Come on, let's put on some tunes while we finish these…" She poured fresh alcohol into each glass. "Then we'll show Rainie to the Ruby Room."

Cheers of agreement joined Roxie as she fumbled for the phone further down the table. Drinks, dancing, and good company. She couldn't ask for more.

THIRTY-ONE

THAT WASN'T WHOLLY TRUE. She could ask for more. One thing more. Xander.

The Ruby Room was Roxie's private playground. Well, okay, so all of Crimson was probably that, but Roxie was modest with her power, believe it or not. Music, drinks, who got granted entry, it was all down to Roxie. The woman had a fortune at her disposal, yet she was happiest singing along and dancing with her friends as thousands of other women would be doing across the world at that same moment.

It was a miracle she even felt her cellphone buzz, there would be no chance of hearing a caller. Except when she read her screen, she didn't want to miss the call either.

Answering, she slipped out the door marked for the restrooms into a stairwell and raised the phone to her ear.

"Alex?"

"Button?"

A smile curved her lips. "Hey."

Oh, it felt good talking to him. They'd talked before she went for her workout. That was less than a day ago, yet it felt like forever had passed by.

"How are you doing, baby?"

Some of her contentment turned to contrition. "I'm—"

"With Roxie, I know," he said, a smile in his voice.

"I should've called you. I should've checked—"

"It's okay. After the way you reacted to her name, asking her to drop by was the least I could do. I didn't really ask—"

"She eavesdropped, I know."

They were in sync, and she loved that about them.

"She's like that. Are you getting along?"

"Yes! She's amazing. She just sucked me into her orbit and it's like we've been friends forever."

"Good. That's good. Maybe I can be your plus one to the wedding."

She laughed. "How are you? How are things going in Sydney?"

"Getting there," he said. "There's a bunch of hospitality bullshit pissing me off."

"Hospitality?"

"Drinks, glad-handing. I want to get to the damn contracts, not have a party."

"You have to play the game. If you're impatient, they'll see that, and maybe take advantage. Don't get screwed on the deal just because you're thinking about screwing my deal."

A groan of pleasure vibrated the line. "I've been thinking a lot about that."

"Mm, I bet you have. I've been thinking a lot about wasted opportunity..." The heat of flirtation cooled. "I'm sorry if I was an asshole, baby."

"An asshole? This about the creep, Demetri, again?"

"No," she said. "I don't care about Demetri, I care about you. Xander Gauge is an incredible man. You're loyal and hard-working, maybe a little misguided sometimes, but who isn't?"

"How much have you had to drink?"

Maybe too much. "Roxie said I can stay at her place upstairs. They have a huge penthouse." Which he probably knew, duh. "Rox says we're always safe at Crimson."

"You are. But take it easy, okay? Roxie is a full-time partier, it's literally her job. Don't try to keep up."

"You don't care that I worry about you? That I'm sorry?"

"You have nothing to be sorry for," he said. "I don't want you sweating the serious stuff, I want you to have some fun."

And there was no better place for that than Crimson.

She leaned back against the wall. "Is your friend Xavien Rourke seeing anyone?"

"I… don't know. Why? You want his number?"

Her smile quirked. "Dyce said something about a woman in his life."

"Dyce?" Xander asked, confused. "He's in California. I thought you were in New York."

"He didn't say it to me, he said it to Roxie, or in front of Roxie anyway."

"I don't know, but I can find out."

The bass of the new Ruby Room track thumped against her back. "It's not important. I was just curious."

"You'll meet them all, you know, and you'll be around when any of them settle down."

"They're your friends, I was just—"

"They'll be your friends too," he said. "I like that

you're fitting in."

"You thought I wouldn't?"

"No, I knew you would."

"Was that the point?"

"Like I said, Roxie's a kind of ambassador for the group. It can be daunting. It's my life, so I'm just used to it. Roxie knows what it is to come in from the outside. Sometimes the mystery of it can be intimidating. I wanted you to see that our life wouldn't be any different, that we don't have to be any different to integrate our lives."

She sighed. "Getting to know Xander Gauge is about more than just our alone time, I get it, I do, and…" Her mouth was a little dry, maybe it was nerves. "You ever hear the expression that you don't know what you've got 'til it's gone?"

Silence lingered for a few seconds. "Do you want me to come get you?"

"No!"

"I can be in the air within an hour, but it'll be—"

"You don't have a home," she said, her heart heavy. "You dedicate all your life to your work."

"And to you," he said with a note of concern. "Button, if something's scared you or someone said something—"

"It's the things I should've said. I'm sorry, Alex."

"Hey," he said. "Please don't get upset. I'm coming home soon."

Home. That was what she wanted and why her heart ached. Work was important to him and nothing would change that. Nothing should change that. She'd said she didn't want to turn around in six months and not recognize herself. She didn't want Xander doing that either.

"I just want you to know that you have a home.

With me… if you want it."

"I do, baby," he said, his voice dropping to that smooth drawl again. "You know I do."

Her lips curled. "Maybe one day we can come to Crimson together? Find a corner somewhere to make out. Do you know Roxie and Zairn have done it right here? Like in the club."

"On the main dance floor?" he asked, snickering.

"In the restroom, but maybe that too. He could shut down the whole place for her."

"I can have him shut it down for us, if that would make you happy."

"Being with you would make me happy," she said.

"You have no idea what it means to hear you say that."

Could be the alcohol or the mood of the night, but she just didn't want him to go another day alone, thinking about her and them with uncertainty.

"I should get back to the party."

"Okay, baby."

Pushing off the wall, she grabbed the door handle, but the door didn't budge. "Oh, uh, well, I would get back to the party if I hadn't just locked myself out."

He laughed. "The Ruby Room?"

"Yeah, oh God, do you have Roxie's number? She probably won't hear her phone over the music."

"She won't even have her phone, Button. If she does, it won't be charged. One sec, I can do it."

"Do what?" she asked, drawing a fingertip around the glowing panel on the handle.

"Press your thumbprint to the reader."

Is that what it was? Okay. She knew that. Totally knew that. She did and it scanned. Then there was a pause. It flashed and the door popped open an inch.

"How did you do that?"

"Magic," he said. "You're in the system, you won't get stuck anywhere again. Go back to the party, Button. I want you to have the time of your life."

THIRTY-TWO

THE TIME OF HER LIFE was right. New York was an incredible city, made even more incredible with Roxie as a tour guide.

But it couldn't last forever. She and Roxie flew back to Chicago in time for her to get to work on Monday. It didn't feel like she'd been dragging, though that might've been the adrenaline still pumping. By the end of the day, it was wearing off, and she needed a nap.

Like Stacey just knew she could do without the hassle, she'd tossed her another couple of assignments later in the day. It was almost eight p.m. when she finally shut down her computer.

She stood up, stretching her shoulder as she put her purse on the desk. Customer Relations worked in their own group office, although there was no one around. Not that she wanted to see anyone.

No, she wanted to get home, take off her shoes, and maybe see if Xander was free. She didn't like interrupting his rhythm at work, but sharing lunch over a video call just wasn't the same as having him there with her. They might see each other for the same amount of time, but the potency wasn't equal when her skin couldn't touch his.

He'd joked about jonesing for her. Or she'd thought it was a joke. Now she wasn't so sure.

Going into the corridor, she tossed the strap of her purse over her head, eyes on the elevator. It was a clean shot out.

At least until Stacey leaped out of her office into her path.

"I'm going home," she said. "No more last-minute assignments, please. I had a long weekend, a fun weekend but—"

"I just need to talk to you," Stacey said. "This will only take a second."

Did "talk to her" ever end well? Doubtful. Shit. Had they somehow found out about her and Xander? She hadn't called him from any company phones or emailed him from her business account.

Rounding into the office to find Stacey wasn't alone was chilling.

"Mr. Donal? Both of you need to talk to me?"

Stacey went behind her back to close the office door.

"Sit down," Eric Donal said.

They'd arranged three chairs in front of the desk, all facing each other. Two were clearly closer than the other. Donal sat in one and Stacey scurried around to sit in the other, leaving her in the hot seat.

"What's this about?" she asked, lowering herself slowly. "Is there a problem?"

"No," Donal said, but glanced at Stacey, becoming more somber. "But it's not good news, I'm afraid."

"Not good news," she muttered, her focus switching between them. "What's going on?"

Had someone died? Was there anyone in her department who'd been sick or absent for a while? Why wouldn't someone—

"We have to let you go," Stacey said.

"Let me go where?" And the moment the words were out of her mouth, she got it. "Shit," she whispered and dropped against the back of the chair. "You're firing me."

"I'm sorry," Stacey said, screwing up her face. "I know it's a shock."

"Yeah, because the Northberg debt was settled."

Donal frowned. "How do you know that?"

"It doesn't matter how I know that. I thought if they paid their account that we'd be okay, that Viva would be back in the black."

"It's a difficult time for all companies at the moment. You are excellent at your job, but Customer Relations is not a required department."

"You're letting everyone go?" she asked. "The entire department?"

"We can redistribute the workload and—"

"Fuck the rest of us," she said, surging to her feet.

Stacey leaped up too. "There's no need to be like that," she said. "This is a very difficult thing to do."

"Uh huh, sure, I feel so bad for you. Let me ask you this, are you going to make rent this month? Will you have money to feed yourself?"

"We'll give you a reference," Donal said, rising beside them. "And your last paycheck—"

"Yeah, because I've busted my ass for this company." Now the last-minute extra assignments took on a whole new meaning. "And you better pay me for my overtime, don't make me come back and cause a scene."

"Don't threaten us."

"Shit," she said, running a hand over her hair. "I can't believe this."

"We thank you for your service and—"

"Oh, whatever," she said, turning on her heels to throw the door out of the way. "Fuck." Storming down the hallway, she jabbed the elevator button, fighting to restrain the moisture threatening her eyes. "Shit."

What the hell was she going to do?

God knew how she got back to her apartment. The walk was nothing but a blur. She didn't even remember walking out Viva's doors for the last time. This was, it was… fired?

Unlocking her door, she walked in and immediately stopped.

Something was different.

What was it?

Was she just paranoid?

Maybe it was—Gwen came striding out of her room and paused, sniffing hard. A small duffel hung in her roommate's hand.

"Gwendolyn," she said slowly, careful with her words. "What's going on?"

Her roommate's eyes were red. They weren't puffy and horrible or anything, but something wasn't right.

"You look sad," Gwen said.

"*I* look sad?" she asked, taking a long step to move out the way of the door that she tossed into its frame behind her.

"Yeah, what happened?"

"Well, I got fired, but—"

"You got fired?" Gwen asked, dropping the bag to hurry over and hug her. "Oh my God, I'm so sorry. Why did you get fired? They can't fire you! You're the best employee they have."

"As my friend, that's what you're supposed to

say," she said, easing out of her friend's embrace. "But what's going on with you? Don't tell me nothing because I know it's something."

And if two of them were without jobs, rent would be impossible to come up with.

Gwen didn't even disguise it. Her friend stepped back and breathed in, raising her arms. "I'm moving out."

With that, Gwen spun on the spot to go back to her bag. She couldn't… moving out? Why would she move out? Why would…?

Gwen was in the bathroom, tossing bottles in the bag, when she got with it enough to chase after her.

"You can't move out. You're not moving out. What is this? I didn't even know you were dating anyone. Who are you moving in with?" Had she been a horrible friend? "I know I've been caught up in this Alex stuff and I went to New York without you, but—"

"It's not you. I just don't want to live here."

"Because?"

On a mission, her roommate grabbed the last of her things from the vanity and zipped up her bag. "Because I don't want to live with Bryan."

"Bryan?" she said in disbelief.

Gwen squeezed past her, but she stayed hot on her heels this time and followed her into her bedroom. A suitcase was open on the bed, already half full.

"It's Tia's choice, I get it, but I just can't. I can't live with him. He'll start throwing his weight around, think he's in charge. And you know he'll use Tia against us. He'll upset her and we'll want to make her feel better… It just won't work; I can't see how it ever could."

"I don't want to live with Bryan either. Tia wants to move him in here? How did that happen? She hasn't mentioned it to me."

"She doesn't want him to live here, he already does. They showed up with a bunch of his stuff yesterday."

"They can't do that," she said. "They can't just make a unilateral decision—"

"Her bedroom, her rules."

"And does he plan to pay his fair share of rent?"

"Tia said they'd split her share, that it should be by room."

"That's bullshit."

"Nothing we can do to stop it. We could try, but it would be a mess. We say no, he stays anyway. What are we going to do? We can't manhandle him off the premises. Even if we did or the cops removed him, changing the locks won't make any difference if Tia just lets him back in."

"Why can't they move to his place?"

"He doesn't have a place. Him and his idiot roommate got evicted."

"For?"

Moving around the room, Gwen tossed things in her suitcase. "Non-payment of rent… and weed, I'll bet, but who knows? I just know I can't put up with it. I already talked to the landlord. I'm going down there to sign myself off the lease. We only have a couple of months left on it anyway. Tia and Bryan can play happy families as much as they like. I don't want to live with the drama."

Their entire relationship was drama. "You can't abandon me to it. You want me to live here with them alone?"

"You have Alex."

"I've been with Alex five minutes," she said. "I'm not going to dump myself in his life after five minutes. We're not moving in ready yet. Where are you planning to go?"

"I'll get a hotel tonight and check online for a new place. Anywhere is better than with Bryan."

And it was on her that Gwen had been dealing with these stresses at home alone. "Okay," she said. "Then I'm coming with you."

Gwen stopped. "What?"

"If you're going, I'm going. I just got fired anyway, and I can't afford this place by myself. If Bryan didn't pay in one place, why would he pay here? Tia made this bed, she can lie in it herself."

Her friend blinked. "You… you'll come with me?"

"Yes! Geez, woman, what did you think I'd do? Can you give me an hour to pack up?"

"Be quick. I don't want another argument. I just want to get out of here."

"Absolutely. There's no point wasting the emotional energy on a fight that no one can win. And we can go to Alex's tonight. Just not long term. I don't want him to think I'm a crazy, you know?"

Gwen had brightened enough to smile. "Yes, I get it. Okay…" She laughed. "Go! Go get packed."

Okay, her whole life in as small a package as possible. Moving wasn't a great idea when she'd just lost her job. Money was tight and they probably wouldn't get their security deposit back, not while there were people still living in the apartment.

At least staying at Xander's was rent free. Not that she'd take advantage. She didn't want him coming home from Sydney only to find out she and her friend had taken over his life.

Almost an hour later, she was still tossing clothes into a gym bag when her cellphone rang. She fished it out of her pocket and tucked it between her shoulder and ear to free her hands for folding. Semi-folding, she was in a rush, what else was there?

"Hello?"

"Hey, honey," Roxie chirped. "Want to come to Crimson tonight?"

"New York?" she asked, frowning. "Didn't we just come from there this morning?"

Roxie laughed. "Yes, but I meant Crimson Chicago. I have a meeting with the contractors tomorrow, but I want to sneak in tonight and take a look around before then, so I can freak them out with my knowledge. Not such a bad thing for them to suspect they're being watched at all times."

"No, that's a good plan, and I'd love to, but I can't."

"Okay. What's going on?" The thread of awareness in Roxie's voice was wary. "Everything okay? You sound all breathy."

"I'm packing. My roommate and I are moving out."

"Of your apartment? Why? You didn't mention that this weekend."

"No, it just happened, like literally just happened. We're trying to get out of here before our other roommate shows up with her jerkoff of a boyfriend."

"Ah, like a midnight flit."

"But at whatever time it is now, yeah."

"Where are you going?"

"Xander's, but just for a night or two, we're not moving in."

"Because…?" Roxie asked, drawing it out.

She exhaled a laugh. "Because I am not a crazy bunny boiler intent on taking over his life. It's only a one-bedroom anyway and there are two of us."

"Come over to my place."

"Your place?"

"Yeah, it's a three bedroom."

She paused. "You're not staying in a hotel?"

"I'm in my apartment," Roxie said. "We keep saying we're going to give it up and we never actually bite the bullet. I have a feeling Knox already bought it. Zairn bought the apartment next door. Maybe Gauge can buy the one above us and we'll build ourselves a castle."

"Are you sure?"

"Of course! There is so much space and I'm not used to knocking around here on my own. I'll send Trevor over with the boys to do the heavy lifting, and they'll drive you here."

"I don't want to put anyone out, but I guess it wouldn't hurt to have another guy around if—"

"The jerkoff boyfriend comes back," Roxie finished for her, "yes, yes, exactly. See, perfect!"

"Okay, I'll finish packing and then we have to go down to the landlord's office. He already said he'd let Gwen sign off the lease; I hope he'll let me sign off too."

"He will," Roxie said without an ounce of doubt.

"How do you know?"

"Because my boyfriend knows something about everyone and my ex-boyfriend goes after bad boys, take your pick. All else fails, I'll call him out on my stream, and we'll have a parade for the jerkoff boyfriend."

She laughed. "You know, I always feel better after I talk to you."

"It's Zairn rubbing off on me," Roxie said. "You're not alone, Rainie. I said it, I meant it. Don't forget it again. Something like this happens, you call me. Don't worry about the time either, like I said, it's always happy hour somewhere in the world. I'm on-call twenty-four seven for my girls."

That startled her. "I'm your girl?"

"You're all my girls, honey. Welcome to the family."

Manson or Brady? Maybe somewhere in between. It was a nice feeling to belong, to be cared for, to have support. Maybe it was too much too soon; Xander might not like it. But he'd encouraged her to accept Roxie and the woman was a force to be reckoned with. Right then, that was exactly what she needed.

THIRTY-THREE

"GET READY. Come with me," Roxie said, swinging into her bedroom.

"Come with you to Crimson?"

After a night under Roxie's roof, the shock had given way to determination. Work. She needed work.

"Yeah, I have this meeting and want you to meet the contractor."

"Why?" she asked. Her legs crossed under her laptop, she rested against the headboard. Toria's headboard actually. "Is he cute?"

Roxie laughed, resting her temple on the hand she had curled around the doorjamb. "We have a whole squad working on the building. Bet there's one in there who'll distract you from Gauge."

"Oh, that's what I need, more men in my life." She put her laptop aside to scoot to the edge of the bed. "I need a job."

"And I'm giving you one," Roxie said.

Wait, what? "You're…?"

"The internal construction is mostly complete,

we're onto the fun part of refurbishment. We have plans but need someone on site we can trust. Someone to make quick, tasteful decisions, when to forge on, when to pull back."

"And you trust my taste?"

"It's the same as Zairn's," Roxie said. "Z picked me, so I know his taste is top-notch. He also picked Gauge, who picked you."

"So it's a six degrees thing?" she asked on a laugh. "You don't owe me anything. I appreciate it, but—"

"This is not me doing you a favor, you'd be doing me one. And Zairn one too. He asked me to oversee the club opening and then we went and got engaged and moved to New York."

"He didn't think to pull the plug?"

"It still means something to me, my city. We might live in the Big Apple, but Chicago will always have a place in my heart. Z knows that. He cares 'cause I care."

"What else can you make him do?"

Roxie cackled. "I plan to spend the rest of my life finding out."

"Next time we take a weekend trip, I want to meet this Casanova. I'm not sure there's a mortal man capable of containing you."

"Maybe he's not mortal. You know, I never asked."

"Not something that comes up much in the course of a date."

"You know we don't really do that either." Roxie bent a knee to raise a foot. "Huh, not much of a relationship, is it?" Her foot hit the floor again. "We have a lot of sex."

"That's the main thing," she joked. Her cellphone rang. "One sec." Lying on the bed, she stretched to the other side and dragged her phone across, hitting answer as she did. "Hello?" She pressed speaker. "Hello, sorry."

"Button?"

"Hey!" she called, her grin matching Roxie's. "Are you calling to break up with me?"

"Calling to break—no, why would you think—"

"These things come in threes," Roxie said.

"Ms. Kyst," Xander exclaimed. "Sticking around in Chicago?"

"For another day or two," Roxie said. "'Til I can be sure you'll treat this gem right."

"You better be bringing her over to our side. You poison my girl and I poison your guy."

"Good luck with that. I know where my guy's bodies are buried and have all kinds of kinky sex tapes to blackmail him with. He'll be in my bed for a thousand years. And if you break this beauty's heart, I'm taking her to California as my sister wife. I call him Casanova for a reason, trust me, he can handle it."

"I take care of all those duties, Roxanna."

"Take care of them quickly," Roxie said, pushing off the doorframe. "We have an appointment with a gang of hotties."

Roxie winked and closed the door as she departed.

"Button?"

"She's gone," she said, picking up the phone and taking it off speaker as she lay down. "How are you?"

"How am I? What was she talking about things in threes?"

"I've had an eventful twenty-four hours. Not even twenty-four hours. It would be like twenty hours. No, damn, less, closer to twelve hours. God, that's depressing. How life can just—"

"Babe!"

"I got fired," she said, leaving enough time to

sigh before continuing. "It's embarrassing. I never thought I'd be embarrassed to tell you. I didn't do anything, it wasn't some dramatic exit. Though, it could've been. Maybe I should go back there and make a scene." She laughed. "It hit me out of nowhere, you know? It's crazy. One minute you're secure, never thinking twice about how you'll make rent, then wham, you're a day away from a box in the street."

"They fired you?"

The depth of that growl was new.

"It's no big deal," she said. "I wasn't madly in love with the company or anything. It just sucks to give your loyalty to something that spits it back at you. And then, as if that wasn't bad enough, Tia announced Bryan's moving in with her."

"She announced it? Why didn't you say no?"

"I doubt Bryan would let anyone say no. He does what he wants when he wants."

"I'll get security to—"

"It's okay, Gwenie and I moved out."

"You're at ours?"

"We're at Roxie's. She called when we were packing and invited us to stay."

"I gave you the key to our apartment, Button. I want you to use it."

"It was easier to be here, Roxie has more room. Besides, I don't want to be one of those limpet people. I'm not a limpet type person. We have never established what we are, but whatever it is, I don't think we're at a place where it's time to move in together. If we get there and decide we want to do that, we have to decide together. I don't want to do it because I'm out on my ass with nowhere else to go. Your place only has one bed anyway, and I wouldn't want to leave Gwenie or make her think she might be a burden."

"She's there with you?"

"She's at work. One of us has to earn a living if we're going to be apartment hunting."

"You have your credit card."

"I can figure this out. Roxie's been amazing. She helped out with the landlord getting both of us signed off the lease. At least we don't have to worry about that chasing us down." She caught a length of hair and slid her fingers down to toy with the ends. "And I know we were kidding, but thank you for not being the third shock. If my best guy friend was to call and dump me right now—"

"I will never dump you," he said. "Have you heard from Demetri?"

"No, why?" She frowned. "Should I hear from him?"

"No, I don't want him sneaking back in while I'm out of town."

"We said no other guys, didn't we? You don't have to worry about that. Losing my job and apartment in one night blindsided me, but Roxie may have me lined up for a job already."

"You should've called me, babe. I was worried when I didn't hear from you last night. Damnit, I should've just got on a plane."

"We're fine, it's fine," she said, looping her hair around her finger. "We had a few drinks and just crashed last night. Anyway, it's like I said, it's embarrassing."

"Embarrassing that you lost your job?"

"You're out there taking over the world one corporation at a time and I can't even get my shit together for a nine to five. I was the one who told you Viva would be fine if we just got the Northberg bill paid. Now it's like I wasted your money."

"You didn't ask me to do that, and it's just money. I don't give a shit about that. I give a shit that they cut you off for no good reason."

"They wouldn't have if they knew we were together, and I don't want to trade off your name like that. It is what it is."

Even if Roxie employed her to help with the Crimson Chicago opening, it would be a temporary gig. Eventually the club would be complete, the doors would be open, and she'd be hunting the job market again. Still, beggars couldn't be choosers, she couldn't refuse work, any work. They'd need a deposit and rent for wherever they moved to next.

"We're supposed to be doing honesty. And I'm your guy, Rainie. You tell your guy when things like this happen."

"You're right. I'm sorry. I should've called."

"What job is Roxie offering?"

"Crimson Chicago," she said. "Zairn bought it for Roxie and asked her to oversee its completion and opening. Then—"

"They got engaged and started jetting off all over the place."

"I'm not sure it's a real serious thing that they were worried about, but Roxie's been nice enough to take me along. I'm looking forward to seeing it. I've never seen an empty nightclub… I should go get ready, I don't want to hold Roxie up. She wanted to go over there last night, but with everything that went down, we missed it."

"You want off the phone?"

"I don't *want* off the phone, I just…"

"You just what?"

"It's like the middle of the night there, isn't it?"

"Just hit midnight."

Rolling onto her side, she breathed out and closed her eyes. "And you're about to lie down in your bed… I dreamed about you last night."

"Oh yeah?" he said, dripping with swagger.

"Want to tell me about it?"

She laughed, though her body relaxed. "When I came to bed, I couldn't stop thinking about you. About how I needed your arms around me, how much I wanted to just lie with you."

"I'm sorry I wasn't there," he said, solemn. "This is why I didn't want to leave you. I want to be there for you when shit happens in your life."

"These things… when these things happen, you learn who really cares."

"I really care."

"I know. But you also learn about yourself, about what's really important to you."

"Am I on that list?"

She drew in a breath, enjoying a few seconds of just breathing with him. "I miss you."

"I miss you too, Button."

"Did we take each other for granted?" No, that wasn't the right question. "Did I take you for granted? I know I want to be with you, to be close to you, but is it damaging? Am I damaging to your life?"

"How would you get there? No, you're not damaging."

"I don't want to slow you down. I want you to progress, to stay on your trajectory. Your work is so important."

"You are so important," he said. "You're everything, Rainie. You are what's important. I'm so pissed you went through losing your job and your apartment to—was Bryan there when you left? Did he hurt you?"

"No. He wasn't there. Gwenie and I packed and left while he and Tia were out."

"You should've used your credit card for security, for movers, for whatever you needed."

"Trevor's been kind. He and his people came

over to watch our backs and help us out." Her lips quirked. "And they may have been loitering in the background when we were in the landlord's office. I'm not sure if Zairn made a call or if Trevor was enough."

"Trevor is…"

"Roxie's Chicago security," she said. "Did you know Zairn bought the apartment next door to Roxie's to act as a security base?"

"I might've, I don't know. Sounds like him though. He's protective of her. They've lived a lot of their relationship in the limelight."

"People love Roxie and she's so good with them. I know people say you shouldn't meet your heroes, but she lives up to the hype and then some."

"If you need someone to make a call, ask your boyfriend, not hers."

"I didn't mean to step on your ego. I didn't ask Zairn to make a call, he and Roxie talk a lot and—"

"It's okay. You're not stepping on my ego. I just wish I'd been there for you."

"You're here now," she said, drawing up her knees toward her chest. "And you're making me feel better. If only…"

"I was there with you. I know, Button. Me too."

"You can sleep through. We don't have to meet for lunch today." Would she go back to the coffee shop now that her job wasn't just around the corner? "But will you call me when you wake up?"

"Yes. I want to know how things went at Crimson."

"Thank you, baby. Sweet dreams."

Boyfriends in the past, for the most part, tended to only half listen. Demetri especially. Xander wasn't like that. Engaged, aware, proactive, he was more than a go-getter. He'd been there and got everything there was to get. Yet, he still cared about her. Was it because they were at the beginning? Would he care as much after six months? After six years?

Picturing their life together was difficult. What did she want? How could they make it work? It wouldn't be business as usual, not for her, and not for him either, if it involved a home base. They'd figure it out. If something was important enough, people made it happen, and Xander Gauge was definitely worth it.

THIRTY-FOUR

"IT'S SO BIG!" she said, opening her arms as she turned on the spot.

Most of the internal construction upgrades had been done, yes, but it was far from club ready. From the bare walls, wires hung from holes, and there wasn't a bar or stage in sight.

More than half a dozen individual spaces made up the club, some bigger, some smaller. It was difficult to picture how it would look at the end, but Roxie said there were plans and renderings to help.

"New York is the flagship venue," Roxie said, "but every Crimson is important. We don't do things by halves."

"No, I see that." The construction guys had left them alone at Roxie's request. "So what do you think? Do you want to take it on for me?"

"I'm clumsy."

"We're not asking you to do the actual work, just supervise it. I don't know exactly how long it will take to finish. These things tend to take on a life of their own.

But it will need a manager too, once it's up and running. And someone will have to deal with the launch."

"Sounded exciting and fun and way better than a stagnant customer relations job, but she had to be honest. "I don't have a lot of experience with running nightclubs. Any experience actually. My experience comes from dancing in them, not managing them."

"You'll learn, and I'm always at the end of the phone. Though, truth is, I don't have experience managing nightclubs either. Zairn has a lot of contacts. A zillion of them. We can help you employ a strong team, people who will support you, no backstabbing and Shakespearian games, promise."

"You're doing this because of Xander. Did he ask you to do this?"

"No one has to ask me. I'm an excellent judge of character… most of the time. Z and I have been talking about it for a while. It's difficult for me to maintain a close eye on things while we're zipping around all over the place. Think of it as being my eyes and ears, if that helps. Once you have your sea legs, we'll take off the training wheels. Phew, that's a lot of idioms." They shared a smile. "If you hate it and you don't want it, that's fine, say that. But don't think Gauge is the be all and end all. I met you, I like you, I trust you."

"You must know other people in Chicago."

"Yeah, my family, but there's no way I'd let my sister near this. Her or her freeloading boyfriend. My girls, Jane and Toria, are on opposite sides of the country. It's no easier for them than it would be for me to keep a handle on it." Roxie came to take her hand. "But you're not tied down by this either. If things with you and Gauge move on or involve traveling or relocating, your happiness is what's most important. This won't restrict you. It doesn't have to restrict you."

"And if things don't work out with Xander? If

we have a fight and hate each other?"

"Then he can fuck off to some far-flung corner of the world. Yes, we like to keep things in the family, but we're not the mafia. We don't cut people off because they stop having sex with a specific person." Except they hadn't had sex. Was that relevant? Something she should tell her new employer? "And Zairn has other friends anyway. If Gauge turns out to be an asshole, I'll send you another."

The broad grin on her new friend's face wrought a laugh from the back of her throat. "It's tempting…"

"You don't have to decide right now. Take a few days, a week, to think about it, weigh up any other offers you have. You don't have to jump in the deep end straight away. We're not ball-busting employers either. Most everything can be undone, providing you don't kill anyone, nothing is unfixable. We pay really well too."

"I'm not playing hardball, I just don't want to let you down. I want everything to be perfect for you."

"Perfect can take many forms," Roxie said. "Think about what's best for you… And you can stay at my place too, for as long as you need to stay there. You and Gwenie. I can't say we won't drop in and visit every once in a while, but you won't have to pay rent."

"Oh, I would definitely—"

"Zairn wouldn't accept it."

She frowned. "I thought Knox owned your place."

Roxie waved that statement away. "We don't care about that shit in our group. Wouldn't it be fun to be part of the Crimson adventure? We have clubs all over the world. As soon as you have your security pass, I'll authorize it everywhere and… Oh! I almost forgot."

Dropping her hand to walk away, Roxie went to her purse on a workbench and rummaged inside before returning with something hidden behind her back.

"What is it?" she asked. "You've already done so much, I don't need—" Roxie brought it around and… "A passport."

"Your passport," Roxie said, showing her the last page. "Now you're unrestricted. You can go anywhere in the world."

And Sydney was the first place that came to mind. She wouldn't really go jetting over there, but it had something she craved.

"This is amazing. How did you do this so fast?"

Roxie shrugged. "We know people. And money gets you about anything you want in this world."

She paled. "Did it cost a lot? I'm so sorry. God, I tell Xander I'm not interested in money and then spend his best friend's money instead."

"You get used to it," Roxie said on an exhale. "I was the same. I spent so much time obsessing about the money, about how I didn't want the lifestyle, about how I wouldn't use Zairn's means."

"And…?"

"Then I realized you just have to go with it."

"Go with it?"

"Go with it. The money is there. It's a part of their lives. Providing they value us more than the dollar signs, that's what really counts. Does Gauge value you more than the dollar signs?"

"Yes."

"Then that's it. Just think about it as another quality. If he was a football nut, you'd go along to games in support. A concert pianist, you'd clap the loudest even if you couldn't play a note. They embrace what we are and the baggage we come with. We have to do the same. You can do good with it too," Roxie said, her lips curling again as she gestured at the passport. "Like this. Sometimes it's the little things that matter most."

She'd never thought of a passport as something

freeing, but that was how it felt. Now if she needed to get to Xander, or he wanted to whisk her away, she wouldn't hold him back.

"I guess this means I'll be able to come to your wedding, no matter where in the world it is," she said, flicking through the pages and peeking up at her friend. "You know I'll expect an invitation now."

"At this juncture, you know as much about the wedding as I do," Roxie said and looped their arms together.

"Doesn't that worry you?"

"Not with Jane at the helm." Roxie started across the club. "She's wedding crazy. It'll be bigger than anything Zairn or I would ever plan, but we can handle the spectacle."

"It's weird, isn't it? If she's so into weddings, why was hers so low-key? She and Knox did it in the Bahamas, didn't they? Were any of her family there?"

Roxie rolled her lips into her mouth, taking a second to subdue the apparent amusement behind them.

"Z is going to like you," she said, pulling their linked arms tighter against her body. "He's definitely going to like you."

THIRTY-FIVE

"*RAINIE TAIT, CRIMSON MANAGER*" had a nice ring to it.

She shouldn't still be lounging in bed mid-morning, but it had been a crazy few days and she needed the rest. Gwen was at work. Her friend got no extra rest, but she hadn't been clubbing in New York all weekend or fired after a slog of work.

The Crimson job could be something to build on. A foundation that would show her just what she was capable of. Was it possible for her to take on such a mammoth task and not fail miserably?

The bedroom door handle moved. Roxie must— Xander.

She sat up, her mouth opening. Was that…? Was he really standing there?

"Alex," she gasped as he tossed the door back into its frame. "Oh my God, what are you doing here?" He toed off his shoes, threw a leather binder to the end of the bed, and took off his jacket. "What happened? Oh my God, what was it? Is it business? Seven? Did you and

Lance fight? Did you fire him? Did you do something crazy? Please tell me you didn't fire your friend for me." He came onto the bed beside her, sitting close, propping his weight on a fist at the other side of her legs. "How are you here…? I mean, I know how you're here, you have a plane. Your own plane. I guess that means you can go wherever you want whenever you want? Oh, God, please tell me. Are you going to break up with me now? Did you change your mind? I'm more trouble than I'm worth, I get it—"

"We go through this shit together," he murmured, sweeping her hair from her face.

Leaning in, his mouth found hers. Everything slowed down. Or maybe it did. He cupped her cheek, tilting it higher to deepen the kiss. Whatever shit was happening in their lives, they should go through it together. But she hadn't in a million years expected he'd come back. Just yesterday morning, she'd been in roughly the same place talking to him on the phone with half the planet between them. Now he was with her. The real, true, flesh and blood Xander Gauge, there at her side.

She pushed back. "What happened with Bingham Bright?"

"It doesn't matter. I'm here now."

"It matters," she said, stroking his stubble. "Please tell me."

"We walked away."

"You—"

"Don't give me shit for it. My gut told me it wasn't right. Not then, not in that moment. If they want it bad enough, they'll figure out a way to bring us back to the table."

"If you still want it, you should've stayed."

He grabbed the binder and his jacket from the end of the bed. After fishing a pen from the inside pocket, he unzipped the binder and gave her the pen.

"I want this more," he said, putting the binder on her lap on a specific page. "Will you sign this?" What was he up to? What did he want her to sign? She didn't have to ask. "You trust me?"

"Yes."

He smiled and nodded at the pages. "Then sign."

Hmm, okay, it wasn't fair that he distracted her with such an amazing kiss and then asked her to be smart and sensible. One signature wasn't enough. He pointed to another page and then another, asking her to initial some places too.

"What is this?"

"I'll tell you later," he said, zipping up the binder to toss it onto the floor. "How are you holding up?"

"I'm okay," she said as he took the pen to put it aside too. "Nobody died."

"I know," he said, sliding down the bed, gathering her into his arms. "That doesn't mean it hasn't been a tough few days."

With her face buried against his chest, his arms so tight around her, she felt safer than she ever had. She'd dreamed of having him there, having his comfort, and without asking, he delivered. If she hadn't been sure before, though she probably had, then there was no denying her love for him in that all-encompassing embrace.

It wasn't the money, the flash, the luxury, it was the man. Just like Roxie said. Xander was worth more to her than anything else, he was all the luxury she needed.

"Was Lance mad?"

"No," he said, his fingers combing down the length of her hair at her back, his breath warm on her head.

"Was Ethan?"

"No one was mad."

"They must think I'm a ridiculous, pathetic—"

"No one thinks that," he murmured, still finger-combing. "You didn't ask me to come back. You didn't need me. I needed to be here. I wanted to be here… with you."

"Roxie offered me that job. She said I could stay here too."

"Is that what you want to do?"

What she wanted to do? In that exact second, there was only one certainty. Pressuring her folded arms against his chest, she put enough space between them to meet his eye. From a content smile, his expression became confused.

She wasn't confused. Not even a little.

Wriggling higher, she caught his mouth with hers again. Life was too short to pass up chances like Xander Gauge. She wanted a love that was easy, one that gave her freedom to be herself, and didn't come with drama. Whatever drama might be in her life, whatever craziness they lived with, what they had was uncomplicated.

Pushing him onto his back, she climbed up onto him, leaving just enough space between them to unfasten the buttons of his shirt.

Sweeping her hair from her cheeks with both hands, he held it at the side of her head, using the hold to break their kiss.

"We're not in any rush," he murmured, the thick weight of bass in his voice revealing his desire. "This should be special."

"You just flew across the world for me."

"You don't owe me anything."

"I don't," she said, opening up his shirt and rising to take her own top off. "But you just proved to me you get it." Taking his wrists, she guided his hands to her breasts, letting them explore what lit his gaze. "All my life I've wanted a relationship with honesty, with faith, and above all else, loyalty and love. I can be open with you, Alex. I can tell you anything." He nodded. "I want a man who'll keep my heart safe. A man I can give my love to and know he'll cherish it and not take it for granted."

"Baby, I'll cherish it, but you've gotta know…"

She almost didn't want him to shatter the peace, but she couldn't ask for honesty then hide from it. "Know what?"

"You'll never be able to love me more than I love you. There's nothing I wouldn't do for you. Nothing I wouldn't do to make you happy. I told you I'd never say no. I will always give you anything you ask."

"I don't have to ask," she said, sliding her hands over his to squeeze her breasts beneath. "You came all the way back here for me because I said I wanted to be in your arms."

"I came all the way back here because you said you knew you wanted to be with me. You referenced us being together. You're reaching all these conclusions while I'm on the other side of the planet." He shook his head once in the pillow. "No. That's not how I want this to work."

"How do you want it to work?" she asked, descending to kiss him again. "How do you want…" Another kiss. "Us…" A quick kiss. "To work?" Pushing downward, her hips moved lower to meet the solid evidence of what worked right there and then. "I want to be with you, Xander." Her hips moved in slow circles. "I want to be yours." She pushed harder. "For you to be mine."

Throwing his arms around her, he flipped her onto her back. "I am yours, Rainie." His hand slithered down her body and under the elastic of her shorts. "No one else's." His fingers slid between her folds as his legs parted hers. "Never again."

"Mm," she purred, undulating with his fingers, stimulating her clit. "And I want this." She squeezed his shoulder beneath his shirt. "I want to know what you feel like inside me, how it feels to have you—" His finger plunged into her. Her body arched, breathing into the invasion. "Like that. More like that."

"Open your eyes."

She did. "Alex…"

"Fuck, you're beautiful."

"Take your pants off," she said, still moving with his hand as he pleasured her. "Please."

"Are you sure?"

"I don't want to wait," she said, shoving the shirt from his shoulders. As he freed himself from it, she unbuckled his belt. "I want this. Now. I want you."

More than just the physical, she wanted the release, but also wanted the clarity. Holding back, hesitating, it might seem smart, but some things had to be taken on faith. He had to be taken on faith. This man was it or he wasn't, but she'd never been so sure of the former. What he gave her was more than she'd wished for, more than she'd dreamed of. It was time to stop punishing him, and herself, for the missteps of their beginnings.

Xander lived wherever the business demanded. She'd never envied his corporation until that moment. The pull it had, his love for it, would she ever match up to Venture?

"Alex," she whined his name, but only just.

The slide of his fingers, the pulse of his want. She was losing herself, slipping into a black hole of forever that she never wanted to escape.

He kissed her. His lips gliding to her jaw and her neck, he played with her, learned her, while he stayed just out of reach.

"With me, baby," he growled. "Open your eyes."

"Oh, I'm with you," she said, her pelvis rising as his stimulation ebbed. "Where are you going?"

"Nowhere," he said. "Nowhere, baby." The urgent pressure of his cock was slow, but necessary, in its need. Exactly what she craved. "I'm right here."

And she welcomed him with a drone of pleasure that rumbled from the back of her throat.

"Right there," she said, breathing out her pleasure. "Yes, right there. Alex… Alex, God, that's it. Oh, that's it."

He moved faster than her heart could beat. Blood rushed through her veins, hot, pulsing, stretching her boundaries, tearing her limits to shreds.

There was no more. No ceiling. No summit of his value.

"Alex," she said again.

His breath beat on her face as he pounded into her, giving himself to her desire.

She wanted his mouth on hers, to envelop herself in him. To live there with him, in him, as a part of his being, an extension to him.

"You feel so good." She inhaled a sharp spear of pleasure. "Like that. Shit. Oh, Alex!"

Calling for him as she tumbled into climax, she couldn't get enough air into her lungs. All life came from him and flowed through her as ecstasy completed her circle.

"Oh, Alex," she panted again, her chest expanding with each deep breath.

He lay at her side and scooped her head closer to kiss her temple. His struggle seemed as real as hers. In the bliss of their bubble, no one rushed them, nothing was urgent. They just lay there, in silence.

"I'm not sure that was real," he muttered.

Maybe it was a dream. Maybe they weren't really there. If that was the case, she still wanted to stay.

Providing he was around, that was all she needed.

"I've never been happier," she whispered as the truth dawned on her. "That's crazy." Exhaling a laugh, her lips curled, and she shifted her head to face his profile. "I have no job. No apartment. Nothing is for sure except…"

When she didn't follow up, he turned his head in the pillow to look at her. "Except…?"

"You." Scooting closer, she rested a hand on the center of his chest. "I always wanted to be secure, completely secure, in a relationship. I didn't want tension and uncertainty."

"There's no uncertainty here." With his forefinger, he caught a tendril of her hair to hook it behind her ear. "And anything you want, you get. Such as…"

Rolling away from her, he leaned over the edge of the bed to get something from the floor. The binder.

"What is in that? Will you tell me what I signed now? Please? You didn't buy us an island, did you?"

"You want an island, I'll get you an island." He unzipped the leather. "But this is a transfer of ownership."

Where was he going with this? "Ownership of what?"

"You are now the proud owner of your very own marketing company."

"A marketing company?" He handed her the binder and she got her first real look at the paperwork inside. "Viva…" Her attention jerked to him. "You bought Viva?"

"For you," he said, leaning over to kiss her hair then propping himself on an elbow.

"You bought the whole damn company… for me."

THIRTY-SIX

"I NEED A SECOND to process this," she said, sitting up to lean back on the headboard. "Is it too early for wine?"

He laughed and sat up next to her. "You want wine, you get wine."

"I can't believe you did this, that you bought... Why?"

"Why not?" he asked. "They fucked you and I am more than happy for you to fuck them... figuratively speaking."

His smile suggested a tease, but she was just... in shock. "You bought it so I could ruin it?"

"You can do whatever you want with it, Button. Run it, delegate it, lay off the people who laid you off. Whatever you want."

"If they're laying people off, doesn't that suggest they're not a sound investment?"

"Sometimes it's not what they are, it's who they are. Most any ship will run aground eventually if there isn't a skilled captain at the helm. If you want to make it work, we'll make it work."

"We?"

Another smile and he pushed her hair from her cheek. "We. Everything is we. Venture is half yours now anyway. This is just another plume in our portfolio."

Panic raced her heart again. "I don't want your company. Oh my God, please don't say you had me sign something about that too."

As she scrambled to check every page, he laughed.

"No, though if you want me to, I will. As soon as we get married, what's mine will be officially yours anyway. Though there won't be a divorce to split assets anywhere down the line, you'll be in charge after I die."

"Married?"

"With the kids, of course."

"Kids?"

This wasn't making plans, it was…

She swallowed. "You want to get married?"

"I want our future to be whatever you want it to be."

"Rainie!" Roxie called from somewhere in the apartment.

Shit, yes, her friend was there, and she was lounging in bed screwing her apparent fiancé.

"I'm a horrible friend."

She jumped up and grabbed her robe from the footpost and tied the belt on the way out.

Roxie was in the kitchen, a suitcase by the door. "Everybody made up," she said, closing the fridge. "Everything you need for Crimson is in the top drawer of the desk."

She joined her friend who kissed each of her cheeks. "You're leaving?"

"Going back to California. Zairn's surrounded by happy couples at the minute. I really can't have him getting ideas. It's my job to remind him the fairytale isn't always so rosy." Roxie looked past her. "Take care of her."

"Always," Xander said. He must have followed her from the bedroom. He appeared around her to give Roxie a kiss. "Dennis on the tarmac?"

"Ready and waiting," Roxie said, tossing her hair over her shoulder. "Trevor and his crew just hang next door. Zairn's paying them, so you can use them for security. They should do something." Xander nodded. "Our car service is on constant notice. Make use of them too. Tibbs has given Topher all the details."

"Thanks, Rox. Tell that guy of yours to keep a closer eye on you."

"Yeah, that won't be happening," Roxie said. "Remember what I said about living here too. The apartment's just sitting here doing nothing anyway. It will be good for this place to have some life in it again."

"Zairn and Kintyre are in Knox's place in LA."

"Yeah, well, Knox is there too, and he bought this place for Jane. He's housing everyone. What a guy." Roxie's playfulness would be missed. Her friend laid a smile on her. "You okay?" She nodded. "I'm always just a phone call away if there's anything you need. What's ours is yours, anywhere in the world."

And now that she had her passport, the possibility of that was even more real. "You've been amazing. You kept everything together, me included. But I still want to meet your guy."

"You will," Roxie said, gesturing around. "Someone will get married first, somewhere in our circle. Zairn loves a good wedding."

"No, he doesn't," Xander said on a snicker.

Roxie's mouth closed in a glare. "He's never been to one with me. Weddings make me horny."

"I'll remember that."

"Wasn't he at Jane and Knox's wedding with you?" Roxie and Xander made eye contact. What were they…? Their smiles sloped slowly and eventually became laughter. "Okay, so what am I missing?"

"Take care of yourself," Roxie said, leaning in to hug her. "I'll see you soon."

Xander held the door open for her, and then their friend was gone.

She sighed. "I'm gonna miss her."

"She's a force. I said so, didn't I?"

"You were right," she said, going into his arms after he closed the door. "So what's next?"

"What do you want to do next?"

Oh, that was an easy question. Her eyes rolled to the top corner of their sockets. "Roxie said I could take a couple of days off… So I guess I'm on vacation."

"Really?" he drawled. "Where'd you want to go? I'll take you anywhere in the world."

"I was hoping you'd say that."

"Yeah? Where do you want to go?"

Stepping out of his embrace, she twined their fingers together to lead him across the room. "To bed." She tossed a sultry look over her shoulder. "At least until it starts raining… You have some making up to do, businessman."

"Anything you say, Button. I am yours to command."

"Don't you forget it."

Their beginning was hardly conventional and things got rocky in the middle. They'd ridden the storm and come out stronger. Tomorrow might be a mystery, but she knew one thing for sure. Xander Gauge was her man. Now and forever.

THIRTY-SEVEN

"OH, WE SHOULD MOVE."

"Oh, I don't think so," Xander said, mimicking her tone, his fingers moving through her hair.

Lying on top of him, she was more used to naked and horizontal than upright.

"When Roxie said I should take some time off, I don't think she meant spend two weeks in bed with my hot boyfriend." Rolling off him, she forced herself to put some light between them. Not much, but more than there had been for a while. "Aren't you worried about the business?"

"Seven?" he asked, shifting onto his side, propping a hand on his temple. "No. Lance owes me, and Ethan worries enough for all three of us."

"They'll think I'm leading you astray."

"They won't—"

"Because I am leading you astray. I am. You were all about the business, and I know I said I wanted you to have a home, with me, but we should be able to do both. Can we do both? Can we have a relationship and still take care of our responsibilities. Though, I suppose…" Her fingertips found his chest. "I don't have responsibilities. Bills here seem to be taken care of, and I'm not used to— I pay for my cellphone. I don't have a car or—"

"Button!" His shout startled her, but he was already smiling when her gaze touched his. "I love you."

"Do you think Roxie will fire me?"

"No," he said, snickering as he swept her hair from her body. "You think her and Zairn have never gone off the grid? Kintyre did it with Lilya when they first got together too." Except the couple were now split up for… reasons. "It happens. It's allowed."

"It's not my experience. I've never been… I've never had…"

"Well, you do now," he said, bowing to kiss her. "Just think of it as making up for lost time."

No work. No gym. No fresh air. They'd been locked in the apartment, together, enjoying each other, and she just couldn't bring herself to regret it.

"Oh my God!"

Her hand leaped to his shoulder when the shout came from within the apartment. Gwen.

"Wait here," she said, scrambling out of bed, grabbing her robe to put it on as she departed the bedroom.

The shocked Gwen stood by the breakfast bar. And she didn't have to ask for the cause of her exclamation, not when she saw Tia just inside the closed front door.

"What is going on?" she asked, tightening the tie of her robe. "Tia, how did you get here?"

"Were you hiding from me? I haven't heard from either of you for two weeks. What kind of friendship is this? And your security guard? Why the hell do you have a security guard?"

Her eyes met Gwen's. "Trev let her in?"

"He asked me, I said it would be okay." Gwen's attention snapped to Tia. "But we can remove that invitation any time."

"Why do you have a security guard?"

"Why are you here?" she asked, ignoring their former roommate's question. "What do you want?"

"I don't understand what happened. Why are you mad at me?"

"Because you moved your boyfriend into our apartment without talking to us about it," Gwen said. "You knew we weren't fans of the guy. Did you really think we'd stick around?"

"So you're abandoning me because of my boyfriend?"

"It's a mistake," Gwen said. "You and him, living together, the guy is going to tear you down. I, for one, didn't want a front row seat."

"Button?" his voice rose behind her at the same time Tia turned.

She twisted to look at him. "We're okay. Can we have a minute?"

The concern of his frown contradicted his nod. "Shout if you need me."

She nodded and he disappeared back down the hallway.

"Who was that?" Tia asked. "Your new boyfriend?" Her hands jumped to her hips. "So it wasn't about my boyfriend, you moved for yours. Is this his place?"

"No," she said, shaking her head. "This is a friend's place. Someone who's letting us stay here while they're out of town." Not a lie. "Did you just come here to check up on us?"

"I was worried. How long is your friend going to be out of town?"

"I don't know."

"Why do you care?" Gwen asked.

"How many bedrooms does this place have?"

"No," she said. Was Tia really suggesting they live together again? "Absolutely no way."

"Why not?"

"Have you broken up with Bryan?" Gwen asked. "For good?"

"No, but I—"

"Alex wouldn't have it," she said. "He'd hire an army before he'd let your asshole of a boyfriend move in here."

"Alex?" Tia said, the line between her brows deepening. "Your friend Alex? I thought he was gay. Are you sleeping with him?"

"You didn't come here to talk about my boyfriend. You want to live with yours, great, go to it, we wish you every happiness in the world."

"We don't want to be around to say we told you so," Gwen said. "Bryan is going to break your heart. You can't deny he's done it a dozen times already."

"He's passionate."

"He's a sociopath. You have to get away from him."

"But I can't live here?"

"No, because we can't trust you not to bring him along. We're living here at someone else's hospitality."

"Alex's? Is this his place?"

"No," she said, disliking the questions.

Roxie had granted them rights to stay there, but she wouldn't take advantage of that kindness by bringing drama to her friend's doorstep. Especially not after the woman had shown such trust in her. If Bryan showed up or Tia tried to bring him inside, Trevor and his crew would throw him out. At her request, or Xander's, sure, but it would still be a spectacle she'd rather avoid.

Tia's interest still tracked around the space. "So

whose is it?"

"Is that it? All you came to quiz us about?" Gwen said, gesturing at the door. "You should go now."

"What? You're kicking me out? What happened to our friendship? We used to be so close."

"That changed when you stopped respecting our wishes. When you prioritized your guy over your friends. I'll say it straight out," Gwen said. "He's going to destroy you; I won't let him destroy me too."

"Our relationship is real. Our love is real."

"Okay, no one said it wasn't." And her friend's presence was becoming more confusing by the second. "Did he send you here?"

With a deep breath, Tia glanced between them. "We can't afford that big apartment by ourselves." Ah, and now the truth came out. "You need to move back in."

"No."

"Bryan isn't all bad. You need to give him a chance."

"You don't think we gave him a chance every time you brought him back into our lives after a breakup. We can only see our friend crying and heartbroken so many times before we say enough is enough. He hurts you over and over again." Gwen was so adamant precisely because she cared, even if it did come off more as anger. "You chose him. You chose to go back to him. We've bitten our tongues, but come on, T. He's an abuser."

Tia's mouth opened in an offended gasp. "He's never hit me!"

"Abuse comes in different forms," Gwen said, folding her arms. "And I'm not sure he never would. The guy has a temper."

As they'd seen and heard in the many arguments they had witnessed. Either it was an anger problem, or the guy really got off on hurting Tia.

"Look, it doesn't matter," she said, trying to play peacemaker, raising a calming hand to each of them. "There's no point us escalating this. Tia, you want to be with Bryan?"

"Of course! I love him."

"We don't want to be with Bryan. We have as much right to make that decision as you do to make yours. I'm sorry. Really, I am. And maybe we can still meet for coffee and drinks," without Bryan, "every once in a while."

"So that's it? You're abandoning me?"

It felt harsh to say it, but their problems were their own. As Gwen had pointed out, Tia made this bed herself.

"We're right here," Gwen said. "We're talking, aren't we?"

"But you don't care that you just walked out and left me to handle the whole rent on a place we got together."

Gwen threw up her arms "Get a new place! That's not the only apartment in the entire city."

"We can't!" Tia snapped and then seemed to second guess herself, losing her anger. "Our credit isn't good enough."

Gwen scoffed. "This is nothing to do with our friendship or us abandoning you. Bryan sent you here, didn't he? He sent you here to get us back for his benefit."

"You're my friends. Aren't friends supposed to help each other?"

Somehow that sounded like a line from Bryan's persuasive mouth. "Friends are supposed to care about each other too. Bryan was happy to fight with you, with us, when he felt in charge. Now we've left, and he can't assert his dominance, he's freaking out."

"He's freaking out because we'll be on the street," Tia said, tears brimming. "We'll have nowhere to live. Nowhere. What are we supposed to do?"

"What about his friends? Go live with them. Wasn't he living with them before?"

Seeing her friend upset wasn't easy and she didn't want Tia destitute. What made it harder? If she walked in and asked Xander to buy a place for her friend, he would without thinking twice about it.

Gwenie raised her voice as Tia did. She retreated. Her friends' focus was on each other, presenting a chance to sneak back into the bedroom.

Xander sat on the edge of the bed in sweats and a tee-shirt, doing something on his cellphone.

Her weight sank back against the door, closing it. "I don't think I can do this."

"Do what?" he asked, tossing his phone onto the bed.

"Be with someone who has money."

His frown snapped on fast and he shot to his feet. "Oh, I don't fucking think so, Button."

"No," she said, pushing away from the door to rush over and lay her forearms on his torso. "I'm not breaking up with you, I'm… How do you do it?"

"Do what?" he asked, a little calmer.

"Deal with the guilt? Tia's out there, she and Bryan can't afford the apartment. They'll be kicked out and have nowhere else to go."

"And you want to do something about that?"

"If it was just Tia maybe, but I don't want to enable her asshole of a boyfriend. Except how can I say no? Doesn't that make me a horrible person? A terrible friend?"

"You don't have to say no, I'll say it. If they're asking for money—"

"No one's asking for money, they don't know

you have money."

"But you could tell them," he said. "It will come out eventually."

That they were together or that he was a one-percenter?

"Then Bryan will just think the faucet is on. He'll gouge us whenever he can. And he'll manipulate Tia with it. In spite of that, right now, I could help. I could stop their stress and give them security. I could help."

"You mean I could help."

She shook her head. "It sets a dangerous precedent."

"You want me to talk to this guy?"

"No! God, I don't want you anywhere near Bryan. I wouldn't wish him on anyone." She sighed. "This whole situation could be cleared up in a heartbeat."

"Except it wouldn't be. Giving them money now guarantees they'll keep coming back for it."

"So how do you do it?"

"Deal with the guilt," he asked, "of knowing I can help but choose not to?"

Effectively, yes, that was exactly what she was doing. "It's so... If it was Tia, I would, but if their relationship is going to last, they have to be able to ride the waves together." She groaned and stepped back, her face dropping into her hands. "That's easy for me to say when we're at such an advantage."

"We don't have to worry about money," he said, stroking her upper arms. "But we've ridden our own waves. You also have to consider..." Her hands dropped as her head fell back. "Helping Tia now, opening that door for Bryan, it could prolong the relationship. If he's as terrible as you say, and they're facing this financial hardship, it could be time for him to move on."

"So the relationship could be over, but if we bail them out, he'll never leave. And Tia will be stuck with him forever, not because he loves her, but because he wants to stay on the gravy train."

With a half shrug, his head dipped in a nod. "I can be the bad guy. I'll say no."

But she just exhaled. "You said you couldn't say no to me."

The moment lingered, but eventually his lips curled. "Okay, you're right, I can't say no. If you want to do this, I won't object."

"I can't do that to you. I can't open your wallet to every stray who wanders by. It's not even my money."

"It is your money, but you're right, you do need boundaries. Zairn's the biggest advocate of that."

"I love you," she said, her logic swirling. "You are my priority." He squeezed her shoulders. "Yes, I want to help Tia, but she is not more important than you. If I have to help and protect anyone, it should be you."

"And there's your answer. Don't feel guilt that you're not giving them a handout, be proud that you're protecting us."

Throwing both arms around him, she squeezed him tight. "Oh, where have you been all my life?"

He snickered and kissed the top of her head. "What matters is I'll be around for the rest of it. You want me to talk to Tia? I can't say no to you, but I have no problem saying it to anyone who tries to manipulate you"

"No," she said and tipped her head back. "Gwenie's not in a giving mood either. Maybe you're right and this will be when Tia sees Bryan's true colors."

"The truth always comes out eventually."

"Yes, it does."

Tia might not like what she had to say, she didn't like Gwen telling truth either. It was tough love, in a way. They'd played the sympathetic and supportive roommates throughout Tia and Bryan's relationship. It hadn't worked to show Tia the truth of him. Maybe being faced with it, steeped in it, at this difficult time, their friend would start to see the real Bryan. And that wouldn't be such a bad thing.

THIRTY-EIGHT

XANDER WOULD BE BACK in a minute. He'd asked her to wait in the apartment. She'd wait… though what she was waiting for—the ring of her phone startled her. She snatched it out of her purse to answer without reading the screen.

"Hello?"

"Hey, honey!"

Roxie. On an exhale, she smiled. Contrition quickly replaced happiness. "I'm sorry, I know, I've been slacking. Xander and I—"

"Are entitled to lock yourselves up for a couple of weeks," Roxie said. "I'm not chasing you, just checking in. How are you doing?"

"Well," she said, relaxing against the end of the breakfast bar. "Right now Xander's talking to Trevor in the hall… or in the security apartment, I don't know. He asked me to wait in here."

"Is there a problem?"

"No, we're going out and… there's a reporter outside."

"Mmm, yeah, the lurker. He shows up every once in a while. The car on the curb would've been clue enough to get him salivating. If you're going out, I guess you're using the car service." That was a logical conclusion, though it hadn't occurred to her. "Don't worry about him. You get used to it."

"It's not me; no one would recognize me. But if he recognizes Xander…"

"Even if he doesn't and sees you both going out under Trevor's protection, he'll dig."

Her trepidation rose to high alert. "And find out Xander and Zairn are friends."

Roxie laughed. "Honey, don't worry so much. Yes, they'll find out eventually that you and Xander are together and it might be a story on some blog or in a gossip mag, but who cares? Who are you hiding from? Gwen knows you're together and who Xander is. Are you worried about your family?"

"No, I just… don't want to embarrass you all."

"Oh, well, that's nothing. Jane, Lilya, and I are doing some secret sleuthing at CollCom this afternoon. If we get caught, we'll wipe you off the headlines for sure."

"Secret sleuthing?"

"It's a long story, just don't tell your guy."

"Okay."

"I like to keep track of my girls, I don't forget about you just because you're not here in front of me. I just want to check you're okay."

"I'm okay, but… The last couple of weeks have been amazing. With Alex anyway. Tia showed up at your apartment yesterday, which caused a little drama."

"Good drama?"

"Got Xander and I talking about friends, people in our lives and his money. He said something about Zairn and boundaries."

"Yes," Roxie said, drawing out the word on an inhale. "Casanova's all about clear boundaries. It was one of the first things he shared with me. He says you get a nose for it, for the people who are genuine and those who are not. He's right, I think. I'm certainly more aware of it now than I was then. Set boundaries early and stick to them, that's his advice."

"Good advice."

"I'll tell him you said so. How did you leave it with Tia?"

"The only way we could leave it. She wanted us to go back to the apartment because she and Bryan can't afford it alone and…" She stopped. "You don't care about this. Sorry. I ramble sometimes. A lot."

"Jane's the same and I do care."

"I promise I'll go to the club this afternoon. I'm on it, I really am, just… Xander did something sort of crazy and I need his back up to deal with it."

"Something crazy? That's always encouraged. What did he do?"

"Bought the company that laid me off."

There was a pause and then a burst of laughter. "Oh my God, I love it!"

"On top of that, he put it in my name so…"

"Oh, this is good. So good! You're a CEO now. Not a bad switch from redundant to in charge."

As if she wasn't already nervous enough. Shit. A CEO? She hadn't thought of it that way.

"I'm not sure how I feel about striding back in there."

"Do they know you're with Xander?"

"I… I don't know what they know."

"What would Roxie do?" her friend said, full of confidence.

"What would—"

"It's something Jane uses when she's nervous or

uncertain. Don't doubt yourself. Own it. You're the boss. Who cares what they think? Go in there and tell it like it is. Xander will back you up."

"This is what he does all day, every day." When they weren't lounging in bed day and night. "He's a pro."

"And he'll teach you, if that's what you want. I told you Zairn has a network, Xander does too, and he has access to my guy's. You'll have support if you want to make this a success."

"If?"

"Yeah, well, I'm sure Xander won't mind if you take it apart and sell it off. He bought it so you could have your revenge or redemption. I can hire someone else to deal with the Crimson—"

"No! I want the job, if it's still available."

"Of course it is, I wasn't firing you, but this CEO thing…"

Could take up a lot of time. "I want to go in there and show face. After I talk to them, I'll figure things out." In theory anyway. "I am looking forward to seeing Xander in boss mode. It's funny."

"They're different in front of the board than they are with us. Agreed. It's definitely hot."

She laughed. "It is."

"There was something else, a reason for my call, but… I'm not sure I should bring it up now."

"Yes, bring it up. Sorry, I didn't even ask how you were doing."

"It was just an idea, to take your new passport out for a spin."

Well, that was intriguing. "A spin?"

"Yeah, if you're going to be part of the Crimson team, and be designing our newest club…"

"Yeah?"

"How would you feel about a tour?"

"A tour?"

"That was my introduction to Crimson, and it sure had a lasting effect. I can have Astrid arrange everything. It's up to you how far and wide you want to go. Check out the North American clubs, throw in South America, Europe, whatever you want."

"You want me to…" The concept was astounding. Was Roxie suggesting that she jet off around the world? On Zairn's dime? "I'm not sure I'd be comfortable. That's got to be expensive, and I don't have—"

"Money's not a problem. Zairn has accounts with Grand hotels around the world, but I guarantee Xander does too. That guy doesn't even have a home base."

"He does now," she said, a flash of a smile flickering across her lips. "His home is wherever I am."

"Aww, God, that's so romantic. You and Jane are like peas in a pod."

Romance was less her notion than the love that backed it up. "It feels like I've woken up in a movie."

Her friend laughed again. "And it will for a while. I get that feeling every time I look at my Casanova. Sometimes he doesn't feel real."

A sensation she was familiar with too. "What does he think about the tour idea?"

"Oh, he loves any idea that involves his friends traipsing around his clubs."

Good point. Maybe Xander wouldn't want to put his life on hold for her to live out a fantasy. "I… If Xander wasn't with me, I—"

"He'll follow you. Trust me. Besides, the hotels are the closest thing he's had to normality. Now he can show you what they have to offer." But she didn't want to just announce to Xander that they were touring Crimson. Though he'd made a few unilateral decisions of his own for them. "Z has a place in London. You're welcome to stay there as long as you want. Just tell them to change the sheets."

Uh… she didn't even want to ask. "I've never been to London."

"It's a great Crimson too… or so I've been told. My memory's sort of fuzzy on that score and I refuse to look at the video evidence." This wonderful woman lived an incredible life. It was amazing she'd stayed so down to earth. "But this is all a backup plan. Being a CEO, you have other responsibilities now."

"Let me talk to Xander, see what he thinks."

"Sure! Call whenever."

"Just not this afternoon."

"Right," Roxie said, a smile in her voice. "And you know, if I don't pick up, or it goes straight to voicemail—"

"You'll call back."

"Yep, I will."

The apartment door opened and Xander appeared. "Ready to go?"

"Ready," she said to him. "I have to go, Rox. Good luck with… your thing."

"Good luck to you too, honey. Just remember…"

"What would Roxie do? I will." She hung up and dropped her phone into her purse. "Okay, let's go own it."

THIRTY-NINE

"DON'T BE NERVOUS," Xander said, taking her hand from her thigh.

She snatched it back. "My palms are sweaty."

A laugh backed his words. "Baby, there is nothing to be anxious about."

"Easy for you to say, this is your daily fare. I've never been anyone's boss. Like ever. What if I get drunk with power?"

"Then we'll take over the world," he said. "I did this because I thought it would make you happy. If you'd rather I take it apart for you—"

"No," she said, pouncing closer. "You did make me happy. You do, I just…" Closing her eyes, she tried to clear her thoughts. "Need to think about something else."

He glanced at the privacy screen, then tucked her hair from her face. "We're only a few blocks away, but if you want me to…"

His fingertips glided up her thigh, under the hem of her dress.

She caught them. "You do that, we'll never get to the meeting."

He laughed and pulled her head to his lips. "Okay. After."

Just looking into his eyes relaxed her. "Yes, after."

But she got what Roxie meant too and pinched him.

"Ouch," he said without pain. "What was that for?"

"Just checking you're real." Sliding even closer, she wrapped his arm around her to lean against him. "Roxie asked if we want to go on a Crimson tour."

"A tour of which one?"

"As many as we want."

"A world tour? Like her and Zairn?"

"I think so," she said, picking up his hand to kiss his fingertips. "I couldn't go if you didn't come with me."

"If that's what you want, that's what we'll do."

"We'll see how today goes, I guess. But I am excited about helping Roxie out with the club here. I'd hate to abandon that responsibility. Roxie was there when I needed someone."

"We can do both. It's no problem. Whatever you want our life to be, it will be. I can work from anywhere in the world."

Most of the time. She tipped her chin her way. "Unless Australian counterparts are being difficult. You didn't tell me what happened there, were they just wasting your time?"

"I have history with Bingham Bright. Their CEO made a pretty hard play for me a few years ago."

"Hard play like to work with them or are we talking personal?"

"It was both. She had some wild idea about—it doesn't matter. This negotiation was further proof I can't work with that kind of volatility."

"She wants you," she said, and shifted against him. "I sent you to your ex-girlfriend? That's creepy."

"It's not as clear cut as that."

"With you, I'm getting used to that," she said, pressing his palm against her. "And I can sympathize with being obsessed with you. I'm obsessed too."

"Yours is love and reciprocated. Hers was… pathological."

Funny how the two could be interchangeable, depending on the situation.

"Is that why you walked away?"

"I walked away because continuing the negotiations didn't make business sense. Kicking my heels down there took me away from more important things." He kissed the top of her head. "Like the woman I love."

The car came to a stop and the tension ratcheted up again. "This is it."

"We'll go in together. I asked for all heads of department in the biggest room they have. You know where that is?" She nodded, her head still against him. "We'll go up. You wait outside, I'll introduce you."

"I don't know what to say."

"I'll take care of that. You just have to show your beautiful face." His finger curled around her chin, forcing her to sit straight when he drew around until their eyes met. "We're doing this together."

"Everything together."

He smiled. "Exactly. All you have to do is give me orders and I'll make it happen."

"Damn," she murmured and he frowned. "Now I wish we'd had sex."

Laughing, he kissed her forehead. "After, Button. Right there in the parking lot, if you want."

Would he deny her anything? No more than

she'd deny him. They got out and up to the largest conference room in double-quick time. Too quick.

"Wait," she said, pulling on his hand before he could go inside. The noise from within suggested there were a lot of people there. A lot of people waiting for her. Maybe for her to fall on her face. "Thank you."

"For?"

His people weren't far behind, she didn't know them all, but could feel them there. They'd never had such an audience for an intimate moment.

"This. Being you. Being my future… I love you."

His smile inspired such pride. "I love you too." Touching her chin to tip up her mouth, he kissed her quickly. "We'll get this over with and then head to a beach in Barcelona."

A dream was right.

Her fingers drifted from his as he strode into that boardroom. Damn, Roxie was so right. Xander might be different in the board room, but he was no less hers. No matter the guise, Xander Gauge was her man.

The room quieted before he said a word.

"Thank you all for being here," Xander said, taking his place at the front of the room.

With the door open, she could see him, but not his audience. "Baby," she whispered to no one.

"You may have heard that Viva has been purchased. What you may not know is the identity of your new owner. My company, Seven, will underwrite every adjustment, but you're leader, the person in charge…" He glanced her way. "Is someone you know well. Someone who also happens to be the woman I love. We're a team, in everything. I'll walk you through the current state of Viva and some potential avenues it may take. Ultimately, the decisions lie with your new CEO. Please welcome her. Rainie Tait."

The whispers started and she held her breath

before striding in. Xander was there, she'd keep her eyes on him. And pray she didn't say anything inappropriate. This would work. She was cool. Own it.

What would Roxie do?

***

"DID YOU SEE the looks on their faces?" she asked, still running a high when they got back to the apartment. "I can't believe it. I can't get over it. That was such a…"

"Rush?" he asked, repeating the word she'd used fifty times since leaving Viva.

Yeah, okay, so she was running on adrenaline. What was wrong with that? This man had flipped her world upside down in incredible ways she could never have dreamed would be part of her life. Xander was nothing but generous, wise, extraordinary love.

Spinning around, she tossed her jacket and purse aside and kicked off her shoes. "Let's have sex again."

Running to him, she leaped up into his arms. Although he accepted her kiss, his fury didn't quite match hers. So when she found herself sitting on the couch at his side, confusion dominated.

"What's wrong?" she asked. "You don't want sex?"

"I do want sex." Though they'd had it not long ago in the car parked in an alley by Viva. Containing her excitement just hadn't been possible. "More sex. You want to spend the next two weeks in those sheets?"

Man had a point. If they kept getting caught up in their physical desire, their futures, and their friends, would suffer.

"I need you to teach me," she said and his brows rose. "Some of the people at Viva are responsible for its current state. But not everyone there is bad. We don't have to keep it forever, but I want to watch you bring it back from the brink."

"I can do that. Starts with a full audit. We'd usually do that before purchase, but I've seen enough of the books to know what we'll find. We'll call Ranby Kearns in."

"They audit? And archive?"

"Yeah," he said. "Seven have in-house services, but I think we deserve a vacation."

"Touring some Crimson sites?" His smile was answer enough. "If you're willing to take care of Viva for me, I can work with Roxie. Toria used to work in marketing too, Roxie's friend in Manhattan. I'm sure if anything was needed on site, while we were out of town…"

"She can be your number two," Xander said. "It's important to surround yourself with people you trust. Your team will be with you through everything, you have to know they want the same thing… Without wanting your job too. You take care of your people and they will take care of you."

"What about you?" she asked, climbing into his lap. "What about us?"

"We take care of each other. You'll always be okay with me, Button."

"No more lies. Ever."

He frowned. "No, baby, I—"

"That wasn't an accusation. I just… have to tell you something."

Which he seemed to steel himself for. "Okay."

"I can't marry you until you prove yourself."

"Prove myself?"

"Yes, prove you're committed to me. That it's really me you love."

"How do you want me to do that?"

Leaning in, her lips touched his ear. "I hear it's supposed to rain tonight."

The rumble of his laugh vibrated through her chest. By the time he cupped her face, her eyes were already closed, her lips parted in expectation of his.

"It would be my pleasure," he whispered against her mouth and gave her exactly what she needed: him.

Read more from the Roxiverse in *Nothing in Between: Three...*

Thank you for reading this tale!
If you can, please take the time to review.

~

Ask your local library for more Scarlett Finn
novels!

~

For all things Scarlett Finn
check out:

www.scarlettfinn.com

Next in the Roxiverse:

www.ingramcontent.com/pod-product-compliance
Lightning Source LLC
Chambersburg PA
CBHW060801190726
48285CB00002B/514

9 781914 517426